PRAISE FOR THE NOVELS OF
#1 NEW YORK TIMES BESTSELLING AUTHOR
BARBARA FREETHY

"In the tradition of LaVyrle Spencer, gifted author Barbara Freethy creates an irresistible tale of family secrets, riveting adventure and heart- touching romance."

*-- NYT Bestselling Author **Susan Wiggs***
on Summer Secrets

"This book has it all: heart, community, and characters who will remain with you long after the book has ended. A wonderful story."

*-- NYT Bestselling Author **Debbie Macomber***
on Suddenly One Summer

"Freethy has a gift for creating complex characters."

*-- **Library Journal***

"Barbara Freethy is a master storyteller with a gift for spinning tales about ordinary people in extraordinary situations and drawing readers into their lives."

*-- **Romance Reviews Today***

"Freethy's skillful plotting and gift for creating sympathetic characters will ensure that few dry eyes will be left at the end of the story."

*-- **Publishers Weekly** on The Way Back Home*

"Freethy skillfully keeps the reader on the hook, and her tantalizing and believable tale has it all– romance, adventure, and mystery."

*-- **Booklist** on Summer Secrets*

"Freethy's story-telling ability is top-notch."

*-- **Romantic Times** on Don't Say A Word*

Also By Barbara Freethy

ONCE YOU'RE MINE

The Callaway Cousins #4

BARBARA FREETHY

HYDE STREET PRESS
Published by Hyde Street Press
1325 Howard Avenue, #321, Burlingame, California 94010

Printed in the United States of America

Cover design by Damonza.com

ISBN: 978-1-944417-31-4

One

⟶⟫⟪⟵

Tori Hayden had had the prickly feeling at the back of her neck since she'd returned to San Francisco three weeks earlier after a decade of being away from the city where she'd grown up. Since she'd taken a reporting job at the *Bay Area Examiner*, a digital and print newspaper known for in-depth stories on local and state issues, she'd felt as if someone was watching her every time she left her apartment or the office, but she couldn't imagine why.

Her current assignment reporting on the homeless population and the efforts being made to help the thousands of people sleeping under freeway overpasses and in front of buildings had taken her into some dicey areas, and she'd rattled a few city officials with her probing questions, but why would anyone be following her? It didn't make sense.

She flung a quick look over her shoulder, seeing nothing out of the ordinary. She'd just left a meeting at City Hall, and the neighborhood wasn't the best, but it was three o'clock on a Wednesday afternoon and there were plenty of people around. Shaking her head at her always overactive imagination, she saw a coffee house up ahead and decided a shot of caffeine would probably help clear her tired brain.

She was almost to the door when her phone buzzed. Pulling it out of her bag, she saw her brother's number and smiled. Despite the four-year age difference between them, she'd always been close to her big brother, Scott. Even when they'd been living thousands of miles apart from each other, they'd kept in touch. Now, with his wedding rapidly approaching, he seemed to find her to be his best resource for help and sanity.

She sat down at an outside table and answered the phone. "What has Mom done now?"

"She rearranged the seating chart and Monica's mother is going nuts, which means Monica is upset—"

"Which means you have to make her feel better," she finished.

"Exactly," Scott replied, tension in his voice. "I keep telling myself it's three more days, and then we're off to the honeymoon. But right now Saturday feels a million years from now. I thought we were past all the problems, but our mother and Monica's mother might be two of the most stubborn people on the face of the earth."

"I don't know Monica's mom, but I've had a lot of experience with ours."

"You need to talk to her, Tori."

"Me? She's not going to listen to me. If anyone can get through to her, it's you. Or maybe ask Ray to intervene. He seems able to calm her down."

"Ray is spending a lot of time golfing these days," Scott returned. "Our stepfather knows the best way to deal with her is to leave the house."

She'd noticed Ray's absences since she'd moved back to town and wondered if her mom and stepfather were as happy as they'd once been. But that was a discussion for another day. "Fine, I will call her and see if I can find out what the problem is."

"The problem is that she wants to have her own table at

the reception, and Monica's mother thinks the parents should sit together. I told Mom she needs to suck it up and do what Monica's mom wants because they're paying, and she got offended."

"I can't imagine why that would upset her," she said dryly.

"Well, it's the truth. Sorry, but I'm out of patience, and I do actually have a job to do besides all this wedding planning."

She knew her brother's work as an environmental lawyer was very important to him and also kept him quite busy. "I understand. I'll talk to her. But maybe if the parents aren't getting along, it would be better to have them sit separately."

"Monica and her mom say it's traditional for the parents to be together, and they don't like bucking tradition. So you have to find a way to convince Mom that she can sit with them for the hour it takes to have dinner."

"I'll give it my best shot. In return, I would appreciate it if you didn't stick me at the lonely singles table."

"I have no idea where you're sitting, and at this point I don't really care."

"Thanks for nothing."

"So how are things with you?" Scott asked, sounding more relaxed now that she'd agreed to help him. "Is San Francisco starting to feel like home again?"

"Not really, but I'm living in a part of the city I never spent much time in when we were growing up. Childhood memories for me are all from the neighborhoods around the Great Highway and Ocean Beach, and the cute restaurants in the Avenues. Now I'm in Hayes Valley, which is charming but crowded, and it feels very urban. However, I am extremely happy to have found a one-bedroom apartment that doesn't completely blow my budget. It's small, but I love not having roommates. Plus, I can walk to work."

"You're not walking through the greatest area," Scott said, a warning note in his voice. "The *Examiner* offices aren't in the best location."

She smiled at his protective words. Since their father had died when they were teenagers, Scott had always watched out for her. "It's not that bad." She wasn't going to tell him about the weird feeling she got when she was walking around the city.

"Just be careful. You often take too many risks, Tori. You're a lot like Dad. Sometimes, I wish you hadn't decided to follow in his footsteps and be a hotshot reporter."

"Dad didn't die while covering a story; he just had an accident," she reminded him.

"I know. I've been thinking about Dad a lot lately."

"Probably because of the wedding. It's only natural that you'd miss him more at this moment."

"I guess. He'll be out of my mind for years at a time, and then suddenly I feel his presence all around me."

She licked her lips, wondering if the prickly feeling had something to do with her father, but she'd never really believed her dad was watching over her the way Scott did.

"You used to feel that way when we were kids," she said. "I never felt his presence, but you did. Especially at your baseball games—remember?"

"Yeah, because baseball was what we did together. It's strange to think he died seventeen years ago. It's a long time."

"Most of our lives." She'd been twelve when their father had passed away, and some days the memories were hard to hang on to, but other times she could see her father in her head as clearly as she could see her own reflection.

"I have to run. I have a meeting," Scott said, bringing her back to the conversation at hand. "Talk to Mom."

"I will. But whatever happens with the seating, it's going to be fine; the wedding will be perfect."

"After all this stress, it better be."

As her brother hung up, she put her phone in her bag. That's when she saw a man across the street. He stood under the doorway of a building, and he wore bulky clothes, a big coat over a sweater, baggy pants, and a baseball cap on his head. When he caught her looking back at him, he suddenly jerked, turned away, and headed down the block.

A shiver ran down her spine. She told herself the man was probably harmless. He could be homeless. His clothes were too heavy for a warm May day. Had she run into him at one of the homeless encampments she'd recently visited, one of which was only a few blocks from here?

She'd tried talking to people there, hoping to get personal stories for her articles, but most people had shied away from conversation. Had someone perhaps had a change of mind but then bailed out at the last second? Was this man the reason why she'd had the tingly feeling at the back of her neck? Had he been watching for a while?

As questions ran through her head, she got up and crossed the street, impulsively deciding to see where the man was going. He'd already turned the corner, so she quickened her pace, hoping he wouldn't just disappear.

She didn't really know why she was following him, except that she couldn't seem to make herself stop. She told herself at any moment she could turn around and go back to her office, but at the moment she was curious as to where he was going. Her curiosity had always driven her—sometimes into trouble, but equally as often into an important story.

She came around the corner and saw him two blocks ahead of her. He was going up the steps to a three-story building. As she drew closer, she realized it was a residence hotel, but like the other run-down structures on the block, it had definitely seen better days.

She hesitated at the bottom of the steps, then went up to the front door. It was partly ajar.

Whatever security lock had been on that door was long gone. She tentatively pushed it open and stepped inside. She was immediately overwhelmed by a thick stench of rotting garbage.

Taking a few steps toward an elevator and a dirty stairwell, she saw a sign tacked on the wall from the Board of Health condemning the building as unfit to live in.

Based on that notice, the building should be empty.

Glancing down the hall, she could see that some of the doors to what had once been rooms were missing or hanging off their hinges.

Where had the man gone? Was he a squatter? Was he staying here until they tore the building down?

It wasn't uncommon for the homeless population to take advantages of buildings like this to take shelter in as long as they could. It was just another part of the problem.

She was impulsive and somewhat fearless, but she also had enough sense to know when to back off. It was too dangerous to follow him farther into the building, when she had no idea who else was inside.

Turning around, she moved toward the door. But she'd barely taken a step when she heard a loud bang. Her heart stopped. She glanced over her shoulder. *Was that a gunshot?*

She'd barely formed that thought when a rocketing blast knocked her off her feet, throwing her out the door and down the steps in a blazing fire of heat, plaster, and glass.

It was only a little after three o'clock, but it had already been a long, busy shift at Fire Station 36 near the San Francisco Civic Center.

Dylan Callaway hopped off the truck as they returned to the firehouse from a motor vehicle accident that thankfully had resulted in no fatalities. He hoped that the rest of the afternoon and evening would be less eventful. But quiet days seemed to be rare this month, with more than the usual number of suspicious fires, motor vehicle and workplace accidents.

"Looking forward to your chili tonight," his cousin Burke told him as they made their way into the common room with the rest of the crew. Like himself and most of the Callaway men, Burke had dark hair and blue eyes. They were close enough in looks that some people thought they were brothers instead of cousins.

"We'll see if I get time to make it," he returned. "It's been one call after another today."

"You're making your chili tonight, aren't you, Callaway?" Pete Holden asked, as he flopped down on the couch. "I've been looking forward to it all shift." Pete was a blond-haired, brown-eyed, thirty-year-old firefighter who'd transferred to the station a few months earlier and had brought an easygoing energy to the house. But one thing he hadn't brought was any skill at cooking.

"Yes, but one of these days you're going to have to step up and make us a meal," Dylan said dryly. "No free rides around here."

Pete laughed. "I'll order in pizzas next shift."

As Dylan headed into the kitchen, Burke followed him. He was a little surprised since Burke's job as battalion chief often kept him busy in his office in between calls.

Burke was two years older than him and was the oldest of his generation of Callaway cousins, many of whom had followed the family tradition of firefighting. They'd been working together the past five years, except for a few months when Burke had been rehabbing his hand after an injury. Dylan had nothing but respect for his cousin, who had been a super-achiever since birth.

While Dylan hadn't risen to Burke's level yet, he wasn't far behind. He also felt a connection to Burke because, like his cousin, he was the oldest in his family of six siblings, and he often felt the pressure to set the bar high for everyone who came after him.

"I hear Ian just got engaged," Burke said, referring to one of his brothers.

"Yes, things are moving very fast for him." He was still surprised that his super smart, genius of a brother, had found love before he had.

"Have you met his fiancée?"

"I have. Grace is wonderful. She's a teacher, very creative, quite different from Ian, who has always been about science and logic and reason. But they complement each other."

"That's what it takes sometimes. Maddie and I are opposites, but we balance each other out."

That was true. The free-spirited Maddie had definitely softened Burke's rougher edges. "How's her restaurant going?"

"Very well. It's booked almost every weekend."

"She's a great chef."

"She is." Burke smiled. "But it makes her a little crazy that you still make a better chili than she does. She really wants the recipe."

He laughed. Maddie had tried to pin him down more than a few times. He didn't make a lot of things well, but he did make one mean, spicy chili that got better every year. "Chef's secret."

"She doesn't like that answer."

"I know she doesn't, but that's the way it is."

"Well, don't count on her giving up trying to get it out of you. She can be stubborn."

"So can I."

"We should go out one night. Are you still seeing that blonde from the fire a few months back—"

He shook his head, cutting off Burke's question. "Nope. Nothing going on there." For a few weeks, he'd dated a woman he'd rescued during a car accident, and it had been a very bad idea. He'd known better, but he'd done it anyway. He wouldn't do that again.

"Too bad."

"Not really." Opening the refrigerator door, he was about to start pulling out ingredients when the alarm bells went off in the house, followed by the dispatcher relating the details of their next call.

He immediately closed the refrigerator door, and went into action. The chili would have to wait. It was back to business.

The fire was only two miles from the station house, and the billowing black smoke was not a welcome sight. As they pulled up in front of a three-story structure, he saw flames shooting out of the windows on the upper floor.

The dispatcher had told them the building was condemned and should be empty, but from his experience, abandoned buildings were often havens for the homeless. Hopefully, no one had been caught inside.

A crowd was gathering along the sidewalk as they pulled up. As he jumped off the truck, a dark-haired woman came running toward them. Her long hair was covered with ash and pieces of drywall, and there were cuts on her face. But it wasn't her injuries that surprised him; it was her very familiar dark-blue eyes.

"Tori?" he asked in amazement. He hadn't seen his friend Scott's little sister in probably a decade.

"Dylan?" she said, her shocked gaze turning even more confused.

"Are you all right? Were you inside?"

"Something blew up," she said, waving her hand at the fire.

"Is anyone else in the building?"

"There was a man—I don't know if he got out."

He looked past Tori to Burke, who'd heard everything she had to say.

"You and Holden, check it out," Burke said, then continued his instructions to the rest of the crew.

"Dee," he said, motioning for the paramedic, who'd just arrived. "Can you check her out?"

As Tori was attended to, he and Pete headed into the building.

The fire was intense, getting hotter by the second. He and Pete went room to room, calling out for victims. They'd only had a chance to clear the first floor before Burke ordered them back outside.

He'd barely made it to the street when the building was rocked by another blast and a raging wave of fire. His lips drew into a tight line as he contemplated the odds of anyone surviving the explosion. If someone was inside, they probably weren't coming out. He hoped that Tori was wrong, that whoever she'd seen in the building had gotten out.

For the next hour, his crew, along with firefighters from three other stations, attacked the blaze from every angle, eventually able to contain it and put it out.

When the fire had subsided, he and Pete went back inside to check for bodies. They went through each room, and in the back room on the third floor, they found a man buried beneath the debris from the ceiling and the roof, his body burned beyond recognition.

His stomach rolled with anger and frustration. Dying from fire was one of the most brutal ways to go. "Damn," he muttered, wishing they'd been able to get him out.

After reporting the deceased to Burke, they finished checking the rest of the building, but thankfully found no more victims.

At the bottom of the stairs, near the back door, he found a billfold that was partially burned, but there was an ID inside—maybe it belonged to the man upstairs.

Once they had determined there was only one victim, they bagged the body and took it outside. He ran a hand through his hair as he watched the ambulance drive away.

"You did what you could," Burke told him.

"It wasn't good enough."

"Unfortunately, some days it's not."

"Yeah." He glanced down the sidewalk and saw Tori. "I need a minute. That's Scott's sister."

"What was she doing in that building?" Burke asked.

"No idea. I'd like to find out."

"Go ahead. We've got this under control."

As he walked down the street, he could hardly believe that the woman in the figure-hugging gray skirt, cream-colored top and high heels was Tori. In his head, she was still twelve and annoying as hell as she followed him and Scott around, driving them crazy with her incessant questions. Back then she'd had a silver grill of braces on her teeth, and big black glasses framing her eyes.

There was no sign of the braces or the glasses now, and she'd filled out her skinny frame with some nice female curves. Her dark hair was long, thick, and flowing around her shoulders, although right now it was tangled and chalky with ash from the fire. Even with cuts on her face, there was no denying her beauty or the irresistible pull of her dark-blue eyes.

He frowned at the direction of his thoughts. This was Scott's little sister. He needed to remember that.

"You okay?" he asked her.

She nodded, but he could see the tension in her gaze.

"Yes," she said, folding her arms across her chest. "I saw you bring out...a body. That was a body, right?"

He could hear the tremor in her voice and knew she wasn't as calm as she was pretending to be. "Yes."

"It was a man—an older man?"

"I don't know. It was a bad fire."

She stared back at him in confusion and then his words slowly registered.

"You mean you couldn't see his face." She shuddered.

"Sorry."

"The explosion threw me out the front door and down the steps. I couldn't go back inside and look for him."

His gaze narrowed at her words. "What were you doing in there? The building is supposed to be abandoned."

A somewhat guilty gleam flashed through her gaze. "I followed him inside. I didn't realize the building had been condemned until I saw the sign on the interior wall."

"You followed him? Did you know him?"

"No, but he was watching me, and there was something about him that made me curious."

His brows drew together as he tried to make sense of what she was saying. "You followed a random stranger who was watching you? Why the hell would you do that?"

She frowned at his sharp tone. "I'm a reporter. I was following a hunch, but when I got inside the building, I had a bad feeling, so I turned to leave. Then something blew up."

"You were lucky you made it outside, Tori."

"I know," she said, blowing out a breath. "I can't believe he's dead. It happened so fast."

Her words reminded him of the billfold he'd found. He pulled it out of his pocket. "I did find this by the back stairwell." The address had been burned away, the man's face and name were smudged but somewhat visible. "Neil Hawkins. Is this the man you saw?"

She stared at the ID, her eyes widening again. She put a hand on his arm, as if she were about to collapse.

"What's wrong? Do you recognize him?"

She swallowed hard, still staring at the photo. "It can't be."

"Can't be who?"

She lifted her gaze to his, and the pain in her blue eyes made his gut clench.

"What's wrong?" he asked.

"My father," she whispered. "That man looks like my father."

Two

—➤➤◄◄—

Tori couldn't believe the face staring back at her, but the longer she looked at the grainy, smudged ID photo, the more her doubts grew. This man did share her father's features, but now that she was getting past the shock, she could see that he was older than the dad she remembered. This man's hair was completely gray and her dad's hair had been a dark-brown. Her dad's eyes had been blue like hers; this man's eyes were brown. This man had a scar over his right brow and a slightly crooked nose. Her dad's nose had been straight, and he hadn't had a blemish on his face. Then there was his name—Neil Hawkins—that wasn't right.

She blinked her eyes a few times. Her logical brain told her this man was not her father, but she couldn't shake the uneasy and disturbing feeling running through her body.

"Your dad died a long time ago," Dylan said, giving her a doubtful look, as his words drew her gaze to his.

She'd seen that skeptical expression on Dylan's face many times in her teenage years. Her brother's friend had always thought she was a little crazy and far too impulsive.

Obviously, today's adventure hadn't done anything to change that opinion.

"Seventeen years," she said, then decided to change the subject. "So how did the fire start?"

"Fire investigators are just getting inside now."

"Something blew up. It wasn't a slow-starting fire. The force of the blast literally picked me up and threw me out of the building."

"You were very lucky."

"I was. I'd like to know what happened."

"The investigators will figure it out. I'm sure they'll want to talk to you."

"I want to talk to them."

He nodded. "Your brother said you were thinking of moving back here. I didn't realize that had already happened."

"Three weeks ago."

"Just in time for Scott's wedding?"

"It was good timing," she agreed.

"I'm sure your family is happy to have you home."

"Yes. I think so."

"I'm going to need that back," he said, tipping his head toward the ID. "I have to turn it over to the investigator."

"Sure." She handed him the ID, feeling oddly reluctant to part with it.

"Do you want me to call someone to come and get you, Tori?"

She suddenly realized she was still holding onto his arm with her other hand. "Sorry." She immediately let go, feeling a little dizzy when she did so.

He frowned. "You should go to the hospital. Did you hit your head?"

"No, I'm fine. The paramedics checked me out."

"At least let me call Scott."

"I don't need you to call anyone. I'm okay."

"You don't look okay."

"Well, I don't almost get blown up every day." She tucked her hair behind her ear, the gesture knocking a chunk of plaster loose. "Thanks for trying to save him—whoever he was."

"That's my job. I'm just sorry we didn't get to him in time."

His lips drew into a tense, angry line, another familiar Dylan expression. He'd never been a guy comfortable with failure, especially when that failure meant someone else got hurt. He'd always been a natural-born protector. He'd also always been extremely good-looking.

She didn't know how Dylan could be more attractive now than he had been in high school, but he was. He had a square face, with strong male bones, brown hair and light-blue eyes that seemed able to look into her soul.

She felt a shiver run down her spine for a very different reason.

Dylan had always been her brother's friend, the four-year age difference making him way too old for her when they were teenagers, but she'd secretly had a little crush on him way back when. Not that he'd ever seen her as anything but a pest.

"Dylan," another firefighter called, motioning him forward.

"I have to go, Tori."

"Of course."

"Take care of yourself. Maybe next time think before you follow someone into an abandoned building."

She didn't particularly care for the scolding reminder, but he was right, and as he left, she drew in a breath, trying to calm her racing heart. It was a difficult task, considering how close she'd come to death, and all because she'd followed a curious impulse.

She glanced at the building, which was charred and smoking, large open spaces where the walls had once been. The fire was out now. The man she'd followed into the building was dead—a man who kind of looked like her dad. She didn't know what to make of that, but she needed to know what had happened, how the fire had started, who Neil

Hawkins was. But she wasn't going to have any answers until the investigators had a chance to do their work. She would have to wait.

Frowning, she turned and walked away. She'd never been good at waiting...

—➤◄—

When Tori entered the newsroom of the *Bay Area Examiner* twenty minutes later, she was met with a shocked and worried expression from the editor-in-chief, Stacey Kinsley, a tall redhead in her early fifties, who had thirty years of news experience behind her and was rarely rattled by anything.

With Stacey was the assignment editor, Jeff Crocker, a thirty-nine-year-old blond-haired man with piercing brown eyes and a cynical edge that Stacey said had sharpened since his wife had left him a year earlier.

"What on earth happened to you?" Stacey asked. "You text me you're in a fire and will be back later? And then you don't answer any texts or your phone? What the hell was that about?"

"Sorry, I was a little shaken up. I wasn't thinking straight."

"I thought you were dead," Stacey said.

"You look like shit, Tori," Jeff said, his gaze narrowing on her face. "Was it the hotel fire about a mile from here?"

"Yes."

"What were you doing there?" he asked. "I thought the building was condemned."

"It was, but..." She licked her lips, not really wanting to tell them about her impulsive actions. "I thought there might be a homeless population inside. You know those old buildings often have squatters." She was happy with her quick thinking, and her statement wasn't completely false.

"Was anyone hurt?" Stacey asked.

"Yes. Someone died." She drew in a breath as another

wave of shock ran through her. "A man."

"How did it start?" Jeff asked. "We heard what sounded like an explosion."

"You heard it from here?"

Stacey nodded. "We didn't know what it was. We got on the phone right away to the police and they told us it was a fire."

"I don't know how it started. The fire investigators were on the scene when I left. I tried to get information, but I was told it was too early."

"Always a reporter," Jeff murmured. "Sticking around to get the story."

She'd actually stuck around because she'd been too shocked to move, and, of course, she'd wanted to find out if the man she'd been following had gotten out. But she hadn't actually thought about covering the fire for the paper, which she really should have considered.

"Did you see Katie down there?" Stacey asked. "I sent her to look for you and cover the fire when you didn't text me back."

"I didn't see her. There were a lot of people around."

"Well, when she gets back, maybe the two of you can compare notes," Stacey added. "Unless you'd rather go home? You don't look good."

"I'm going to be fine." She pushed past them to sit down at her desk before she made a lie of her words by passing out. Now that the adrenaline rush was fading, she was feeling lightheaded.

"You're not fine. You need to go home," Stacey said.

"I can drive you," Jeff offered. "You usually walk to work, don't you?"

"Yes, but I just need a minute."

"You need more than that," Stacey said decisively. "It's almost five anyway. Go home, get some rest."

"I should talk to Katie about the fire."

"I'll have her call you if she needs any info. Now get out of here."

Seeing the steel in Stacey's eyes, she got to her feet. "Okay, thanks." She hated to look weak in front of her new boss and coworkers, but she'd bounce back stronger tomorrow. She just needed to catch her breath.

Jeff's car was parked in an underground garage and within minutes, he was pulling into traffic. Although she didn't live far away, with the afternoon rush hour in full swing, it was going to take a few minutes to get home.

"You're one of those, aren't you?" Jeff asked, breaking the silence between them.

"What do you mean?" she asked warily. Since she'd started at the paper, Jeff had been the least approachable and welcoming person on the staff, and she didn't know why. She usually got along really well with people. Katie, one of the other reporters, had told her that Jeff had wanted Stacey's job, but she'd been hired from another paper when the position became open. Maybe that's why he had a chip on his shoulder.

"You're one of those reporters who has to break down doors, climb over barricades, go where no one has dared to go before," he drawled. "Am I right?"

"That's what reporters do. That's what you do or did," she said, realizing a second too late that she'd probably just antagonized him more.

"I did do that, until I realized that the reporter can become the story if they're not careful."

His words hit close to home but she decided to turn the conversation back to him. "What happened to you?"

"It doesn't matter. But I know what it's like to want to break the big story like Bernstein and Woodward, Calvin Harte, Charles Pennington, and Ben Hayden." He shot her a glance as he ended with her father's name. "Do you think I don't know you're Ben's daughter?"

"I wasn't trying to hide it, but I don't trade off my dad's reputation." She'd never brought it up at her two previous news jobs, but they had been on the other side of the country, and her father's reputation was certainly bigger in San

Francisco, where he had done his most impressive work.

"Your dad was a legend in this city. He went where no others would go. He used his pen as a sword. He was determined, ambitious, sometimes reckless, but he was one of the greats. I worked with him the year before he died."

"You did?" she said in surprise.

"Yes. The *Herald* was my first newspaper job. I was twenty-two, fresh out of college. Your father was inspiring. He was a hero to all of us."

"I wish I'd been more aware of his work back then, but I was a kid. Most of what I know about his big stories, I've read about from others."

"Well, I didn't spend much time with him, but I do know that when he got a lead, he didn't let go of it. I think you're like him. I know you won't follow my advice. But just remember, you can't be great if you're dead."

"That's good advice. A little depressing, but I get your point." She paused. "When did you get cynical, Jeff?"

"Me? Oh, hell, who knows? This job shows you the worst of people."

"I know that, but sometimes it shows you the best."

"Just don't make the job your whole life."

She had a feeling now he was talking about his marriage. "That's my street. You can turn right. It's the third building." As he pulled up in front of her four-story apartment building, she said, "We should get a drink sometime. I'd like to get to know you better."

"I'd like that, too." He paused. "I had a friend in mind for the job you got. Sorry if I haven't been overly friendly."

"I hadn't noticed," she lied.

He smiled. "Take care of yourself."

"I'll see you tomorrow."

She got out of his car, thinking that taking the ride home had actually helped break the ice between them, and now she understood that his attitude toward her wasn't as personal as she'd made it.

She checked her mailbox in the lobby, and then went up

the stairs to her second-floor apartment. She'd barely gotten inside when her phone rang. Seeing her brother's name on the screen, she had a feeling she was about to get more unwanted advice. *What was it with the men today?* Everyone seemed to want to tell her what to do. First Dylan, then Jeff, now Scott.

"I haven't had time to talk to Mom yet," she said, as she answered the call, hoping her brother was following up on the reception seating issue and that he hadn't gotten a call from one hot firefighter. Of course, she was wrong.

"I'm not calling about that. Dylan said you were in a fire. What the hell happened, Tori? Are you all right? Where are you?"

"Slow down, Scott. I'm fine. I'm at home now. I wasn't injured, and I can't believe Dylan called you." She set her bag down on the coffee table and flopped onto her couch.

"He said you were following some random stranger into a deserted building. What were you thinking, Tori?"

"It wasn't exactly like that, Scott. Look, I appreciate your concern, but you don't have to worry about me."

"I don't have to worry about you? Dylan said you looked at some guy's ID and thought it was our father."

"Dylan has a big mouth," she retorted. "The man did have features similar to Dad. And you're one to talk. You've been seeing Dad our whole life."

"Not actually seeing him, just feeling him around me. There's a difference."

There was a difference, and the last few hours had been so surreal, she couldn't trust her memory or her impression of the man's photo. She needed to find out more about him. "Do you know the name Neil Hawkins?"

"No. Why?"

"That's the name of the man I was following."

"The one who died in the fire?"

Her lips drew together at the reminder. "Dylan told you that, too."

"Was it the same man?"

"I think so. And he did look like Dad, Scott. Or at least

like a relative."

"He doesn't have relatives in this area."

"I know that. I'm just telling you what I saw."

"I can't deal with this right now, Tori. I'm getting married on Saturday."

"There's nothing for you to deal with," she told him, hearing the stress in his voice.

"You said that once before, and the next thing I'm bailing you out of jail."

"That was one time. I was sixteen, and it was just a misunderstanding. I wasn't vandalizing school property; I was investigating a story for the newspaper."

He sighed. "You and your investigations."

"Hey, it's my job."

"Fine. But I cannot handle any misunderstandings now. I've got enough on my plate. I want this weekend to be the happiest time in Monica's life."

"I'm not going to screw up your wedding," she assured him. "Don't give any of this another thought."

"You're sure you're all right? Do you need to see a doctor?"

"No. I'm relaxing at home. I'm thinking about binge watching something on television while eating a half gallon of ice cream."

"I believe the ice cream but not the television marathon. You're going to get on your computer and start digging into this man's life."

Her brother knew her too well. "Well, I can't get into trouble on my computer, so take a breath, and go be with your fiancée. I'm not going anywhere tonight. In fact, as soon as you hang up, I'll call Mom and see if I can talk her into sitting with Monica's parents."

"I would appreciate that."

"I just need one thing from you," she said impulsively.

"What's that?"

She hesitated, then went with the idea brewing in her head. "Dylan's phone number."

"Why?"

"I want to follow up with him about the fire. I need to know how it started."

"Tori—"

"Look, if I talk to Dylan, I won't have to go digging on my own. Which means I'll probably get into less trouble."

"Why do I bother to argue with you?"

"I have no idea."

"You know, there was a time when I was excited about you moving back home," he said wearily.

"It's not that bad. You're just stressed about too many things right now. Don't let me be one of them."

"All right. Here's Dylan's number."

She jotted down the number. "Thanks. I'll talk to you later."

"Be careful, Tori. Think before you act. I know that's not your usual style—"

"I do think," she interrupted. "I'm not a little kid."

"In my head you are."

"Good-bye, Scott." She ended the call, then debated who to talk to next. Her mom or Dylan?

There was really no choice to make.

—————

Dylan didn't recognize the number ringing his phone, but his gut told him it was important to take the call. They'd just gotten back to the firehouse and he'd been about to start making the chili, but instead he headed outside for a little privacy.

"Hello?"

"Dylan? It's me, Tori."

Her husky voice made his body tighten. "Tori? Everything all right?"

"Yes. You didn't need to call Scott," she said with annoyance.

"You didn't look so good, and I didn't think you were

going to call him yourself."

"I wasn't. In case you hadn't noticed, I'm all grown up now. I can handle myself."

He'd noticed she was all grown up—he'd definitely noticed. In fact, he hadn't stopped thinking about her since he'd seen her, and it hadn't been in a friend-of-her-big-brother kind of way. "I was just concerned about you."

"I'm fine. Do you know what caused the explosion?"

"Not yet, but it's early. We just got back to the station a short time ago. The investigation will take at least a few days, if not weeks."

"I heard a loud bang before I was knocked off my feet. I don't know if that helps."

"Be sure to relay that to the investigator when he calls you."

"Will that be tonight?"

"Probably tomorrow. Why are you so interested in how it started, Tori?"

"Because I was almost killed. I've never been that close to something like that before."

He could hear the edge in her voice and doubted she'd be getting much sleep that night. He knew what it felt like to relive the events of a day over and over again. "You just have to breathe your way through it," he advised.

"I'm trying. What about the victim? Do you know anything more about him?"

"No. I turned the ID over to the investigator, and I'm sure they'll work with the police department to locate any relatives." He paused. "You still thinking he looked like your father?"

"I know it seems crazy, but I need to find out who he was, why he might have been watching me."

Her words reminded him of their initial conversation. "You said you followed him. Why would you do that?"

"I'm writing an article for the *Bay Area Examiner* on issues with the homeless population and some of the growing violence in various encampments. I've been reaching out to people, hoping to get an interview; I thought he might be someone who wanted to talk to me but then got scared off."

"So you went after him?"

"I wanted to see where he was going. I just can't believe he's dead now. I keep seeing that body bag come out of the building…"

He still felt bad for not having been able to save the man, whoever he was. "You have to try to stop thinking about that."

"Tell me how to do that," she said with a sigh.

He wished he could. "Try to focus on something else. You have Scott's wedding coming up."

"That's true," she said, but then quickly returned to the subject that was on her mind. "I really wish I could talk to your investigator tonight."

"Even if you could, he's not going to tell you anything about an ongoing investigation. In fact, you might find yourself under suspicion for being so interested in the fire. It's not uncommon for arsonists to get too close to their own fires or to stick around and follow the investigation."

"You don't seriously think I started the fire?"

"Of course not. I'm just stating the facts."

"I can see your point," she said. "What if you spoke to the investigator and shared whatever information you could with me? Then I could stay out of it, which I'm sure would make my brother happy."

Against his better judgment, he found himself agreeing. "I'll talk to the investigator tomorrow and get back to you."

"Can we meet after work? Will you be at the firehouse?"

"No, I'm off shift tomorrow morning." He thought for a moment, thinking he was probably about to make a big mistake, but he couldn't think of a good reason not to see her. "I'll meet you tomorrow night at Brady's Bar and Grill."

"I haven't heard that name in a while. Brady's is still going strong?"

"Yes, it is," he said. Owned by a former firefighter, the bar had long been a hangout for firefighters and cops. "How about six thirty?"

"That's perfect. And you don't need to alert Scott to anything else, Dylan. He has enough stress getting through all the pre-wedding events. I don't need him worrying about me."

"Then don't give him anything to worry about. See you tomorrow, Tori."

As he went back into the firehouse, he didn't feel remotely guilty for having told Scott about Tori almost getting caught up in a fire. He had three younger sisters, and he'd want to know if one of them were in trouble. But he did appreciate the fact that Scott had a lot going on, so he'd be a good friend and look out for Tori himself. Hopefully, he could keep her out of any more trouble.

That thought made him smile. Tori had always been a force of nature. He had a feeling that hadn't changed.

Three

---⇒≫≪⇐---

Gary Kruger, an investigator with the San Francisco Fire Department, showed up at Tori's office a little after four on Thursday afternoon, after having set an appointment with her earlier in the day. Upon his arrival, she took him into the conference room for a little more privacy.

Gary was an attractive man with short brown hair and shrewd brown eyes, who appeared to be in his early thirties. "Thank you for seeing me," he said politely.

"Of course. I'm happy to help with your investigation." She was hoping that in addition to providing Gary with her information, she might get some answers of her own.

"So, I understand that you were in the lobby of the building when the fire started. Is that correct?"

"Yes. I was actually on my way out."

"Why were you there? The building was supposed to be empty."

"I'm reporting on the homeless population. I thought there might be squatters in the building."

"Did you see anyone?"

"I saw a man. He had on a lot of clothes, like someone who lived outside. I think he was in his fifties or sixties. I wasn't close enough to get a good look, although I did see an ID recovered by one of the firefighters."

"Yes, I have that ID for Mr. Neil Hawkins. That was the man you saw in the building?"

"Yes, it was." She drew in a breath and let it out. "I can't believe he's dead. Everything happened so fast. Do you know how the fire started?"

"It's an ongoing investigation."

"But there was a blast. It was deliberate, wasn't it? It's not like a heater blew up or something, right?"

"As I said, we're looking into all possibilities."

She frowned, not liking his very vague answers. "Do you know anything about the man who died? Has his family been notified? Or maybe he didn't have family? Was he homeless?"

"Unfortunately, I can't share any information from our investigation. Did you see anyone else in the building or perhaps outside?"

"There were people on the sidewalk, but I didn't notice anyone in particular."

"Did you hear anything before the fire started? Were there voices?"

"No, I didn't hear anyone talking."

"And no one else inside?"

She frowned at the repeated question. "I already said no. Was there someone else in the building?"

"Not to my knowledge," he replied. "I'm just trying to cover all the bases."

"I did hear a loud bang right before the bigger blast. It almost sounded like a gunshot, but maybe that was just a smaller explosion before the bigger one."

He nodded, but didn't offer a reaction. Instead, he said, "Anything else you'd like to share?"

"No, but I wish I knew more," she said. "What about the owner of the building? Have you spoken to them?"

"We are in touch with the owner of the building. Thank you for your time, Ms. Hayden."

"You're welcome. I don't think I've been very helpful."

"Every fact helps us put together the bigger picture."

"Do you think you'll be able to catch who did it?" she asked, as they stood up.

"I hope so. That's my job," he said, for the first time cracking a small smile. "I can see myself out."

"All right." They parted ways after leaving the conference room, and she returned to her desk. As she did so, Stacey came out of her nearby office with a quizzical look in her eyes.

"Who was that?" she asked.

"The investigator looking into the hotel fire."

"Does he have a cause, a suspect? Was it definitely arson?" Stacey asked.

"If he does, he wasn't willing to share it with me," she replied. "I answered all of his questions; he did not answer any of mine."

"That's probably protocol."

"I'm sure. I'm going to talk to another firefighter tonight, a friend of mine from years ago. We're meeting at Brady's Bar and Grill. He was on the scene yesterday, and he might be able to tell me more."

"Good. If you get more information, you can do a follow-up story. But I don't want you to get too distracted by the fire. There's nothing that interesting about an old building burning down before it would be torn down. I want your focus on the housing/homeless article. How is that coming along?"

"I should have a draft early next week."

"I want something different and new in this piece," Stacey told her. "Everyone in the city knows there's a problem. I want us to tell them who's working on a solution, and what creative ideas are being floated out there. If there's an individual or a department who's stonewalling possible solutions, the citizens of this city need to know that, too."

She frowned, realizing she really didn't have what Stacey

wanted. "It's a complicated issue. I haven't found any one person or department standing in the way of anything. But there's definitely a lack of agreement on solutions."

"I know it's complicated, which is exactly why I wanted you on this article," Stacey said. "I've read your work. You know how to dig, so get out your shovel. If you need more time, take it. I'd rather put out something great in a few weeks than a half-assed story now."

"Got it. And I never do anything half-assed," she said.

Stacey smiled. "Good to know."

As Stacey returned to her office, she went back to her cubicle. She tried to get into her article again, reading through the first few paragraphs of her piece, but Stacey's desire for something groundbreaking made her realize that she really didn't have enough for even the roughest first draft. She needed to do more research. Checking her watch, she realized it was almost five—too late to touch base with any city officials. That would have to wait until tomorrow, which might be a good thing. She was distracted by the fire and her conversation with the investigator. Not to mention, she still needed to talk to her mother about Scott's problem with the reception seating, and her mom had been avoiding her calls and texts all day.

Since she had an hour and a half before she had to meet Dylan, she decided to make a stop on the way. Grabbing her bag, she headed out the door.

She walked home as quickly as she could, unable to stop looking over her shoulder at every corner. Occasionally, she felt as if someone were on her heels, but no one stopped her or bothered her in any way. She was just being paranoid.

When she got home, she dashed upstairs to change into jeans and a clingy knit top, run a brush through her hair and touch up her makeup—because she was meeting Dylan, after all—and she'd like to look better than she had yesterday. Plus, she wanted to make sure the scratches she'd gotten in the fire were not visible, or she'd be answering questions from her mom.

As she drove across town, she realized it was the first time she'd actually driven anywhere since moving into her apartment. She'd either been walking, taking the bus, or using a car service to get around downtown, but her mom's house was on the most western edge of the city, and parking was more prevalent on the street that ran next to the Great Highway and directly across from Ocean Beach.

Going back to her old neighborhood known as the Sunset brought forth a lot of memories that she didn't have anywhere else in the city. It was these blocks where she'd ridden her bike and played with her brother and her friends.

When she spotted the shimmering blue of the ocean, a wave of wistful nostalgia ran through her, as she remembered all the times she'd gone to the beach with her dad. He'd taught her to bodysurf, and they'd built sandcastles and collected seashells as the sun set. He'd spent those dusky evenings, sprawled out on the sand, talking about his dreams and her dreams and all the amazing turns her life could take.

She had never imagined then that one of those turns would take her dad away from her. The pain of the loss had dimmed over the years, but it was stronger here, which was one of the reasons why she'd left home to go to college back east and hadn't returned until now. It had been easier to build a life for herself away from the memories. She'd thought she was ready to be back in San Francisco, but yesterday's events had definitely rattled her, and there was a part of her that wondered if she'd made the best decision, but it was too late now.

She pulled into a parking spot across the street from her mom's two-story house and got out of the car. She rang the bell, because even though she'd grown up in the house, it didn't feel like her home anymore. It actually hadn't felt that way since her mother had married her stepfather Ray and moved him into the house. Ray was a good guy, but he just hadn't seemed like he belonged in the house her father had bought.

In the end, she'd been the one to move out, and Ray had

been in the house fourteen years now.

"Tori," her mom Pamela said with a delighted smile, as she opened the door. "Did you say you were coming over? I thought I wasn't seeing you until tomorrow night."

"No, I didn't say I was coming over, but you haven't returned any of my calls or texts," she said, as she entered the house.

In the entry, she was immediately assailed by the scent of gardenias, a beautiful batch of which sat in a vase on the hall table. Her mother was a landscape designer, and in Tori's mind, she always smelled like flowers. Today was no different.

"I've been so busy with everything," her mom said, not quite meeting her gaze.

Her mother was taller than she was by a few inches, and they didn't look anything alike. Her mom had short brown hair that was layered and angled around her face, light brown eyes, and a thin frame. Tori looked more like her dad with her dark hair and dark-blue eyes and curvier figure.

"That's not the reason, Mom," she said gently but firmly.

Her mother gave her a somewhat guilty look. "I knew why you were calling, Tori."

"Yes, you did. It's about the seating chart. Why are you giving Scott a hard time?"

"I want to sit with my friends, with people who have known Scott his whole life. Why does it matter?"

"I don't know why exactly. But it matters to Monica's mother, and that means it's important to Monica, and Scott wants his wife to be happy. I would also think you would want your daughter-in-law to be happy. You like Monica, don't you?"

"Of course I do. Her mother is a different story. Just because she belongs to the Olympic Club and has more money than I do, she thinks she's in charge of everything," Pamela added on a cranky note.

"You have to find a way to get along with her, Mom. It's not just the wedding. Scott and Monica will have children, and you'll be sharing those grandchildren with Monica's family, too. Don't put Monica in the position of having to choose between you and her own mother. You're not going to win."

"I know. I know. Do you want something to drink? I made some fresh lemonade after working in the garden all afternoon. It's so nice to see spring arrive after such a rainy winter. The flowers are coming to life."

"Lemonade sounds good."

As they headed down the hall to the kitchen, her mom added, "I was just starting dinner. Do you want to stay and eat with us? Ray went golfing today with Monica's father and uncle, but he should be back soon."

"So Ray is making nice with the soon-to-be in-laws?"

"He was trying to make peace. That's what Ray does," she said with a smile. "I've also got Joanie and Mitch Hedden coming over for dinner, as well as Jim Beacham. He's been a little lonely since his wife Elaine died last year."

She slid onto a stool at the kitchen island as her mother poured her a glass of lemonade. "I haven't seen the Heddens or the Beachams in years." Mitch and Jim had been two of her father's best friends, and the three families had done a lot together when she was a child. "How is Tracy?" she asked, referring to Jim's daughter, who had been a year younger than her.

"She's married with twin babies. Her husband is a computer tech guy and very successful. They just moved into a big house in Hillsborough."

"Nice. I was sorry to hear about Elaine's passing. She was a nice woman."

"She was. You should stay for dinner. I know they'd all love to see you. This is why I've been wanting you to come back for so many years, so we can have impromptu dinners together, and I don't just have to brag about you to my friends, they can actually talk to you themselves. I've missed you, Tori."

"I've missed you, too."

Her mother's gaze narrowed. "What happened to your face? Are those cuts?"

She'd thought she'd covered up her scratches with enough makeup, but apparently not. "I—I got caught up in some thorny roses."

"In the city? I didn't think there was any green around your apartment," her mother said, giving her a suspicious look.

"I walk other places beside around my apartment. Anyway, I can't stay for dinner; I'm meeting someone."

"As in a man? Do you have a date, Tori?"

"It is a man, but it's not a date." She'd successfully distracted her mother from her cuts, but she'd just opened a new line of questioning.

"Well, why not? You're not getting any younger."

"Hey, let's get Scott married, before you start in on me."

"So who is it? Someone from work? Is he handsome?"

"Mom, it's not a potential boyfriend. It's just Dylan."

"Dylan Callaway?" her mother echoed in surprise. "Why are you meeting Dylan? Are you talking about the wedding?"

She grabbed onto the question like a lifeline. "Yes, I wanted to talk to Dylan about…decorating the car Scott and Monica are going to leave in," she said quickly.

"I don't know what car that's going to be. They're heading to the airport straight from the ceremony. Ray might just drop them off."

"Oh, well, I'll talk to Dylan about it."

"Dylan is single, you know."

She saw the gleam in her mom's eyes. "Yes, and he considers me an annoying brat."

"That was when you were kids. He's a good man. Like all those Callaway boys, he lives up to the high example set by his father and uncle and grandfather."

"Do you still see his mom?"

"At least a few times a year. Sharon is still busy working as a nurse, but she comes to our neighborhood Bunco parties. She'll be at the wedding on Saturday along with her husband

Tim."

"It will be nice to see her again. Are any of Dylan's siblings coming?"

"No, Monica's mother limited our guest list, so I could only invite a few of my friends."

"Well, you can't blame her. Weddings are expensive."

"And I am happy to contribute. But she won't take my money," she said with irritation. "By the way, in case you were wondering, Dylan is not bringing a date."

"I wasn't wondering," she said, taking a long draught of lemonade.

Before her mother could press her any further, she heard the sound of the front door opening and people coming down the hall. She got to her feet as her stepfather Ray, as well as Joanie and Mitch Hedden and Jim Beacham, came into the kitchen.

"Look who I found outside," Ray said.

Ray and her mom's friends looked a bit older than when she'd seen them last.

Ray had an olive complexion and dark hair that showed traces of gray, but he'd always been in great shape, and that hadn't changed.

Joanie Hedden was a short, plump blonde with sparkling green eyes. Her husband Mitch was a beanpole, over six foot four, with graying hair and a pair of glasses resting on his long nose.

Jim Beacham was a stocky, former football player, with reddish brown hair and a ruddy complexion.

"Oh, my," Joanie said, her gaze landing on Tori. "Little Tori—I can't believe it. It's been so long, and you're all grown up now."

"It's good to see you all," she said, hugging Joanie and then doing the same with Mitch and Jim, who had been second fathers to her.

"You look just like your dad," Joanie added, turning to her husband. "Doesn't she look like Ben, Mitch?"

"She does," Mitch agreed with a nod, shadows darkening

his eyes.

"Ben should have been here for this weekend," Jim murmured. "He would have liked seeing his son get married." He shook his head, as if he still couldn't comprehend the tragedy that happened so many years ago.

As a pall fell over the kitchen, Ray cleared his throat. "Are you joining us for dinner, Tori?" he asked.

"Unfortunately, I can't."

"She's meeting Dylan," her mother put in.

"Dylan Callaway?" Joanie asked, new interest in her eyes. "Are you and Dylan seeing each other?"

"No, we're just meeting at Brady's to talk about the wedding and some other stuff."

"What other stuff?" her mother asked curiously.

"Nothing important. It was nice to see all of you again. We'll catch up more tomorrow at the wedding." She glanced at her mom. "Remember what we talked about earlier?"

"Yes, I will sit at the head table with Monica's parents," her mom replied with annoyance. "I'll tell Scott tonight."

"Good. I'll see you tomorrow."

"Say hi to Dylan for me. I always liked that boy," her mother said. "I've missed seeing him around the past few years."

"I'll be sure to tell him that."

———

Her mother might still think of Dylan as a boy, but the guy sitting at the bar having a beer was all man.

Tori swallowed hard, pausing by the door as she took a moment to catch her breath and really look at him. She'd been so caught up in the fire and her near escape from death yesterday that she hadn't really taken Dylan in.

But now...

Her heart beat a little faster as her gaze ran across his body. He'd filled out since his late teens and early twenties with broader shoulders, more defined features and muscles that were evident even in jeans and a button-down shirt. His thick, brown hair had always captivated her imagination. She couldn't count the number of times she'd thought about running her fingers through it. His hair was longer now and drifted over his collar, which was even more appealing.

His profile was strong and masculine, and the traces of a beard on his face gave him an even edgier, sexier look. When he turned to look at her with sharp, light-blue eyes blazing against his tan face, her stomach did a somersault, and her palms got sweaty.

She couldn't believe she was reacting so strongly to him. It had been more than a decade since she'd seen him, and it wasn't like they'd ever gone out. He'd been way out of her league when she was thirteen and he was seventeen, but the four-year age difference seemed like nothing now. And while she hadn't known how to make sense of her confusing attraction to him back then, she had a pretty good idea of what she'd like to do with him tonight. There were all kinds of deliciously tingly feelings running around inside her body.

Bad idea, she told herself. *One of her worst ideas ever.*

But she couldn't help but curve her lips in response to the smile on his face. Maybe she'd just let herself enjoy the moment.

Her teenaged self would have killed to be invited to do anything with Dylan. And while she was feeling all kinds of attraction to him, in his mind she'd probably always be Scott's little sister. He'd already scolded her like a big brother for following a stranger into an empty building. She wasn't getting out of the pesky-little-sister-of-his-best-friend zone any time soon.

Forcing herself to move, she joined him at the bar, sliding onto the stool next to him.

"I thought you were going to stand me up," he said. "You're late."

"I was talking to my mother. That always seems to take longer than I think."

"Everything used to take you longer than you thought,"

he said dryly. "Back in high school, Scott and I were always waiting for you when we had to give you a ride somewhere."

She didn't much care for the reminder, and she certainly couldn't tell him that was because she'd spent extra time on her makeup whenever she knew he was going to be around. "That was a long time ago."

"True. You have grown up."

"So have you."

Their gazes clung to each other just a little too long. Dylan suddenly frowned, then straightened and said, "Can I buy you a beer?"

"I'd rather have a glass of Merlot."

"Sure."

As he passed her order onto the bartender, she looked around the restaurant and said, "This place looks better than I remember." Owned by a former firefighter, Brady's had been a popular watering hole for the Callaways. She'd come here a few times for birthday dinners and other celebrations.

"It should look better. It was rebuilt a couple years ago after a fire."

She raised an eyebrow. "A fire in a firefighter's bar?"

"That wasn't a coincidence."

"What happened?"

"It's a long story, but one of the owner's sons had a fascination with starting fires. My cousin Emma was caught up in the middle of it."

"Is Emma also a firefighter?"

"She was, but now she's an investigator."

"Does she work with Gary Kruger?"

"Yes," he said. "Did you speak to Gary?"

"This afternoon. He came by my office, and asked me a lot of questions, but he didn't feel like answering any of mine in return. I'm hoping you have more information?"

"I don't have much, but I can tell you that the fire started in an upstairs apartment—the same apartment where the victim was located," he added.

She thought about that for a second. "Does that mean he

started the fire? But why wouldn't he have set it in such a way that he could get out? And he couldn't have been upstairs more than a few minutes before the explosion. How did he set it off that fast? Do you think he set it up beforehand? But then what was he doing wandering around, watching me?"

Dylan started shaking his head before she got her last few words out. "Damn, you haven't changed a bit, Tori. You can ask more questions without taking a breath than anyone I know."

She frowned. "It's my job to ask questions now. I'm a journalist. I get paid to get answers."

"Well, you certainly found the perfect job for yourself."

"I did. Now, can you answer any of my questions?"

"Let's see. The fire was definitely set deliberately. They found an accelerant and the remnants of a homemade device at the scene. They'll examine the evidence and determine if the fire signature can be tied to any other fires in the city or any known arsonists."

"Is there any information on Neil Hawkins?"

"Not that Kruger was willing to share with me. I barely got the fire information out of him."

"Why wouldn't he talk to you?"

"Because it's his job to investigate fires. Mine is just to put them out. He was very quick to remind me of that," Dylan added, not looking too happy about that.

"So it's a territorial thing."

"Probably. It's also early in the investigation. There's a lot to do."

"I did some research on the Internet. I found three Neil Hawkins in the San Francisco Bay Area. Two were the wrong age, and the third guy was Asian. Do you remember the address on the ID?"

"I'm pretty sure it said San Francisco."

"That's what I thought, too, but I was a little distracted by the guy's face."

"Because you thought he looked like your father."

"Didn't you? You knew my dad."

"A long time ago. I didn't see a resemblance, but to be honest, your dad's face is a little hazy in my mind. He wasn't around that much when I was at your house."

She could understand that. The few years before her dad had died he'd been working a lot, and it was during that time that Dylan and Scott had become good friends. "Do you know if the police have found any relatives to Mr. Hawkins? Has anyone been notified of his death?"

"Kruger told me that the police were working on finding relatives, but no one had been contacted yet." Dylan tilted his head. "Let's get back to you. So you said you followed this man into the building, because you're doing some news story on homeless people. Do you think he knew you were following him?"

"I don't believe so. I first saw him when I was sitting outside of a coffee house a few blocks away. I looked up and caught him staring at me. When he realized I was looking back at him, he took off down the street. I waited a second and then I followed him. He was already around the corner before I started after him, and he was two blocks ahead of me when I saw him enter the building. I went inside just to check things out."

"Do you know how dangerous that was?"

"It was broad daylight."

"And yet you almost got blown up."

"Well, obviously, I didn't think that was going to happen."

"You didn't consider that he wanted you to follow him? Maybe he lured you there."

She thought about that, but it didn't ring true. "I don't believe that's what happened. And I'm still baffled by how he could have set off an explosion that fast."

"He could have set it up earlier."

"I suppose so. Or he surprised the arsonist. Maybe he was squatting in the building. It was a free place to stay until it got torn down, which apparently was going to be soon."

"That makes sense," Dylan agreed.

"See, I can make sense once in a while."

He grinned back at her and that lopsided smile of his made her heart skip a beat. "Apparently so."

"I have to know what happened in that building, Dylan."

"For a news story or because the man looked like your father?"

"For me," she said. "Because I was there. Because I can still feel the blast of that fire, and my hip hurts from where I landed on the sidewalk."

He frowned at that. "You're lucky you weren't hurt worse."

"I know that."

"Look, you may never know what happened, Tori. Do you know how many arson fires are never resolved?"

"I'm guessing a lot."

"Because the evidence is usually destroyed in the fire. We're lucky the investigators found anything they can use as a lead."

"I get it. It's just frustrating."

"It is," he agreed. "So, let's talk about something else. How is your mom? You said you stopped there on the way over here?"

"She's good but stressed about the wedding," she replied, as she sipped her wine. "My mom and Monica's mother are apparently very different people, but they have one thing in common—they both like to be in control. They've had a few bumps. The latest is over the reception hall seating, but I think my mother will give in, and everything should go smoothly. Scott is really worried about making sure this is Monica's perfect day. It's pretty sweet, actually."

"Yeah, he's whipped," Dylan drawled.

"He's in love. There's a difference."

"Is there?" he asked with a laugh.

"Yes. And I've never see him so happy."

"He is pretty damn happy," Dylan agreed, finishing off his beer.

His words made her wonder about Dylan's love life. He

wasn't married or bringing anyone to the wedding, but she knew little else about him. She'd actually made it a point not to ask Scott about Dylan over the years. She hadn't wanted to hear about him and his girlfriends. She'd wanted to keep him out of her head. But now she was curious. She just didn't know how to bring up such a personal question.

Dylan apparently didn't have the same problem.

"You got a boyfriend?" he asked.

"No, not at the moment."

"Really? Is that because you ask too many questions?" he teased.

She made a face at him. "No, it's because I haven't met anyone I wanted to be my boyfriend. And I don't ask that many questions."

"Are you serious, Tori?"

"What? I'm as normally curious as the next person. And if I asked a lot of questions of you and Scott, it's because you would never tell me where you were going or what you were doing."

"Because we didn't want you to ask to come along or know what we were up to."

"I doubt you were doing anything that interesting," she said.

"We probably weren't," Dylan admitted. "We were much more wild and crazy in our heads than we were in real life."

"Except when you were speeding down the Great Highway in some souped-up car you'd just rebuilt. Are you still into the muscle cars?"

"Muscle cars, classic cars…I love them all. I'm working on a Plymouth 1971 Barracuda right now."

"Are you going to race it?"

"Not officially, but I'll definitely take her out on the open road."

"I remember the one race you and Scott took me to up in Sonoma. I couldn't believe how fast you drove."

"That was fun," he said with a nod.

"I really wanted to feel that kind of speed, but, of course, when I said that out loud, you and Scott laughed at me."

"We were jerks, weren't we?"

"A lot of the time." She paused. "I know you like working on the old cars, but why?" It was a question she'd always wanted to ask him.

"See, there's another question."

She laughed at the teasing light in his eyes. "You don't like the question, because you don't want to answer, but I really wish you would. I'm curious."

"I don't have a great answer. I guess I like bringing something old and dead back to life. I see a lot of destruction in my line of work. Restoring old cars feels like something positive." He shrugged. "It's hard to explain."

"Actually, you explained it really well." She was touched that he'd given her a real answer. "But I do know that your love of cars started long before you were a firefighter."

"That's true. I bought my first junk heap of a vehicle because I wanted my own ride, and my parents were not interested in dishing out money for cars. There were too many of us for that. So if I wanted my own wheels, I had to find them. I liked it so much that I helped Hunter and Ian out, so they could get mobile. It became a hobby that I kept up long after I could afford to buy a new car. But now it also provides a nice change of pace from breaking down burning buildings with a sledgehammer and shooting streams of water at a blazing fire."

"I understand. Sometimes it's nice to escape into another world."

"What's your other world?"

"Me? I don't know. I mostly work these days." She finished her wine and then wished she'd taken longer to sip it, because now she should probably go.

"Do you want another drink? How about a burger?" he asked. "I haven't had dinner yet, have you? And Brady's still makes the best bacon cheeseburger you've ever had."

"I've never understood the appeal of bacon on a burger, but I could eat," she said, surprised by the unexpected invitation. In her past experience with Dylan, he was usually ready to get rid of her as fast as possible.

"Let's grab a table."

"Okay." She felt a little flustered, but as she followed him across the room to an empty table, she reminded herself that this was not a date.

Although, it was kind of starting to feel like one.

Four

Tori had changed a lot, Dylan thought. She'd grown out of her braces and glasses and was strikingly pretty with long, thick, brown hair that ran down past her shoulders and big, bright, dark-blue eyes that reminded him of the sea—way, way out from shore, where the colors were the darkest, deepest blue. Her skin, where it hadn't been stung with shards of glass from the explosion yesterday, was creamy and clear, and Tori's lips looked soft and full and very, very kissable.

He mentally put the brakes on that thought. He was *not* going to kiss Scott's sister. That was a crazy idea. He'd never dated the sister of any of his friends. That was just asking for trouble and having grown up with five siblings, three of whom were sisters, he knew enough about women to know who to stay away from.

But they were just having burgers and catching up—no big deal.

After they ordered another round of drinks and two burgers, Tori rested her arms on the table and gave him a long look.

There was something in her direct gaze that made him nervous, which was an odd thing to feel around her. But then she wasn't the quirky little kid who followed him and Scott around anymore. She was a woman—a beautiful woman, and she was smart, too. She was also reckless and impulsive and competitive, he reminded himself, which was why she'd almost gotten herself blown up.

He still didn't really understand her logic, but then she'd never been particularly logical. Tori Hayden ran on emotion. And that was the last thing he ever acted on.

As they stared at each other for far too long, he decided to break the growing tension between them. "So, what's on your mind?"

"Nothing."

"Come on, Tori."

"Well, I have a few questions, but I'm reluctant to ask them now."

"I was just teasing you before. Ask away. What do you want to know?"

"I guess I'm a little curious about you, Dylan."

"Oh, yeah?" He was surprised. He'd thought she'd get right back to questions about the fire. "Curious about what? You already know I'm a firefighter and that I still waste my time fixing old cars."

"What else do you do? Do you have a woman in your life?"

"Not at the moment."

"Interesting," she murmured.

"Is it?" he countered.

"Whatever happened to your high school and college girlfriend—Jenny Meyers? You went out all through college, didn't you?"

"And for a couple of years after that," he admitted, feeling the pain from those dark memories.

"What happened between you?"

"Nothing we need to get into."

He could see she didn't like that vague response, but

thankfully, she moved on. "Well, what about since then? Any other serious relationships?"

"Nope. What about you? You said you don't currently have a boyfriend, but I'm guessing you've broken a few hearts over the years."

"I doubt that. I dated someone for almost two years when I was in New York, but he didn't like my work hours, and when I had a chance to get a better job in Boston, he told me not to go."

"And you love it when people tell you what to do," he said dryly.

"I didn't like his all-or-nothing attitude," she admitted. "I thought he could have supported me in the move. The cities aren't that far apart. We could have done long distance for a while."

"It sounds like you were better off making a clean break."

"Probably. It was freeing not to have to worry about working long hours. I tend to get caught up in whatever story I'm covering. Reporting isn't just a job for me; it's a passion. It's who I am. I want to make a difference—the way my father did. He used to tell me how important it was to have reporters who would fight injustice and be a voice for those who might not be able to speak. That's what I want to do. And sometimes it takes evenings and weekends to do that."

He loved the way her eyes lit up when she spoke about her job. Tori had always been willing to put in more than a hundred percent on anything she was driven to do. "Good for you."

She gave him a somewhat embarrassed smile. "Sorry. I didn't mean to get on a soapbox."

"I like people who care about what they're doing. Work is where you spend a lot of your life; it's great if you can enjoy it."

"I do—mostly. Unfortunately, I've found that sometimes it's not that easy to either get to the truth or have the time to really dig for it. That's one reason I took the job at the

Examiner. They report the daily news, but they also do longer features, and that gives me more time to write a series of articles on one subject, do more in-depth with interviews and opinions."

"And you're focused on the homeless issue."

"Yes. It's a really big problem in this city, Dylan."

"I know. I'm out there every day. It's complex."

"It is. And I didn't mean to imply that you were blind to anything," she said quickly. "What you do is more important than anything I do; you save lives. You run into burning buildings when everyone else is running out." She paused. "How do you do that, Dylan?"

He shrugged, realizing once again that it wasn't just that Tori liked to ask questions; it was that her questions were sometimes too personal. He couldn't just brush her off; she wanted a real answer.

"It's what I'm trained to do," he said.

"But still, you have to have so much courage. Do you love it? I know you followed in your dad's footsteps. Is it what you thought it would be?"

"It's more," he said, considering her question. "I grew up thinking that I would follow in the family tradition, which involves not just my dad, but my uncle, my cousins, and my grandfather. Callaways are born to serve and protect. So I never really thought about doing something else—well, maybe racing cars, but I always knew that was more of a hobby."

"Some people make it a career."

"That wasn't going to be enough for me. Once I became a firefighter, I realized that it wasn't just the tradition that I liked; it was the actual job. It's dangerous and thrilling and the adrenaline rush is addictive, but so is the ability I have to help someone. I like being able to do that. It hurts when I can't."

"Like yesterday," she said quietly.

"One more minute—if I'd had one more minute," he said, his voice trailing away. "But I didn't."

"You tried your best."

"It wasn't good enough."

She stared back at him with a thoughtful gaze.

"What?" he asked.

"I don't think I ever realized you could be so hard on yourself. You were always about fun when you were hanging with Scott at our house."

"I'm still about fun," he said, realizing he'd let her see a side of himself he didn't show very often. "Anyway, that's enough about me."

"What about your siblings? What's everyone up to?"

"Hunter is a firefighter, but he's traveling at the moment. Ian is a scientist. I have no idea what he does, but I'm sure it's going to change the world."

"He always was the smartest kid around. And your sisters?"

"Annie works in advertising and graphic design. She lives in Los Angeles. Kate is an FBI agent."

"No way," Tori interrupted, her eyes widening in surprise. "She's in the FBI?"

"Yes, and kicking ass on a regular basis. She lives in DC with her boyfriend who's an ex-agent turned PI."

"Wow, that's amazing. And Mia?"

"She moved to Angel's Bay and married a guy with a little girl, so she's a stepmother now. She also works at an art gallery in the town."

"I used to love your big family. It seemed like so much fun to have that many siblings around. And then there were all your cousins. Callaway parties were standing room only."

"That's very true. I never knew any different so it all feels normal to me. I actually liked hanging out at your house; it was a lot quieter."

"Except when I was asking you all those irritating questions."

"Even then."

"Really? You're being nicer than I remember."

He laughed at the teasing light in her eyes. He found himself wanting to be nice to her, wanting to be a lot more than just *nice* to her. He couldn't remember when he'd really talked to a woman, not just did the small talk dating kind of conversation but actually spoke about things that mattered. It felt remarkably easy to be with Tori. "I wasn't always nice to you?" he challenged.

"No, you weren't. Although, you were nicer than some of Scott's friends. But you were the big man on campus—the hotshot athlete. All the girls wanted you, so it's not surprising your ego was rather large."

"All the girls wanted me, huh?"

"Well, that's what I heard," she said, a slight flush in her cheeks now. "I was a lot younger, so I didn't know exactly what was going on."

"Your brother was popular, too."

"Oh, I know," she agreed. "Girls used to try to be my friend just so they could come over to the house and flirt with you and Scott."

"Who did that?"

"Too many to name."

"How about one?"

"Melody Price."

"Melody," he murmured, thinking the name was familiar, but he couldn't quite place her.

"Blonde hair, big boobs, skinny legs," Tori said tartly.

"That could describe a lot of girls in high school."

"That's true. You did have a type. Jenny Meyer had the same blonde centerfold look to her."

"Jenny was very attractive."

"She was. I wanted to be just like her. I could see that blondes were having a lot more fun than me, so I actually tried to dye my hair blonde. Unfortunately, it came out orange. I couldn't leave the house for a week. Even my mother agreed that it was too embarrassing for me to go out in public, so she let me stay home sick until we could get a salon to fix it." She paused. "I did some stupid stuff back then."

"That does sound stupid," he agreed.

She rolled her eyes at him. "You didn't always make the best decisions, either, Dylan."

"We don't need to get into my bad decisions." He sat up a little straighter as the waiter set down their burgers. "Saved by the bacon burger."

"For now," Tori said, as she eyed her cheeseburger with avocado and onions. "I don't remember the burgers being this big." She took a bite, then added, "Or this good. It's amazing."

"They got a new chef about a year ago."

"Well, he's great."

"He is."

As they worked their way through their burgers, they chatted a little more about old times and mutual friends. Tori had a great memory—too good at times. She seemed to recall every bad decision made and every stupid thing he'd ever done.

By the end of dinner, he realized she knew a lot more about him than he knew about her, and now he was intrigued to know more. He was sorry when the waiter brought their check, and Tori said it was time to head home.

"I'll walk out with you," he said. "Did you take a cab?"

"No, I drove. It actually felt good to be behind the wheel," she said, as they walked out of Brady's. "I hadn't gotten the car out of the garage in the three weeks I've been here. Not easy to park around where I live, but out here, there's more space." She paused. "Where do you live?"

"In the Marina, near the Presidio and the Golden Gate Bridge. I run there in the mornings."

"That's right. You like to run," she said with a grimace.

"What's wrong with running?"

"It just seems so boring," she said, as they walked down the street. "I like fitness classes better—music, movement, people around."

"Well, you can find plenty of those in the city."

"I can. Now I just have to find the time—what the hell?"

He frowned as she crossed the street, wondering what

had suddenly startled her. When she pulled a piece of paper out from under the windshield wiper of what had to be her car, he saw her face tighten. She looked up at him, then turned her head quickly from one direction to the other, as if someone were watching them.

"What is it?" he asked sharply.

She handed him the piece of paper.

There were only three words on it: *Stop Asking Questions.*

His gut clenched, as his gaze took in the empty street. There wasn't much open this time of night and not a lot of people around.

"What's this about?" he asked.

"I don't know."

"The fire?"

"Or maybe my homeless story. I've been to a lot of homeless camps, to City Hall, to shelters, to groups developing new plans to fix the situation. I've been trying to make sense of what funds are set aside for housing and how they're being used. I've been turning over a lot of stones."

His lips tightened. "So you could have pissed any number of people off."

"Apparently you're not the only one who thinks I ask too many questions," she said, trying to be light and funny but falling significantly short.

"This is a threat, Tori."

"Not much of one. It's just words scribbled on a piece of paper."

He didn't like the way she was downplaying it. "Someone knew this was your car. And how did they know you would be here? Did they follow you? Did you tell someone you were meeting me here?"

"Now you're the one asking too many questions."

"Tori, come on. Who did you tell about our meeting?"

She thought for a moment. "I told my editor I was meeting you to see if you had more information on the fire," she said. "But she likes me to ask questions, and she's not interested in the fire story; she wants me to get back into my research on the homeless article."

"Who else?"

"I mentioned it to my mom and Ray and some of their friends."

"What friends?"

"The Heddens—Joanie and Mitch. You remember them, don't you?"

"Sure. Was anyone else there?"

"Jim Beacham. But I've known the Heddens and Jim since I was a child. Our families have been super close. They wouldn't do this."

"No," he agreed, coming to the only other conclusion. "Then someone followed you."

"They would have had to follow me from my apartment to my mom's house to here. That's a long tail over several hours. And I was at my mom's house for at least a half hour. Why wouldn't they have left me the note then?"

"I don't know, but you need to report this to the police."

"I can, but it's not going to matter, Dylan. It's just words scribbled on a piece of paper. I've been threatened before. I know the drill. The police take a report, and that's it."

"You've been threatened before?"

"It goes with the territory of being an investigative reporter."

He frowned at her answer. "What happened the last time?"

"Nothing. It was just a warning. I'm sure this is, too. But I'm not going to let anyone scare me away from doing my job."

He could hear the determination in her voice and while he was impressed, he also didn't like it.

"If you're thinking about calling Scott, forget it," Tori warned him. "He's getting married on Saturday. I'm not going to ruin that."

He didn't want to stress Scott out, either. "I wasn't planning on calling him. But I do think you should talk to the police. Maybe they can pull security footage from a camera around here." Tori's car was parked in front of a hair salon and a dry cleaner. There was no obvious sign of an exterior camera but there could be one on any of the other buildings on the block.

"I guess I can call them, but I'm telling you, they're not going to do anything."

He suspected she was right. "Okay, hold on," he said, as she took out her phone. "I have a better idea. My cousin Emma's husband Max is a detective with the SFPD. Let's start with him. He can hopefully advise you on the best action."

Tori's eyes lit up. "Emma, the fire investigator? I know she's not assigned to the hotel fire, but if this note has anything to do with the fire—"

"She'll want to know," he finished. "So will Kruger. But let's start with Emma, because I really want to get some perspective on this note." He took out his phone and punched in Emma's number. He thought the warning had more to do with Tori's news story than the fire, but he couldn't be sure. Either way, he wanted to get the police involved. He owed it to Scott to keep an eye on Tori.

He told himself that was why he was getting so involved, but as he looked into Tori's beautiful blue eyes, he knew that wasn't the only reason.

Five

Emma Callaway Harrison had short blonde hair that perfectly framed her face and warm, friendly, blue eyes. Tori had met her a few times in her teenage years, but she doubted they'd ever said more than a few words to each other.

Emma had definitely changed since Tori had seen her last. She was seven or eight months pregnant, for one thing, and married to an attractive, tall, dark-haired man with intelligent green eyes, who gave her hand a firm shake upon introduction.

With Max and Emma was a cute freckle-faced, red-headed child of about seven, who was introduced as Shannon.

"It's so good to see you again, Tori," Emma said.

"It's great to see you, too. And congratulations on motherhood."

Emma patted her round stomach. "I can't imagine that I can get any bigger, and yet I do." She put her arm around Shannon. "But this little girl is a big help and she's going to be an amazing big sister."

"I bet she is," Tori said, giving Shannon a smile.

Emma glanced down at her daughter. "But it's time for you to get ready for bed, honey. Brush your teeth and pick out a book, and Dad or I will be in soon to read to you."

"Okay, night," Shannon said, an Irish lilt to her voice.

"She's adorable," Tori said, as they all walked into the living room. She took a seat on the couch next to Dylan.

"Our little angel," Emma agreed, as she and Max sat down in chairs across from them. "We found her in Ireland with a little help from my grandmother. It's a long story."

"I'd love to hear it sometime."

"And I'd be happy to tell you, but Dylan said this is about the fire at 23rd and Harrelson Street," Emma said. "What's going on?"

"I was in the lobby of the building when it was exploded. I was thrown out of the structure, but the person I had followed into the building died."

Emma's gaze turned sober. "I heard about that. I'm really glad you're all right, Tori."

"Me, too. I spoke to an investigator in your office today, Gary Kruger, and I answered his questions, but he couldn't tell me much. So Dylan and I met up tonight to talk about it at Brady's Bar and Grill. When we got to my car after dinner, there was a note tucked under the windshield wiper." She handed the note to Emma, who read it, then passed it on to Max.

"We thought we should talk to you," Dylan cut in. "Tori doesn't think the police would be that interested in following up on this, but I'm hoping you might tell us differently, Max."

"And you think this is related to the fire investigation?" Max asked.

"It might be," Dylan said.

"Or it might not," she added. "I'm an investigative journalist, and I've been working on other stories that involve city officials, government agencies and homeless shelters. I don't know that I've made any enemies, but apparently my questions in some area of my life have bothered someone. As a reporter, I've been warned off before, but I usually have a better idea of who's upset with me. I have no idea if I've inadvertently stumbled into something and someone thinks I know more than I do, or what."

"Who knew you were going to be at the bar?" Max asked, repeating Dylan's earlier question.

"My editor, my mom, my stepfather, and some family friends; that's it."

"Do you live alone? Did you see anyone when you left your apartment?" Max continued.

"I do live alone, and I didn't notice anyone following me tonight, but..." Her voice trailed away as she thought about the prickly feeling she'd been getting lately.

"But what?" Dylan pressed, his gaze narrowing at her hesitation.

"It's going to sound silly, but since I moved back to the city three weeks ago, I've had a weird feeling that someone is following me or watching me."

"You've only been in town three weeks?" Max asked.

"Yes. I moved back here from Boston. It was time to come home and the right job opened up. It's hard to believe I angered someone so fast that they would leave me a threatening note."

"Can you see if any security cameras in the area around Brady's might have caught whoever left the note?" Dylan asked Max.

Max nodded. "I can look into that tomorrow."

"I'd also like to know more about the man who died in the fire," she put in quickly. "I'm assuming the police are investigating that. I know his name was Neil Hawkins, because Dylan found his ID."

"Why are you so interested in this man?" Emma asked, her gaze speculative.

"Because I thought he was watching me before I followed him to the hotel."

"So that's why you think this warning note could have something to do with the fire," Emma said. "I've got it now.

I'll talk to Gary tomorrow and see what he knows." She looked at her husband. "Would Tony be investigating the fire victim?"

"Probably," Max said. "Tony Phillips is the police liaison with the arson unit. I'll ask him what he knows about the victim."

She was thrilled at how willing Emma and Max were to help. "I really appreciate your help."

"So you both have your assignments," Dylan said lightly. "Sorry to drop all this on you, but I didn't know where else to turn."

"You don't have to be sorry," Emma said, with a wave of her hand. "You're family, Dylan. We help each other out when we can."

"Well, I owe you one," Dylan said. "I'm a little surprised you're still working. Isn't the baby due any minute?"

"Not for seven more weeks," Emma said. "But the finish line is getting closer. I'm both sad and excited about it at the same time. I can't wait to meet my baby, but I've enjoyed being pregnant. It took me a few tries to get here, so I want to savor every minute."

"We should let you go," she said. "I know Shannon is waiting for a story."

"We'll be in touch," Emma promised.

Max walked them to the door. "Be careful, Tori," he said, a serious gleam in his eyes. "I wouldn't dismiss the note too lightly, not until we know more."

His words scared her a little, but she nodded. "I intend to be very careful and very aware of my surroundings."

He smiled. "Good. I'll get back to you tomorrow with hopefully some information."

"Thanks," she said.

"Goodnight, Max," Dylan said.

Then they made their way back to her car, which they'd taken from Brady's.

Dylan had insisted they stick together, and his car had been parked farther away than hers.

"Emma looks happy," she said, as she got behind the wheel.

Dylan fastened his seat belt. "She does. She had a rough few years, although I didn't really know about it at the time. Apparently she had a couple of miscarriages. She was worried about ever having children, and now she will have two."

"And that's probably just the start. You Callaways like to procreate."

"Hard to argue that point. It seems like half my cousins are pregnant or have just had a kid. My family is falling behind, something my mom likes to mention every now and then."

"Mine, too," she said, as she drove down the street. "She keeps asking me where her grandchildren are. I suspect it will get worse now that I'm back in town. But I'm hoping she'll keep the pressure on Scott. He's the oldest, and now that he is getting married, he should also go first in the grandchildren department. By the way, I didn't want to tell my mom why I was meeting you, so I said we were going to talk about decorating Scott's car for after the wedding."

"He told me the limo is taking him and Monica straight to the airport and then they're off to Hawaii."

"Oh, well, that's fine. I didn't really want to decorate the car anyway."

"So you didn't tell your mother about the fire?"

"No, I didn't." She sent him a pointed warning look. "And you're not going to do that, either."

"She didn't ask you about the cuts on your face?"

"Apparently I didn't cover them up as well as I thought. I told her I got caught up in a rosebush."

"And she believed that?"

"I changed the subject fairly quickly. Anyway, I just want to make sure we keep all this away from my family and the wedding."

"I understand."

"Good. This weekend has to be perfect for Scott."

"I don't know if weddings are ever perfect, but I'm sure it will be great."

"Have you written your toast yet? I assume as the best man you're going to make one."

"I'm working on it. I'm surprised you're not a bridesmaid." He sent her a questioning look.

"I don't know Monica that well, and she has a lot of friends. I'm not at all offended. In truth, it's been easier not to be in the wedding party. Do you know any of the bridesmaids?"

"I've met a couple of them. The maid of honor is a crazy party girl."

"Really? Monica doesn't seem like that."

"No, but this friend of hers from high school is. She tried to make out with me at the engagement party."

She laughed at the annoyance in his voice. "And you said no? That doesn't sound like the Dylan I remember."

"The Dylan you remember was seventeen."

"And loved making out in the school hallway, or at the football game, or in his car."

"Scott told you that?"

"Seriously? No. I saw you, Dylan. You weren't exactly in hiding. I once saw you make out in a booth at Bob's Burgers for like ten minutes. I thought you were going to suffocate."

He grinned. "High school was fun."

Her high school experience had been a lot different than Dylan's. "For you, maybe. I was awkward and never seemed to wear the right clothes or say the right thing. It was not my favorite time."

"Well, you don't seem awkward now, and I like your look."

Her nerves jangled—not just at his words, but at the look in his eyes when she glanced over at him. She would have killed for an appreciative look like that from him ten years ago. But now—now she had to stay focused, not let herself get caught up in his charm.

He was being nice to her, but that was because he had a

protective streak a mile long, and he probably felt he owed it to Scott to watch out for her. She couldn't let herself think it was anything more than that.

She turned the corner where Brady's was located and said, "Which car is yours?"

"The Mustang at the end of the road."

As she pulled up alongside the blue Mustang, she smiled. "I should have figured. You've always had a Mustang."

"It is one of my favorite cars," he admitted. "Although, I had a better one until my brother Ian crashed it in the woods outside of Lake Tahoe."

"I hope he wasn't hurt."

"No, he was fine. My car was totaled. I couldn't salvage much more than a few parts."

"I'm surprised Ian was driving your car."

"I thought he needed to have a fun ride for a change. He's back to his usual boring sedan now, kind of like this car."

"Hey," she protested, loving her hybrid silver Prius. "I love this car, and it's small enough to fit into most parking spaces in the city."

"It does fit you," he said. "So, I'm going to follow you back to your apartment."

"You don't have to do that."

"Well, I'm going to, so don't try to ditch me."

"It's miles from here and not close to where you live."

"It's fifteen minutes out of my way. I want to make sure you get home safely. Don't argue. It's just going to waste time."

The stubborn look on his face was one she was very familiar with. "All right. Thanks—for everything."

"You're welcome."

As she drove back to her apartment, it was actually somewhat reassuring to see Dylan's lights in her rearview mirror. She was trying not to read too much into the threatening note she'd received, but she had to admit she was a little rattled by the warning. And she was beginning to think the prickly feeling she got every time she left her apartment or work was not just paranoia.

But why would anyone be following her? Warning her? She hadn't discovered anything earth-shattering—at least, she didn't think she had. *Was the warning tied to the fire, to the man—Neil Hawkins? Or was it about her news article? Were they in some way connected?*

She groaned in frustration. Dylan was right. She asked too many questions—even of herself.

A short time later, she pulled up in front of the entrance to her garage. Dylan drove up alongside her, and she rolled down the window. "This is me."

"I'm going to park, and then I'll meet you in the lobby. I want to check out your apartment."

"Dylan, you're taking this too far," she protested.

"I'll just take a quick look around, make sure you're locked in, and then I'll go."

Since he was already pulling away, she drove into her garage, parked in her spot and took the stairs up to the first floor. She let Dylan in, and he followed her up to her apartment.

"It's not decorated yet," she said, letting him inside. "I've been so busy since I moved here, I haven't had time to hang pictures or finish buying furniture."

"I can see that," he said, wandering around the very small living room, which only boasted a couch, a coffee table, and a TV. A small dining table with two chairs was by the tiny galley kitchen, in front of the windows that looked over the street.

As Dylan wandered into the bedroom and bathroom, she moved over to the window. The street was quiet. No cars, no lights, no one walking.

Dylan came back into the living room as she turned around. "All clear," he said.

"I thought it would be, but I appreciate you coming inside to check."

"It's not a problem." He tipped his head toward the window. "Anyone out there?"

"No. I'll be fine, Dylan."

His gaze still held concern and some doubt. "I hate leaving you alone."

"I have a deadbolt on the door, and there's a security door on the first floor."

"People get buzzed in through security doors all the time," he said.

"Well, there are only six units in this building, so it doesn't happen very often here."

Dylan's gaze moved to the wall behind her. "No way," he said, walking over to the cello leaning against the wall. "You still play this thing? It used to be as big as you were."

"I surpassed its height awhile ago. And I do still play. It's relaxing."

"I remember all the times Scott and I had to pick you up from your lessons. I couldn't understand why you didn't play something else, like a flute or a clarinet or a guitar."

"Because I like the cello."

"Why?"

"I don't know," she said vaguely.

"That's not good enough. You asked me why I like to restore cars. What was it about the cello that calls to you?"

She glanced over at her instrument and thought of how she could explain it to him. "The cello lives in the richest and warmest part of music. It's full and vibrant, and there's so much range. You can get a majestic booming bass or a melodious sweet tone. And it's a very physical instrument to play. It takes the perfect balance of movement and posture to play well, and I feel like the cello takes my whole body into the music—if that makes sense." His smile made her realize that she'd probably over-answered that question. "You asked," she reminded him.

"I did. It seems that we both have hobbies we love. Play something for me."

"I don't think so."

"Why not?"

"Well, I think you and Scott used to say my playing

sounded like a screeching parrot begging for its freedom."

"I did not say that," he denied.

"Maybe it was Scott."

"I'm sure it was Scott. Come on. I took you to Emma's. I followed you home. I made sure your apartment was safe. You owe me."

"And you want a cello solo as payback?" She couldn't keep the surprise out of her voice.

He grinned. "Maybe I want to see if you're better than a screeching bird."

"I'm actually very good."

"Then impress me."

"You're serious?"

"And you're stalling." He pulled out a chair at the table and sat down. "Show me what you got, Tori."

"Fine." She took her cello out of its case and sat down in the other chair.

While it felt weird at first to be playing for Dylan, she soon got caught up in the music the way she always did. Music had gotten her through all the hard times in her life, and even now it was starting to release the stress of the past few days.

She probably played far longer than Dylan had imagined she would, and she gave him an apologetic smile when she finally stopped. "Sorry, I lose track of time when I play. What did you think?"

He gazed back at her with his magnetic blue eyes, and she swallowed a knot of emotion. It suddenly became very important to hear his opinion.

"You're not just good; you're amazing, Tori. I guess all those lessons were worth it."

"Thanks."

"Why aren't you playing with an orchestra?"

"Oh, that was a dream a long time ago, but as I got older, I realized that I probably wasn't good enough to make a living, and in truth it was really just something I wanted to do for me. News was what I wanted to work at."

"Was that choice for you or for your father?"

"He was part of it," she admitted.

"Does doing his job make you feel closer to him?"

"Yes. He was always so happy to share his job with me, his thirst for knowledge and truth. When I think of him, those conversations are big in my mind."

"When I think about your dad, I remember him with that black suitcase with the pink ribbons. He always seemed to be on his way somewhere or coming back from somewhere."

"I tied those ribbons on his suitcase. He didn't like the pink, but I did. I said he'd never have to guess which bag was his. He laughed and said he'd never take them off. And he never did." She shook her head. "Funny, the things we remember."

"It is," he agreed, gazing into her eyes. "Memories are tricky things, though. Seeing you now, hearing you talk about the past, makes me realize that what I remember isn't exactly what you remember."

She was confused by his words and even more unsettled by the intensity of his blue gaze. "What do you mean?"

"It doesn't matter." He got to his feet. "I should go."

"Okay," she said, setting her cello aside so she could stand up. "I'll see you tomorrow at the rehearsal dinner. Unless you're working?"

"No, I'll be there."

"Great. If you hear anything from Emma or Max before then—"

"I'll let you know." He walked to the door, then paused. "Call me if you have any problems here."

"I will, but I'm sure I won't."

"I hope not. Good-night, Tori."

"Night," she muttered, closing and locking the door after him.

As his footsteps went down the hall, she let out a breath, not honestly sure which had shaken her up more: the disturbing note, or that she'd spent the evening with Dylan.

But she couldn't let herself think that he was doing

anything more than watching out for her. She couldn't let her old fantasies come back to life now. Just because he was charming and funny and he'd loved hearing her play the cello didn't mean that they were going to be anything more than friends. And even if he wanted more—he had potential heartbreak written all over him. She might be fearless when it came to getting the truth, but with her heart she was a lot more careful.

Six

She was his best friend's sister. She was pushy and annoying. She played the cello, of all things.

Dylan mentally recounted all the reasons he should not be interested in Tori as he made his usual run through the Presidio toward the Golden Gate Bridge Friday afternoon, but nothing was quite sticking. She'd spent a lot of time in his dreams the night before and that had surprised him.

He'd never noticed her when they were teenagers, or if he had noticed her, it hadn't been in a good way. She'd usually just been interrupting whatever fun he was having with Scott. Or they'd had to stop whatever they were doing to go pick her up from somewhere. He'd thought of her as an annoying girl, who asked way too many questions and looked at him with intense blue eyes that always made him feel like he wasn't doing enough with his life, which had probably been true at that point.

After high school graduation, he and Scott had gone to the same college for the first two years, and then Scott had transferred to UCLA. While they'd stayed friends after that, they hadn't been nearly as close as they'd once been, and Tori certainly hadn't been in his life much after that. He vaguely remembered her graduating from high school and going to a family party, but that was pretty much it.

He hadn't thought about her at all in the last several years. He couldn't even remember Scott talking much about her, maybe the occasional mention of her job or where she was living, but nothing that had lingered in his head.

Now she was invading his every thought. And she wasn't a shadow of a girl he barely remembered; she was a vibrant, beautiful, smart woman, who still had one thing in common with her younger self—she was a magnet for trouble. If he wasn't careful, he was going to be in that trouble right along with her. In fact, he was probably already there.

Getting Emma and Max involved had put him right in the middle of the action. But he couldn't take it back, and he knew it had been the right thing to do. Tori had been threatened. However much she wanted to downplay the note, she'd been shaken up by it, and he couldn't blame her. He didn't like the thought of someone following her around the city, finding her car, and leaving a warning. If Tori continued asking questions, and he suspected she would do just that, what would happen next? He didn't want to find out.

Picking up his pace, he sprinted to the bottom of the Golden Gate Bridge. Once there, he slowed down to a walk, giving himself a minute to enjoy the view of the bay, the sailboats on the water, and the majestic bridge. He loved San Francisco. It was his town—the city he protected every day of his life.

That thought took him back to Wednesday's hotel fire. It wasn't the first or last suspicious fire he would fight, but because of Tori, it felt more personal. It also bothered him that he hadn't been able to save the man inside, no matter who he was or what he was doing in the building. Getting there a second too late always haunted him.

Turning his back on the beautiful view, he ran back to his apartment. He needed to shower and get dressed for Scott's wedding rehearsal.

Once he'd gotten ready, he pulled out his phone and called Tori.

"Hello," she said, a somewhat breathless note in her voice.

"It's Dylan. How's it going?"

"Good."

"You sound like you've been running."

"I just got home from work. Do you have any news?"

"No. I haven't heard from Emma or Max."

"That's disappointing. I would have thought we'd hear from them before now. I hate waiting for answers."

He smiled to himself, knowing patience was not her strong suit—or his. "I'm not a big fan of waiting, either. But I'm sure they'll call when they know something. How are you getting to the rehearsal?"

"Driving."

"Why don't I pick you up?"

"I can drive to the church and my mother's house on my own, Dylan."

"I know you can, but why not go together?"

She hesitated, then said, "All right. But I need to leave here in about fifteen minutes."

"I'll head over there now."

"Text me when you get here, and I'll come down."

"See you soon."

He ended the call, grabbed his keys and left his apartment. There was a fair amount of traffic on the way to Tori's house, so it took him about twenty minutes to get there. She came down as soon as he texted, giving him a look of irritation as she got into the car.

"Now who's late?" she muttered.

"Friday afternoon traffic," he said. "We'll still get to the church on time, and it's not like we're the key players."

"You're somewhat important. You are the best man."

"I don't think it's going to take much practice to stand next to Scott and hand him the ring when requested."

"Me, either. I don't know why anyone has to rehearse, but apparently it's a tradition."

As she crossed her legs, he couldn't help but appreciate the beautiful silky skin of her bare legs under a floral dress. She looked pretty, and she smelled like a garden. All of his senses were on high alert, and he had to force himself to focus on the road and not on her.

"Have you talked to Scott today?" he asked. "I left him a message earlier asking him if he needed anything, but he didn't get back to me."

"I spoke to him this morning. He's stressed. Not just with the wedding; he has some project to finish before he leaves tomorrow on his honeymoon."

"Scott never likes to leave loose ends."

"No, he doesn't. Nor does he like to delegate and lose any kind of control. I think he was always like that, but it got worse after my dad died. He didn't want any more surprises— good or bad."

"Is that the way you felt, too?" he asked curiously. "Like you needed to control everything?"

"Not in the same way Scott did. I was more about wanting to right wrongs, fight injustice, which a shrink would probably say had something to do with how unfair it was for me to lose my dad at such a young age."

"That would make sense."

"Scott and I were both impacted by the tragedy in a big way, but I know I can't use it to blame all my bad faults on," she said, giving him a small smile.

He found himself smiling back, liking the way she thought, and how candid and self-aware she was. "Most people would use it."

"Well, I'm not most people."

He certainly couldn't argue with that. Their conversation was interrupted by the ring of his phone, which was lying on the console. He pressed the speaker to answer. "Emma?"

"Hi, Dylan."

"Do you have some information? I'm in the car with

Tori."

"Great. I'm glad I can talk to both of you at once," she replied. "Hi, Tori."

"Hi, Emma," Tori said. "Do you know who put the note on my car?"

"No, unfortunately, Max hasn't been able to locate any security cameras with footage of that area. I'm sorry. But I do have some other news."

"What is it?" he asked, his nerves tightening.

"I was in Gary's office when he got a call from the coroner's office. They ID'd the victim of the fire. It wasn't Neil Hawkins."

"What?" he asked in surprise, glancing over at Tori and seeing the same shocked look in her eyes. "Are you sure?"

"Yes. The man's name is Robert Walker. He's a forty-three-year-old resident of Oakland. He has a long record of assault, burglary, and other miscellaneous offenses. He's basically been in and out of jail most of his life."

"What about arson?"

"He was never charged with that, but it's possible he's done it before. Or it's possible he wasn't the fire starter. Gary spoke to his sister, and she said he's been out of touch with the family for years, that he was bad news, and she didn't know what he was up to or why he would have been in that building." Emma cleared her throat. "But that's not even the most interesting part of this story."

"Go on," he said impatiently.

"Robert Walker did not die from smoke inhalation or burns; he was shot in the chest."

Dylan's pulse leapt. He pulled off to the side of the road, feeling like this conversation needed his full attention. "Are you sure?"

"Yes, Max just confirmed it for me. Walker was shot from a few feet away. The police are now investigating his death as a homicide. It's possible the fire was set to cover up the murder."

"I heard a big bang," Tori muttered. "Right before the

second explosion. So the man I followed into the building...Neil Hawkins. Was he the shooter?"

Dylan didn't like that idea. *To think that Tori had been following a man with a gun, a man willing to commit murder...and apparently that man was still free...*

"Max is looking into Neil Hawkins as a person of interest," Emma replied. "Is it possible this man knew you were following him, Tori? Could he have put the note on your car?"

"I guess he could have. I've been thinking he was dead this whole time."

"You need to be careful," Emma said. "And look, guys, Gary wasn't thrilled with me getting into the middle of his investigation, so I don't know how much more I can do for you. He's very territorial, and he has a chip on his shoulder, because he thinks I get benefits from my Callaway name."

"I understand," he said. He'd had similar problems over the course of his career.

"But I'll still keep my ears open and let you know if I hear anything. And, of course, Max will be in the know, so if there's any information I can give you, I certainly will."

"Thanks, Emma," he said. "We'll talk soon." He looked over at Tori. She'd paled in the past few minutes.

"I can't believe the man I saw wasn't the victim," she said, giving him a confused look.

"He must have run out the back door. That's where I found his ID."

"So who started the fire? Walker or Hawkins?"

"Hell if I know, but Robert Walker didn't shoot himself, so it's likely Neil Hawkins was the shooter."

"Unless there were other people in the building. We don't really know who was upstairs or how many people got out," she said.

"No, but I'm guessing there weren't more than a couple of people at the most." He glanced over his shoulder and pulled back into traffic. He wanted to do nothing more than hash everything out with Tori, but they had a rehearsal to get to. "I wonder if the warning note on your car did come from Hawkins," he said.

"But Brady's was miles away from the scene, and that guy didn't even look like he had a car. He really seemed like someone who lived on the streets."

"Or that's what he wanted to seem like. You said the guy was watching you. Maybe he was watching you for longer than you thought. He might have known where you lived."

"That would explain the weird sensation I had when I left my apartment. But why? I'm just at the beginning of my news story. I've asked some pointed questions, but no one has reacted in any kind of extreme way. I just don't know what I could have done to worry someone so much that they would follow me around."

"That's what we have to figure out."

"We? I don't want to put you in danger, Dylan."

"I can take care of myself."

"Well, you don't have to take care of me, too. I can handle this."

Maybe she could, but he wasn't going to just walk away. "Two heads are better than one. Let's work the problem together and see where we end up."

"I suppose," she said slowly.

"We need to find Neil Hawkins."

"Yes," she agreed. "He's the key to this. If he's not dead, then he can be found. I need to see him. I need to look into his face."

"So you can see if he still resembles your father?" he asked, meeting her gaze. "You've told me that you have doubts about that now, but it still lingers in your head, doesn't it?"

"It does," she admitted. "It's probably because I never saw my dad after he died. One minute he was in my life, and then he was gone."

"It was a boating accident, wasn't it?"

"Yes. He was deep-sea fishing in the Caribbean with Mitch and Jim—his two best friends. It was one of their favorite things to do. They ran into a big storm. Their boat was crushed with waves of water. Somehow my dad got trapped down below, and he drowned before they could get him out. After all the dangerous things he'd done in his life— he'd covered wars and interviewed gang members—he dies on a weekend with his friends. My mom used to tell us we should be happy that he died doing something he loved. But I just kept thinking he shouldn't have died at all. They should have checked the weather. They should have been better prepared." She sighed. "But, of course, none of that happened, and he was gone."

"I can't imagine what you went through, Tori." His thoughts moved back in time. "I remember being at the funeral, feeling terrible for your family, especially you and Scott. I certainly saw how difficult it was for Scott to keep going. He was like a stone statue for months, but then he started to get better. Life felt like it went back to normal."

"It did for everyone else. You can't know how it feels unless you live it, and I'm glad you've never had to live it, because it's awful."

"I feel bad now that I didn't offer more support."

"You were a teenage boy, and I know Scott didn't like to talk about it."

"He didn't say much," he agreed.

"This weekend is going to be difficult for my brother. There are events in our lives where we both really miss our father, and I think this wedding will make us feel his absence even more."

"I wish things were different, Tori."

"So do I. Unfortunately, wishing doesn't get you anywhere." She smiled. "That's actually something my dad used to say. He always told me to put my dreams into action if I wanted to see them come true."

He was beginning to realize where some of Tori's determined drive came from. He turned in to the church parking lot where the rehearsal would be held and saw some friends getting out of their cars. "Looks like we're not the last ones here."

"Thank goodness. My mom hates when I'm late." She paused. "Don't say anything about any of this, okay, Dylan? As soon as we get out of this car, it's all about the wedding. I don't want to take anyone's attention away from Scott and Monica. This is their weekend."

"I won't say a word."

———

Tori sat at the back of the church, watching her brother and Monica and their wedding party rehearse the ceremony.

Scott and Monica were certainly an attractive couple. Scott had brown hair and light-brown eyes like their mother. He was extremely fit, working out every day. He was very disciplined about everything in his life, and he was always dressed impeccably well.

Monica was a good match for him with her cool blonde looks and slim figure. She was also into healthy pursuits— Yoga, Pilates, meditation—and she kept busy with her work at a non-profit foundation. She was a bit reserved, but then Scott could be quiet, too.

She wondered if they'd have children. She thought so, hoped so…it would be fun to have nieces and nephews.

Watching her brother hold Monica's hands and smile down at her with love and tenderness throughout their faux wedding ceremony made her heart swell with happiness. While Dylan might not have witnessed the true depth of her brother's despair after losing their father, she'd had a front row seat. Scott had tried to keep her away from his bad moments, disappearing into his room for hours at a time, but she hadn't been fooled, and now seeing his renewed joy in life, she thought he was definitely starting a new chapter.

As her gaze moved away from her brother and Monica, it landed on Dylan. Dylan had cleaned up nicely for this rehearsal, wearing black slacks and a light-blue dress shirt that reflected the color of his eyes. His face was cleanly shaven, his brown hair styled. Dylan had always had a rougher edge and a bigger personality than Scott, but they were both good guys.

It was impressive that they'd stayed friends all these years. She hadn't kept in touch with any of her high school friends, and most of her college friends were back East since she'd gone to school at NYU.

But not only did Scott have Dylan in his group of ushers, he had also asked Paul Hastings, another high school friend, and David Connors, who had been his college roommate for two years, to be in the wedding party. They were a good-looking group, and she saw some of the bridesmaids eying their matching usher with some interest, including Monica's maid of honor, Ava, who was now walking down the aisle with Dylan. She was quite animated and laughing at whatever Dylan was saying.

Dylan wasn't that funny, she thought with a frown. But it wasn't unusual to see a woman flirting with him the way Ava was. Tori had spent most of middle school and high school watching girls flirt with Scott and Dylan.

She wondered again why Dylan was still single. Why hadn't one of the no doubt hundreds of women he'd gone out with stuck? And what had gone down between him and Jenny—something so bad he didn't want to talk about it? Scott had never mentioned anything, but then Scott and Dylan seemed very capable of keeping each other's confidence. She'd have to find out on her own. Not that she should care at all. In fact, she had a lot more important things to focus on.

As the party made their way down the aisle, she got up from her seat and followed them outside. Her mother was just finishing up a conversation with Monica's mother and thankfully no one seemed to be upset. When Monica's mother walked away, she went over to join her mom. "So far so good," she said.

Her mother smiled. "Yes. I can't believe the day is almost here. It seems like yesterday Scott was just my very small boy."

"Hey, you can't cry yet," she said with a laugh, seeing the teary moisture in her mother's eyes. "Save something for tomorrow."

"I'll try." She put her arm around Tori's shoulders. "I'm so glad you're here. I just wish your father was here as well."

Her mom didn't mention her dad very often. In fact, Tori couldn't remember the last time Ben Hayden's name had come up. She didn't know if her mother refrained out of respect to her second husband Ray, or if it had just been so long since his death that he wasn't on her mind anymore. Hearing her mother say something now made her feel a rush of pain that the family she'd once had no longer existed. But she couldn't let emotion bring down the joy of the weekend.

"I feel the same way," she said. "I'm sure he's here in spirit."

"We used to talk about watching you and Scott get married, playing with our grandchildren, growing old together. That's when your dad said he was going to slow down." She laughed a little at that thought. "I didn't really believe it. He always went at a hundred miles an hour. He had so much he wanted to do. Maybe he instinctively knew he didn't have that much time." Her mother shook her head. "I don't know why I'm saying all this now. Pay no attention to me."

"It's fine. You can always talk to me about Dad."

"Well, right now, I need to find Ray and get to the house so we can make sure the caterers have all the food out when everyone gets there."

"I'll be right behind you," she said, as her mom went to join her husband.

She looked around for Dylan and saw him standing with Ava, Monica and Scott.

Seeing Dylan and Scott with two pretty women reminded her of the past when she'd been the fifth wheel. Ava wouldn't appreciate her interruption. She was definitely trying to let Dylan know she was interested, but too bad. It had been Dylan's idea for them to go together. If she got in the way of them hooking up, so be it.

She walked over to the group and mischievously put her hand on Dylan's arm the way Ava had done earlier, making it seem like they were a little friendlier than they were. "Are you ready to go, Dylan?" she asked.

"Did you two come together?" Scott asked in surprise.

"Yes, Dylan was nice enough to offer me a ride," she replied. "We should all get to the house. Mom has a great dinner waiting."

"Let's go," Dylan said. "We'll see you all there."

"Well, you have a fan," she said, as they headed toward his car.

"Ava?" he asked.

"She's just your type—blonde, big boobs, skinny legs."

He opened her car door. "I don't just date blondes. But even if I did, what's it to you?"

"Nothing. Just making a comment," she said, as he got into the car.

"You sound jealous."

"Don't be ridiculous."

He gave her a questioning look that she'd never seen on his face before. "Is it ridiculous?" he asked.

Her heart skipped a beat. "Of course," she said, stumbling over the words. "You're Scott's friend."

"And you're Scott's little sister," he muttered.

"Always have been," she said, not sure what he meant.

"Maybe I'll get Ava's number."

"You should," she said in annoyance.

She folded her arms in front of her chest as he drove out of the lot, wondering why clarifying where they stood with each other didn't feel better.

Seven

—➤➤◄◄◄—

Ava was the most shallow woman he'd ever met. Dylan tried to look politely interested as she droned on and on about her Mexico trip, but long before she was done, he was more than ready to find another conversation. Unfortunately, Ava had attached herself to him as soon as he'd entered Scott's house, and the one person who could have run interference seemed content to stay on the other side of the room.

Tori had ditched him the second he entered the house, ostensibly to help her mom, but since then he'd seen her talking to just about everyone but him. Now she was talking to his friend, Paul Hastings.

Frowning, he thought if he couldn't date Scott's little sister, then Paul sure as hell couldn't, either. Plus, Paul changed women as often as he changed clothes. He had no interest in being anyone's boyfriend.

Maybe he should warn Tori.

But it wasn't his business. And she wouldn't appreciate his insight. She'd probably tell him to take his advice and shove it. He smiled at that, thinking that she was even prettier when she got a fire in her eyes. That seemed to happen a lot when they were together.

"Isn't that funny?" Ava said, obviously interpreting his smile as interest in her story.

"Definitely," he replied, having no idea of what she'd said. "I'll catch up with you later. I need to talk to Paul."

"Can I come?" she asked with a flirty smile.

"We need to talk about groomsmen stuff."

Disappointment colored her expression. "Fine, but don't take too long."

He walked over to Paul and Tori, who were laughing at something together. It was both nice and irritating to see Tori having a good time. She'd been scared and stressed since the fire, but now she was much more relaxed. That was a positive thing. He was just irritated that Paul had been the one to ease her tension.

"What's so funny?" he asked.

"Paul was just telling me about his skydiving trip, how he was so worried about making sure his chute was on that he forgot to zip up his pants and when he jumped out of the plane, his pants dropped down to his thighs, and those still in the plane got a nice view of his ass."

Paul definitely had a good game, managing to make himself look like a superhero and a self-deprecating charmer at the same time. Dylan would have appreciated the play more if Tori hadn't been the target.

"That story gets better every time you tell it," he told Paul.

Paul gave him a shrug and a laugh. "What can I say? I always remember new details. Can you believe little Tori is all grown up? It has been a long time since we all hung out together."

"Like you guys ever let me hang out with you," Tori said. "At best, you both tolerated me being in the same room, but that was about it."

"Were we that bad?" Paul asked.

"Yes," she said. "But I understand it better now. The age

difference was bigger in your minds than in mine. I thought I should be doing everything you were doing."

"Trust me, you were better off being left behind," he said.

"Dylan is right," Paul agreed. "We made some bonehead moves back then."

"But you guys were always entertaining," Tori said. "I was a little sad when everyone went off to college. It was a lot more boring in this house when you were all gone."

"Hey, what's going on?" Scott interrupted, looking more at ease now that he had the rehearsal behind him.

"Just catching up with your little sis," Paul said. "I'm going to get another drink. Can I get you something, Tori?"

She held up her half-full glass of red wine. "I'm good. Thanks."

"Me, too," he said at Paul's questioning look.

As Paul left, Scott said, "So do I want to know what's going on with that fire you were involved in, Tori?"

"You really don't," Tori replied. "You're getting married tomorrow, Scott. Concentrate on that."

"I am concentrating on that, but I still need to know if you're in any kind of trouble."

"I'm not," she said firmly.

Scott looked from Tori to him. "Is she telling me the truth, Dylan?"

"Why are you asking him?" Tori put in with annoyance. "If I say it's the truth, it's the truth."

"You would lie to protect me," Scott retorted.

"Well, you would do the same," she countered. "And it's not your job to protect me."

"It was."

"Well, I'm not twelve anymore, so consider yourself fired."

Scott frowned. "You can't fire me. I'm your brother. Don't be so annoying."

"Don't be so big brotherly."

"Dylan—can you help me out here?" Scott asked.

He smiled. "Tori is very capable of taking care of herself." He didn't want to lie to one of his best friends about the potential seriousness of the situation Tori was in, but he also wanted to keep Scott's attention on the wedding and not on a situation he could do nothing about.

"That's not exactly the answer I was looking for," Scott grumbled.

"You don't have to worry. I'm keeping an eye on her," he said.

"Oh my God," Tori said, storm clouds gathering in her dark-blue eyes. "Stop it, both of you. I've been looking out for myself the past ten years. Get over yourselves. I don't need either one of you to keep an eye on me. I'm going to find Mom and see if she needs any help."

Dylan saw the warning light in Tori's eyes as she gave him a pointed glance on her way out of the room.

Scott must have seen it, too, because he said, "Okay, seriously, what's going on, Dylan? And don't tell me not to worry about her. I know how she is. She's impulsive and reckless and she doesn't always think before she jumps."

"That's true, but she's also smart, independent, and stubborn as hell."

Scott's brows drew together. "Since when have you gotten to know her so well?"

"Since we reconnected at the fire. I've kept her abreast of the investigation."

"So it was arson? What about the man she followed into the building?"

"It looks like he escaped the fire as well."

"But I thought someone died."

"It wasn't him."

"That doesn't make me feel better. Has she seen him again?"

"No."

"I don't like this, Dylan. I don't know what she was thinking, going into an abandoned building after some stranger."

"She's a reporter and, as she's mentioned a number of times, she's grown up, and she can handle her own life."

"I know she's good at what she does. But, like my dad, she can get tunnel vision on something, and she doesn't see what's around her—including danger signs."

"Did your father get into dangerous situations?" he asked, curious to know more about the man who seemed to keep coming up in conversation.

"Yes. He had some really scary moments in his reporting days. He didn't like to back down, not when he thought that there was an important story to tell. He took reporting to an extremely high level, and I see Tori doing the same thing. I understand her drive to be good, to live up to Dad's reputation, but I hate that she takes risks the way she does. I don't want anything to happen to her."

"Your dad didn't die on the job," he couldn't help pointing out. "It was a weekend fishing trip."

Scott sighed. "I know, and Tori reminds me of that all the time. But sometimes I wonder..."

"About what?"

"If my father was so overworked and stressed out that he didn't put enough planning into that trip. If he drank too much or made bad decisions because he was exhausted. I know he wasn't sleeping much the week before that getaway boating trip. It was one of the reasons why my mom encouraged him to go. She thought he needed a break from work. Relaxing was not an easy thing for him to do."

"Did his friends tell you that he made bad decisions? They were with him, weren't they?"

"Yes. Mitch told me that my father was drinking a lot that day—more than usual. He'd gone down below decks to take a nap. A storm came up suddenly, and they were caught unawares. My dad got trapped below deck." Scott ran a hand through his hair. "Damn, I don't want to be thinking about that now."

"Then don't. I'm sorry I brought it up. This is your wedding weekend, Scott. The only thing on your mind should be getting married and having honeymoon sex with your new wife."

His words brought the smile back to Scott's face.

"Trust you to help me get my priorities straight," Scott said. "In all seriousness, Dylan, I know I'm getting married tomorrow, but I can still deal with a problem if there is one. You need to be honest with me."

Tori would rip his heart out if he said anything about the threatening note, but he was torn; this was Scott he was talking to, and they'd always been straight with each other. He needed to find a way to satisfy his loyalty to both of them.

"I'll tell you this," he said. "I'm keeping an eye on Tori, and I intend to keep doing that as long as it's necessary."

"So there is something going on?"

"Nothing specific. I just want to reassure you that I've got this. You can count on me."

"All right. Thanks. That makes me feel better." Despite his words, Scott suddenly frowned.

Dylan followed Scott's gaze. Paul had his arm around Tori's shoulder and was whispering something into her ear.

He found himself frowning, too.

"Is Paul hitting on Tori?" Scott asked.

"I'd say that's a yes," he said in clipped tones.

"Can you break that up?"

"I'd be happy to," he said, the smile returning to his face. "Anything for you, Scott. This is your weekend."

It was a little before ten on Friday night when the rehearsal party began to break up. Tori glanced at Dylan, who had been by her side all night. Next to him was Ava, who had apparently decided that she needed to be wherever Dylan was. Paul made up their foursome, and while he was fun and outgoing, he talked a lot about himself, and she couldn't imagine a less interesting person than Ava, who was beautiful but had little personality. She was ready to be done with the two of them.

Thankfully, her mother interrupted another one of Paul's heroic adventure stories.

"It's so nice to see all of you back in my house," her mother said. "Dylan, you and Paul used to practically live here in high school."

"Because you made the best cookies," Dylan said.

Her mom smiled. "You're charming, but I did not make the best cookies; your mother did that. I'm looking forward to seeing her tomorrow, and your dad, too."

"They were happy to be invited," he replied.

"Do you need any help cleaning up?" she asked her mother.

"No, no, the caterers have it all under control. Everything went smoothly, don't you think?"

"It was perfect. You did an amazing job, Mom."

"Well, hopefully the wedding will be just as drama free."

"I guess we'll take off now," she said. "If you're sure you don't need any help."

"No, go home and get some rest. I'll see you at the church at four. Don't be late, Tori. You know that makes me crazy," her mom added.

"I won't be late," she said, seeing a small smile play across Dylan's face. "I don't know why everyone remembers me as being late all the time."

"You always got caught up in something when you had to be somewhere," her mom said.

"Scott and I waited for you a lot," Dylan piled on.

"If I was late, I was doing something important," she defended.

"Well, I think you're worth waiting for," Paul put in with a charming smile.

She rolled her eyes at his blatant flattery. "I'm sure you didn't back then, Paul."

"Times change," Paul said with a laugh. "Do you need a ride home?"

"I'm taking her home," Dylan said quickly.

"You're taking her home?" Ava questioned, disappointment in her eyes. "I was hoping you could drop me off. I didn't drive. I guess I can call for a car."

"I'll take you home," Paul said.

"Sure, thanks," Ava said, not looking too thrilled about that.

"I'll see everyone tomorrow," her mom said.

Tori said good-bye to her mother and Ray and some of their other family friends, and then she and Dylan made their way out to his car.

"Ava seemed disappointed that you weren't driving her home," she said, as she took her seat.

"You are really obsessed with Ava."

"I'm not obsessed, but I couldn't help noticing the way she glued herself to your side."

"I'm irresistible. What can I say?"

She wished she could say she didn't find his charm irresistible at all, but that would be too big of a lie. Instead, she changed the subject. "Did Scott grill you on the fire and my involvement in it?"

"He did."

"You must not have caved, since I didn't hear anything from him about a threatening note."

"I told you I wouldn't tell him, and I didn't. But I don't like keeping such an important thing from him."

"There's nothing he can do."

"That's what I told myself. I did assure him I'd keep an eye on you. Before you get all worked up about that, just remind yourself that keeping Scott relaxed and happy is your key objective, too."

He was right about that. "Fine. If that made him feel better, then okay. But you don't have to babysit me. I managed to make it through the day without any problems. It's very possible that nothing else will happen."

"I hope that's true."

There was a heavy note in his voice that told her he didn't quite believe it. "What?" she asked. "What are you thinking?"

"I just have a gut feeling that this isn't over yet."

She couldn't deny that she had the same feeling.

"Scott mentioned your dad to me," Dylan continued. "He seems to be on everyone's mind these days."

"It's the wedding. He's missing an important event in our lives." She paused. "What did Scott say about him?"

"He said your dad could be impulsive and reckless—like you."

She sighed. "I don't think either one of us are that bad."

"I wish I could remember your dad better. Do you have any pictures of him?"

"Sure. I have a photo album at my apartment."

"Would you mind showing it to me?"

She glanced at him. "Why?"

"I feel like it would be helpful to see his face. Especially since you think the mysterious Neil Hawkins bears a striking resemblance to him."

"Maybe that would be helpful," she said. "I don't know why I didn't think of it myself."

"So you don't know everything," he teased.

"I never said I did," she retorted. "You're the cocky one, Dylan."

"You really didn't have the greatest impression of me back in high school, did you?"

She didn't really know how to answer that. Her feelings about Dylan had always been confusing. He'd been so many things to her. He'd infuriated her, charmed her, filled her with desire and spine-tingling fantasies that she didn't know what to do with, but the boy he'd been and the man he was now were blurring in her mind.

One thing was clear: she'd never, ever expected to have his attention the way she had it now.

It was exhilarating and terrifying and made her feel off balance in ways that had nothing to do with any danger that might be lurking in the shadows. Right now, it felt like the most dangerous person was sitting in the car next to her.

"You're taking a long time to answer," Dylan said,

shooting her a speculative look.

"You weren't completely terrible back then. But you're being nicer now. You've definitely matured in a positive way."

"Happy to hear that," he said dryly.

She fell silent for a few moments as he navigated through the city traffic. She glanced at the side view mirror, hoping that no one was following them.

"Don't worry, I've been watching," Dylan told her. "No one has stayed behind us for long."

"That's good."

He stopped at a light. "So, you're not interested in Paul, are you?"

She was surprised by the question. *Why would Dylan care if she was interested in Paul?*

Unless... Her pulse sped up, but she really didn't want to let herself go there.

She should tell him she found Paul handsome and appealing, but she'd never been a good liar. "No. He's attractive, but he talks way too much about himself. And I think a lot of his stories are bullshit."

Dylan laughed. "Not many women see through his stories so quickly."

"That surprises me."

"He does like to talk himself up, but he's not a bad guy," Dylan said. "I've known him a long time. He's been a good friend."

"Do you want me to be interested in him?" she asked. "You're selling him pretty hard."

"No," he said shortly. "I mean, I don't care what you do. I was just curious."

Despite his denial, she thought he cared a lot more than he was saying, and that made her nerves jangle again.

A few minutes later, he parked down the block from her apartment. As they got out of his car and walked down the street, she found herself sticking close to him, appreciating his solid, powerful male body next to hers. She could take care of herself, and she was used to being on her own, but at this moment, she wasn't going to complain about his presence.

They didn't see anyone on the street or in the building and made it up to her apartment without incident, but she still breathed a little easier once they were inside.

"Do you want something to drink? I have decaf coffee."

"No, I'm stuffed from your mother's buffet dinner."

"She did go all out. I think she wanted to show Monica's parents that her portion of the wedding events was first-rate."

"Well, she succeeded. Do you have that photo album?"

"I'll get it."

She went into her bedroom and grabbed the old album out of her bookcase and took it back to the living room. Dylan was sitting on the couch, flipping through the channels on her TV. He paused on the Giant's game.

"Who's winning?" she asked.

"Looks like they're up five-nothing in the top of the ninth." He quickly turned off the television.

"You can watch it if you want."

"I just wanted to check the score. They've got it under control."

"The team is so much better now than it used to be."

"You'll have to go to a game now that you're back."

"That would be fun. I haven't been to a ballgame in years. I hear there's a new stadium."

"Yeah, it's great. You know, your brother has season tickets."

"I didn't know that, but I'm not surprised. He's had a love affair with baseball for as long as I can remember. I'm surprised Monica talked him into getting married during the season."

Dylan grinned. "That surprised me, too, but I'm sure he would have put his foot down if she'd tried to schedule too close to the play-offs."

"My dad loved baseball, too. He wasn't around for a lot of our activities, but he always tried to make Scott's baseball games." She opened the photo album, noting the yellowed edges of the pages. "I can't remember when I last looked at this."

"Not when you were moving?"

"No. I got the job offer and I had to pack up really quickly. No time for any trips down memory lane." The first few photos were of her as a baby, and she skipped ahead to the year right before her father died. She paused on a page of photos from her eleventh birthday. "This was taken at the beach, and that's my dad."

Dylan moved closer to her, and her whole body tingled. She could feel his warm breath on her neck, and it was more than a little distracting.

"You look like him," Dylan said.

"The hair and the eyes," she agreed, trying to forget about Dylan so she could concentrate on her dad's features.

This picture was a little grainy, so she flipped through a few more pages until she found another photo of him with her brother at a Giants game. "Just as we were saying," she said, feeling a wave of sadness. The picture reminded her of how close her brother and her dad had been.

"So what do you think?" Dylan asked. "Does he look like the man you followed, the picture of Neil Hawkins on the ID I found?"

Did he?

She stared hard at the picture. "I wish I still had that ID to compare the two. I feel like there are similarities, but the man I was following was a lot older." Her heart pounded against her chest as the impossible idea flitting around her head began to take root.

"Would he be the same age as your dad if your father had lived?" Dylan asked, obviously reading her mind.

Her head came up quickly, her gaze meeting his. "What are you saying? My father is dead. He was cremated. We had a funeral. He's buried in a cemetery off Skyline." She slammed the photo album shut and jumped to her feet. "I can't believe you're even suggesting that he could still be alive.

That's cruel, Dylan."

He slowly stood up and met her gaze head on. "It was in your head, Tori. I just brought it out."

"It was not in my head," she lied.

"Yes it was, and it *is* a crazy idea. That's why I wanted to get it out in the open so you could see it for what it is—impossible."

She stared back at him, shocked he'd read her so well.

"Now that we've gotten that out of the way, you can move on," he continued.

She wanted to move on. Because if Hawkins had killed Robert Walker, then the man was a murderer, and her father would never kill anyone. "You're right. I need to move past the resemblance, which is doubtful anyway."

"I usually am right," he said. "It's good you finally see that."

She let out a breath as his words eased the tension in her body. "I think once we get past the wedding, my emotions won't be so all over the place. I'll be able to think more clearly, be more objective."

"I'll believe that when I see it. The girl I remember always had a lot of drama going on."

"Are you ever going to see me as anything but that drama-filled, awkward, pushy, thirteen-year-old who annoyed you?"

Something shifted in his gaze, and he hesitated a speck too long. Her nerves tightened. "Forget I asked."

He took a step forward, and she had to fight the urge to step back. This was Dylan. He wasn't going to do anything.

He wasn't going to kiss her—was he?

Her palms started to sweat, and her breath grew shallow as his gaze raked her face, settling on her mouth.

"What are you doing?" she whispered.

"Hell if I know," he said. "But I can tell you one thing."

"What's that?"

"I'm not seeing you like that girl right now."

"No?"

"No. Do you know how beautiful you are, Tori?"

His question stole the breath from her chest. "You think I'm pretty?" The idea seemed completely impossible.

"God, yes." His light-blue eyes sparkled with what looked like desire. "I want to kiss you."

"What's stopping you?" she asked breathlessly.

"You're Scott's sister."

"So what?"

"So, we don't hit on each other's siblings."

"Don't use him as an excuse, Dylan. This isn't about him, and you know it. It's about us—you and me."

His lips tightened. "I wish it were that simple, Tori."

"It *is* that simple." Realizing he was about to choose his loyalty to Scott over the electricity crackling between them, she put her hands on his face and impulsively took the kiss she'd wanted for over a decade.

His lips were warm, and they parted in surprise under hers. He jerked, and she thought he might pull away, but suddenly he was kissing her back, taking control of her mouth, sliding his tongue between her lips, making one of her longtime fantasies come true. His kiss was everything and more than she'd ever imagined.

But it was over far too quickly.

He pulled back and ran a hand through his hair. "You do not make things easy."

She didn't know what that meant, but she had a feeling it wasn't a compliment.

"I can't do this, Tori," he said, regret in his gaze.

"Why not? I saw you once make out with a girl you'd met thirty seconds earlier."

"She wasn't…you."

She swallowed a knot in her throat, not exactly sure what that meant, either. "You're not taking advantage of me. I'm a grown woman."

He shook his head. "I have to go."

"Dylan—"

"Lock the door behind me."

He was gone before she could say another word.

She walked over to the door and turned the deadbolt, then she leaned against it and put a hand to her still tingling lips.

Maybe she'd crossed a line by kissing him, but...she smiled to herself. It had totally been worth it. That man could definitely kiss.

Unfortunately, now that she'd had a taste, she wanted more, and it didn't look like that was going to happen any time soon.

Eight

He'd thought about Tori all night and most of the morning. Not even a five-mile run had taken her image out of his head or the taste of her mouth off his tongue. He didn't know how she'd gotten under his skin so fast. One minute, she was just a childhood friend and the next minute, she was the most desirable woman he'd had in his arms in a long time.

As he drove toward the church where he was going to have to see her again at Scott's wedding, he relived their kiss one more time and firmly reminded himself that it couldn't happen again.

Kissing her had been a bad idea on a lot of levels, some of which had to do with his long-term friendship with Scott, but not all. He hadn't had a great track record with women, and he wasn't good at relationships. He was good at having fun, and Tori and he could have a lot of fun, but she'd want more, and he wasn't good at *more*.

Annoyed with himself and with her for kissing him when he'd had every intention of walking out of her apartment without touching her, he pulled into a parking spot in the church parking lot and shut off the engine.

Taking a deep breath, he grabbed his suit coat from the backseat, shrugged it on and headed toward the church. Today was not about Tori or about him; it was Scott's day.

He found his friend standing to the side of the church with Paul. Scott looked remarkably calmer than he had the last few weeks.

"How's it going?" he asked.

"Great," Scott said. "You're cutting it close."

"Sorry." He couldn't admit that he'd been stalling so he'd have even less of a chance to see Tori before the wedding, which was stupid, since they were going to be together for the next several hours. And, really, what the hell was wrong with him? He could be in the same room with her.

"It's fine. You're here now, and I am not going to stress about anything else."

"Looks like a big crowd," he said, waving toward the stream of people heading into the church.

"Monica has a lot of relatives and friends. My side will not be as crowded as hers."

"Does that bother you?"

"Not even a little bit," he said with a laugh. "I don't care about any of this. This is all for Monica. I wouldn't have cared where we got married or who was there to watch us. But it's important to her to have a big day, so it's important to me. I want to make her happy."

"I'm sure you will. You have a good track record for accomplishing anything you set your mind on."

"I knew I would marry her the first day I met her. She's the right one for me," Scott said.

"How did you know?" he found himself asking.

"I just knew. It was like everything was suddenly easy. There weren't any games, no awkwardness. It felt right."

"I wonder what that feels like," Paul drawled. "You know, Dylan?"

"Can't say that I do," he said, although Scott's words had made him think about Tori, how easy it was to be with her.

But that was because they'd known each other since they were kids. *Wasn't it?* He shook that question out of his head. "Are we doing photos before the ceremony?"

"No, everything is afterwards," Scott said. "And there won't be a long photo session. It was the one thing I made Monica agree to. I hate when everyone is waiting an hour at the reception for the wedding party to arrive."

"I agree," he said.

"I'm going to have a word with Monica's dad," Scott said, walking away to speak to the older man.

"Looks like it's you and me, Dylan, on the bachelor train," Paul said.

"You still on that train after taking Ava home last night?" he asked with a grin.

"She's a man-eater," Paul said with a laugh. "But honestly, all she did was talk about you. You may not have brought a date to the wedding, but I don't think you'll be lonely tonight—if you don't want to be."

"I'm not interested in Ava—are you?" he asked, thinking he'd heard an odd note in Paul's voice.

"No. She talks way too much for me. I need a woman who likes to listen." He paused. "Tori grew up really nice."

"Yeah, I saw you hitting on her last night."

"That was nothing. We were just having fun." Paul gave him a knowing look. "You're into Tori, aren't you?"

"No."

"Yes."

"Definitely not," he said more forcefully.

"Scott wouldn't like it," Paul said.

"I'm very aware of that."

"So is he the reason?" Paul asked.

"There's no reason. She's a childhood friend."

"Who is super-hot now. Maybe I should be hitting on her."

"You just said you need a woman who likes to listen—that isn't Tori."

Paul laughed. "You have it bad. Screw Scott. If you like

Tori, go for it. You're both adults."

"I'm not having this conversation," he said. "There's nothing going on."

"Not yet," Paul said knowingly. "But we've got a long night and a lot of champagne ahead of us."

He ignored that, seeing the wedding planner waving them over. "Game time," he said. "Let's get Scott married."

As they entered the church, he saw the bridesmaids lining up in the vestibule. Ava gave him a flirty wave. He smiled back but followed the wedding planner to the side door. She told them to go down to the front of the church and form a line next to the minister.

When they got there, Scott was waiting. Dylan took his place beside him as the crowd settled in for the ceremony.

As his gaze swept the church, he saw Tori sitting in the front row with her stepfather and her mother. She looked gorgeous in a silky cream-colored dress with tiny straps that revealed her beautiful shoulders and the hint of some even prettier breasts. Her long, dark hair fell over her shoulders in a cloud of rich luxury, and her blue eyes sparkled back at him.

All of his mental prep about staying away from her, keeping her in the little sister friend zone went out the window. He forcibly dragged his gaze away from her.

He saw his parents sitting a few rows back on Scott's side of the aisle. His mom gave him a little wave. He tipped his head in acknowledgement, then turned his gaze toward the back of the church as the music began to play.

The bridesmaids came down the aisle, one by one. Ava gave him another seductive look as she stood across from him. He gave her a brief nod, thinking it was going to be a long evening trying to dodge her, especially once the champagne was poured.

The music hushed, then changed to a different song as Monica made her way down to the altar on the arm of her father. She looked beautiful in white lace, but what really touched him was the love he saw in her eyes as she faced

Scott. Monica was looking at his best friend like he was truly the only man in the world. Despite the large crowd gathered for the ceremony, it felt like they were in their own little world of mutual adoration, their vows and glances feeling intimate and honest and very, very confident that they would be happy forever.

He wondered what it would feel like to be that sure, that certain that the person standing in front of you was the person you would spend the rest of your life with. He couldn't quite imagine it, which was odd. He'd seen solid marriages. His parents had been married for thirty-five years, his grandparents for more than sixty. He knew what that kind of love looked like, but it still felt like something out of his grasp. The one woman he had let himself get involved with had disappointed him on so many levels.

But Jenny had been a long time ago. They'd been too young and too selfish, too ill-equipped to maneuver their way through problems and real life. He'd definitely shied away from committed relationships since then. *Maybe it was time to take another risk...*

The crowd broke into applause as the minister proclaimed them Scott and Monica husband and wife. They walked down the aisle holding hands, and he found himself matched up with Ava as they walked down the aisle and out of the church.

She kept a hand on his arm even when they'd cleared the building, but thankfully the photographer and wedding planner moved them to the side and started breaking up the wedding party and immediate family into photographic groups while the rest of the guests made their way to the reception.

At some point, he found himself standing next to Tori as the photographer took a shot of the bride and groom and their respective parents.

"You did good up there," she said with a tight smile. "You didn't even trip."

"Was that your expectation?"

She shrugged. "Just saying."

An awkward silence fell between them.

"Tori."

"Dylan."

They both spoke at the same time.

"You first," he said.

"I'm sorry."

He was surprised by her words. "I don't need an apology."

"Really? Because you seemed pretty mad when you left my apartment last night."

"I wasn't—angry."

"Then what were you?" she asked, hitting him with a question he didn't really want to answer.

"I was—surprised." That was a lame response but the best he could come up with at the moment.

"Why were you surprised? You were a breath away from me, and it seemed like you wanted to kiss me until you remembered who I'm related to."

"Can we not talk about it here?"

"We don't have to talk about it at all."

"That would be even better," he said with relief.

She rolled her eyes and turned her attention to the wedding planner, who called them both in for a group shot of family and wedding party.

Thirty minutes later, they were released from photos to make their way to the reception at the Marina Yacht Club. A limousine carried the wedding party, but he'd told Scott he preferred to drive his own car. Tori got into a vehicle with her mother and stepfather, so he had no further conversation with her. That was a good thing. Hopefully the next time they spoke, he wouldn't sound like an idiot.

Dylan was an idiot, Tori thought as she sat in the backseat of her stepfather's car. Her mom and Ray were talking about how beautiful the ceremony had been while she silently relived the awkward conversation she'd just had with him. She never should have apologized for kissing him, because she'd just breached the distance between them before he did. He could pretend that kissing her hadn't been on his mind, but she knew that wasn't true. He hadn't been unwilling. He'd kissed her back with great enthusiasm. Her body still tingled at the memory. But then he'd put the brakes on and thrown the car in reverse.

She didn't know why he was so hung up on her being Scott's sister. It was some kind of "guy code" but she didn't get it. It wasn't like she was thirteen anymore. She was twenty-nine years old and Dylan was thirty-three, and if they wanted to have any kind of relationship, it was no one's business. She didn't think Scott would care at all. Dylan was just using her brother as an excuse.

Or maybe she had taken him by surprise or misread the signals, and he'd just awkwardly wanted to put a stop to it.

No. Damn him for making her question her instincts. She wasn't the most experienced person when it came to reading men's intentions, but she knew when someone was attracted to her—at least she thought she did. There was a part of her— the shy, insecure, young teen with a fantasy crush—that still couldn't quite believe Dylan was attracted to her.

Maybe he'd been taken aback by the chemistry between them as well. He'd never seen her in that way before, and he didn't really want to.

She sighed, feeling enormously conflicted. She should probably be sorry they'd crossed a line that would forever change their relationship, but she just didn't feel that bad about it. She'd wanted to kiss him forever, and she had. He'd survive. So would she. They probably wouldn't even see each other after the wedding.

Although, he was still her link to Emma and Max and the fire investigation. She couldn't kick him to the curb yet. If he went on his own, she'd have to chase him down. If he didn't want a personal relationship, fine, but she still had to figure out who'd threatened her and why.

"You're quiet, Tori," her mom said, glancing over her shoulder. "Everything okay?"

"Yes, of course."

"It's an emotional day," her mother added, giving her an empathetic smile.

"It is, but a happy one—for the most part."

Her mom nodded, her eyes blurring with moisture. "Yes—for the most part."

They didn't speak her father's name, but she knew he was on both of their minds.

"Can I just say you both look beautiful today?" Ray put in.

"You can always say that," her mother told him, as she turned back around in her seat.

They arrived at the Marina Yacht Club a few moments later and made their way into the reception. Her brother and Monica made a grand entrance, followed by the wedding party, then it was on to cocktails and appetizers and conversation.

As she maneuvered past a group of old family friends, she ran smack into Dylan. *So much for avoiding him.*

He caught her by the arm to steady her, then immediately stepped back, as if he couldn't stand to touch her for one second. "It's crowded in here," he said.

Apparently they weren't getting past the awkwardness any time soon. She nodded, moving a little off to the side to grab a glass of champagne from the waiter. Dylan did the same.

"Cheers," she said, tipping her glass to his, then took a sip. "I can't believe how many of my parents' old friends and neighbors are here. It's been fun catching up, but it does get a little old hearing how I've grown up so nicely. I'm beginning to realize just how hideous I was as a child."

Her words put a smile on his face. "You weren't a monster, Tori."

"If you'd just heard Mrs. Peters say, *'Oh, my, look at how little Tori turned out, I never imagined you could be so pretty,'* you wouldn't say that."

"Hey, Mrs. Peters told me I was almost as good-looking as my father now, so apparently I still have a ways to go."

"Are your parents here?"

"Somewhere. I saw them at the church but haven't seen them here yet."

"Your mom was always nice to me. One time when I was about twelve, I fell off my bike in front of your house, and she came out and helped me up. She made me come inside so she could bandage me up and offered me double chocolate fudge cookies. They were amazing."

"Those were my favorite, too."

"She was very sweet to me."

"Well, she's a nurse and she has six kids, so she always had a supply of Band-Aids and chocolate cookies on hand—still does, I think."

"Do you spend a lot of time with them?"

"Not as much as my mom would like."

"I think I'm going to feel the pressure to visit my mother more often now that I'm back, but I'm looking forward to it. I used to come home for holidays or they'd come out to visit me, but I missed all the impromptu get-togethers. It will be nice to be around for those. It will be different, though, with Scott and Monica being there as a couple, probably starting their own family one day."

"That's already happening in my family, but it's fun to get new blood in the mix."

"Tori," Joanie Hedden said, interrupting their conversation. "That was such a lovely ceremony."

"I thought so, too," she said, giving Joanie a hug. "Do you know Dylan Callaway?"

"Of course. Dylan was practically in your family the amount of time he spent at your house," Joanie said. "How are you, Dylan?"

"Very well, thanks. Where's your husband?" Dylan asked.

"Oh, he had to take a call. Mitch doesn't seem to understand how to tell anyone he'll call them back. The man never even had a cell phone until a few years ago and now he's on it as much as our grandchildren. Our daughter Lindsay has two children now," she added. "You both remember her, don't you?"

"Yes, she was a really good tennis player," she said.

Joanie laughed. "Yes, she was. She had a lovely college career, but fell in love right after she graduated and decided to get married and be a stay-at-home mom. She does, however, teach tennis clinics a few mornings a week, and she said it's fun to be back in the sport after being away a few years." Joanie paused. "I should go find Mitch. I think they're asking for everyone to get seated."

Joanie was right. The wedding planner stepped up to the microphone, asking everyone to find their tables.

"I'll tell Mitch," she offered. "I was just going to look for the ladies' room. Is he outside?"

"By the front door, I think," Joanie said. "Can you tell him we're at table twelve? Do you know which one that is?"

"I'll help you find it," Dylan offered.

As Dylan escorted Joanie to her table, Tori walked out of the dining room and into the lobby. Through the windows she could see Mitch on his phone. He was standing just outside the door. She didn't want to interrupt him, but she'd promised Joanie, so she stepped outside.

He said, "Hang on," and lowered his phone. "Is dinner starting?"

"Soon. Joanie asked me to tell you they're sitting down. She's at table twelve."

"Got it. I'll be right there. By the way, you look beautiful today, Tori."

"Thanks."

As she went back through the door, she thought she heard Mitch say some rather disturbing words into the phone. It sounded like, *'I can't keep lying to her.'*

Was he talking about Joanie? Her stomach turned over.

She really hoped Mitch wasn't having an affair. Joanie was the nicest woman on the planet. She did not deserve that. Hopefully, she'd just heard him wrong.

With a frown, she used the ladies' room, then made her way back into the reception.

She was seated at a singles' table filled with some of Scott's work friends. She made polite chitchat through the meal, but was relieved when the dinner plates were cleared and the toasts began.

Dylan's toast to the happy couple was warm and funny and weakened her resolve to be mad at him or done with him.

Why did he have to be so attractive? So charming? So sexy?

It just wasn't fair.

After the toasts, the dancing started. She got up from her seat to take some candid shots of Scott and her mom sharing their mother/son dance, smiling as her mom kept wiping tears from her eyes. Scott gave her mother a long hug when the dance was over and then went to dance with his wife while her mom moved into her husband's arms, and couples from various tables began to spill out onto the floor.

"Tori?" a woman said, a questioning note in her voice.

She turned and smiled at the short blonde with the big smile—Dylan's mother, Sharon Callaway. "Mrs. Callaway, it's nice to see you again."

"It has been too long," Sharon said. "How are you?"

"I'm fine."

"Your mother told me you're a news reporter like your dad. Ben would be so proud of you."

"I hope he would be," she said.

Sharon waved over a tall man with pepper-gray hair and light-blue eyes that matched Dylan's. "Tim, look who I found—Tori Hayden."

"Hello," Tim said with a smile, shaking her hand. "We heard you just moved back to town. How are you liking the city again?"

"Very much. I'm living closer to the civic center, so it's

different than where I grew up, but I'm not too far away."

"Your mother is thrilled you're home," Sharon said. "And I know just how she feels. I like when all my kids are nearby. Unfortunately, that doesn't happen very often."

"What doesn't happen very often?" Dylan asked, interrupting their conversation.

"Having all my children in one place," Sharon said.

"Hey, I'm here. That should be enough," he joked.

"You are special, of course," Sharon said. "But I do love my other children just as much." She paused, her gaze moving to the group next to them. "Oh, look—there's Joanie," Sharon said, taking her husband's hand. "Let's say hello, Tim. We'll talk to you both later."

As they left, she turned to Dylan. "Your parents look well."

"They stay active."

"Your dad is retired, isn't he?"

"From the fire department, but he still does construction with my uncle Kevin, and he's gotten very into golf. He's never been a man to do nothing."

"I'm guessing you take after him, Dylan."

"It wouldn't be the worst thing." He cleared his throat. "So you're not dancing?"

"No one has asked me."

"Not one of the single guys at your singles' table?"

"Rub it in why don't you?"

He laughed, and she started to feel like maybe they were getting back to normal.

"Sorry, couldn't help it," he said. "How did you enjoy your meal with Ava?"

"Thankfully, she was across from me, so we couldn't talk much. I'm hoping to keep a good distance between us the rest of the night."

"Then you better move, because she's headed this way."

Dylan saw the purposeful look on Ava's face, and then grabbed Tori's hand and said, "Let's dance."

"Not exactly the greatest invitation I've gotten," she

complained, as he pulled her into the middle of the crowded dance floor. They'd barely gotten there when the song changed from fast to slow, which would have been good since there wasn't much space to move around in. But when Dylan put his arm around her, she felt like she was right back where she'd been the night before.

And so was he…

She could feel the tension in his body as he held her slightly away from him, as if he were fighting some internal battle about whether or not to pull her closer.

She didn't really know what was going on in his head, but she thought there was more behind the wall he wanted to put between them than just Scott.

"Relax," he told her.

She was surprised by the statement. "I was going to say the same thing to you. It's just a dance, Dylan. I'm not going to jump you."

A light flared in his eyes at her words, and she thought maybe he wouldn't mind her jumping him, no matter what he would say about it later. But she'd already put herself on the line once; she wasn't going to do it again.

Dylan looked into her eyes, and she could see the conflicted emotions in his gaze. Then his fingers tightened around her hand as he pulled her against his chest.

He might still be fighting their attraction, but as she inhaled the woody scent of his cologne, she was already surrendering. She closed her eyes and let the music and the magic of being in Dylan's arms run through her.

She could really get used to this.

Of course, Dylan wasn't going to let her get used to it, but if he would, she could…

She smiled to herself as his hand pressed against her back and her breasts tingled with each light brush against his chest.

Dylan was the most attractive man in the room, as far as she was concerned. He looked very handsome in his dark suit, but she'd really like to see him without anything at all. She had a feeling his body was magnificent: rippled muscles, just the right smattering of dark hair along his chest, powerful arms that would hold her tight, strong legs pinning her to the bed...

Her eyes flew open as she realized just how carried away she was getting.

Unfortunately, now she was looking into Dylan's eyes, and she had the distinct feeling that some of her own fantasies had been playing through his head.

Then the music ended.

They broke apart as the dancers applauded, and the band jumped into a fast song. She couldn't do another dance, not even a fast one. Her pulse was pounding and her face felt red and hot, and she needed to put some distance between her and Dylan.

"I—I need a break," she said, dashing off the dance floor without waiting for a reply. She made it through the reception hall, into the lobby, and out the door before anyone caught up with her.

Once outside, she took in some deep breaths of chilly, wet air. The fog had swept over the city while she'd been inside. But she was happy for the cold; she needed something to cool her down.

"Tori?"

Her mom's voice turned her around. "Hi. I was just getting some air."

"Are you all right? I saw you run off the dance floor."

"I'm fine."

Her mother's sharp gaze seemed doubtful.

"Really," she reaffirmed.

"I was thinking this might be a difficult day for you, honey. Your brother is getting married, and the two of you have always been so close."

"I'm happy for Scott. I wish him nothing but happiness."

"I know that. But I don't like how Monica's family has kept you in the background all day. You should have been in the bridal party. We should have been sitting together at the reception. I hated seeing you surrounded by strangers, just because of some ridiculous old-fashioned traditions."

"Don't worry about it." Her mom was getting worked up over nothing, and she needed to put a halt to that. "I had a great conversation with some interesting people, and I didn't have to buy an ugly bridesmaid's dress. It's all good."

"And you're being very nice about not complaining. But I also know this is a day where you're thinking about your dad."

"That's true. I do miss him."

"So do I. I hate to say too much in front of Ray. I would never want him to think I don't love him as much as Ben, because I do. It's different; that's all."

"Ray would understand that."

"He's a good man—so different from your father, though. Ben was exciting, bigger than life, filled with desire and dreams and goals. But he could also be unpredictable and sometimes even a little selfish. No one is perfect, and I'm sure he had complaints about me. We really only fought when we were apart too much and needed to spend more time with each other." She drew in a breath. "Ray is solid—like granite. He's an immovable rock. He doesn't change directions with the wind; he doesn't want to blow things up or change lives; he doesn't talk all the time. He just listens and is supportive, and he wants us to enjoy our day-to-day."

She personally thought Ray was a little dull compared to her dad, but her father had definitely been one of a kind. And how difficult it had to have been for Ray to come after a man like her dad, and Ray had taken on two teenagers as well. She hadn't always been as nice to him as she should have been. "I'm glad Ray makes you happy," she said. "You deserve that."

"Thanks, honey. I want you to be happy, too. I wish you'd brought someone tonight."

"It's actually nice to be free to chat with people. If I had a date, I'd have had to pay more attention to him. Now I can just concentrate on catching up with old friends."

"Everyone is so happy you're back in town. Joanie told me how impressed she is with all you've accomplished. I hope you know how proud I am of you, Tori."

"I do know, and thanks." She paused, thinking about Joanie. "Earlier this evening, Joanie asked me to find Mitch and let him know that we were starting dinner. He was talking on his phone, and he seemed pretty agitated. I heard him say something about not wanting to keep something from someone. Are he and Joanie good?"

Her mother frowned. "Well, I think so, but I haven't spent a lot of time with them lately. Mitch gets a little moody, but I hope nothing is going on."

"He could have been talking about anything. Don't give it another thought." As she finished speaking, she heard a crackle from the nearby trees and saw a flash of light. "What's that?" she murmured.

"What do you mean?" her mother asked.

"Someone is over there."

"Well, we should go inside."

"One second," she said, taking a few steps closer to the edge of the trees that served as a barrier between the parking lot and the club. Two men stood in the shadows, and one of them was the same height, the same build as the guy she'd followed into the building that had exploded.

"Tori, come back," her mom said.

Her mother's voice startled the men. The one who'd resembled Neil Hawkins quickly disappeared into the shadows. The other one came forward with a familiar loping, long-legged gait. It was Jim Beacham.

She stared at him in surprise. "Who were you just talking to? Who was that man?"

"What?" Jim asked, a surprised note in his voice.

"The man you were with. Who is he? How do you know him?"

"Tori, what's going on?" her mother asked, coming forward. "Jim, what are you doing out here?"

"I was just having a smoke," Jim said.

"What is going on?" Scott said.

She turned her head, seeing Dylan and Scott come up behind her mother. She didn't know what everyone was doing outside but at the moment she was more interested in who Jim had been speaking to. "Jim was talking to someone in the parking lot. I just asked him who it was." She shot Dylan a glance. "He looked like Neil Hawkins."

"Who is Neil Hawkins?" Scott asked.

She ignored her brother, turning back to Jim, who seemed to be slow in coming up with any answers. "Who was that man?" she repeated.

"I don't know," Jim said. "He asked me if I had another cigarette. I did, so I handed one over and then I gave him a light. He said something about the fog and how cold San Francisco was in the spring."

"That's it?" she asked.

"Yes, why?"

"You didn't think he looked like my father?"

"Like your father?" her mother echoed. "Tori, what are you talking about?"

"She's talking about the man she followed into the fire," Scott said. "Aren't you?"

"What fire?" her mom said, getting more confused by the moment.

"It's a long story," she said. "Jim—did you think the man looked like my dad?"

"No. I didn't see any resemblance. Why?"

She couldn't begin to explain, so instead she said, "I'm going to check out the parking lot."

"You're not going anywhere by yourself," Scott said, stopping her in her tracks.

"I'll go with her," Dylan offered.

"It will just take a second," she said.

"No. This is my wedding. You're not chasing anyone down. All of us are going back inside, and we're going to enjoy the reception. We have the cake to cut and a bouquet to throw, and Monica will have everything she wants tonight.

Got it?"

She really, really wanted to go after the man she'd just seen with Jim, but she couldn't ruin this day for her brother. "Got it," she said.

"Good. Let's go."

"I still want an explanation," her mother said, giving her a pointed look. "We're going to talk later, Tori."

She and Dylan fell into step behind her mom and brother.

"He's probably gone, Tori," Dylan said quietly. She met his gaze and sensed he understood her frustration better than anyone else, but then, he knew more of the story than the rest of the group.

"I'm sure you're right," she said.

"Sorry if I upset you in some way," Jim said, as they reached the door to the yacht club. "But what's all this about seeing someone who looks like your dad?"

Since Scott and her mom were already heading into the hall, she took a minute to explain.

"There was a man watching me the other day," she said. "I followed him and he led me into a building that exploded shortly thereafter."

Jim's face paled in shock. "Are you serious? Are you all right?"

"I'm fine. And Mom doesn't know about it, so let's keep it that way for now."

"You're going to have to tell her after what just happened."

"I will, but not tonight."

"And you think this guy who was watching you was the same guy I just gave a cigarette to? Maybe I should go look for him. Find out what he's doing—if he's stalking you or something."

If it was the same man who'd been watching her before, then he was definitely following her; she just didn't know why.

"I thought the guy was homeless," Jim continued. "Are you sure it was the same man?"

She let out a sigh. "I don't know. I can't be a hundred percent sure. There were a lot of shadows. Maybe I'm losing my mind. Seeing my dad in every man's face. You really didn't see a resemblance?"

"No, I didn't."

"Then maybe I am seeing things, because you knew him well."

"This is a hard day," Jim said, echoing her mother's earlier words. "I feel bad that Ben isn't here. He should be."

"I agree."

"Do you want me to go look for him?" Jim asked.

"I can go with Jim," Dylan offered.

She shook her head. She didn't know if the man was dangerous, and she didn't want to expose anyone else to harm. Plus, her brother had made it clear he didn't want any drama at his reception. "I'm sure he didn't stick around. Let's join the rest of the party."

"If you're sure," Jim said.

"I am."

"I'll see you inside," Jim added.

As Jim went to join the rest of the party, she looked at Dylan. "I think that was Neil Hawkins."

He nodded, a grim look in his eyes. "If it was, that's not a good thing. I'm going to take a look around, Tori."

"You heard what Scott said."

"He was talking to you, not me."

"He was talking to all of us."

"I'll just be a few minutes."

She knew she should make him stay with her, but she was torn. "Okay, but be careful," she said.

"Don't worry about me. I'll be fine."

As he headed back outside, she really, really hoped that would be true.

Nine

———⟫⟪⟪⟪———

After leaving Tori, Dylan headed outside, walking quickly through the trees and into the parking lot. There was no sign of movement. He moved up and down the rows of cars, checking to see if anyone was sitting inside a vehicle, but they were all empty. He walked out to the street and looked around.

The sidewalk led to the Marina Greens one way and the Presidio the other way. There was no one walking, but there were cars on the road, stopping at a nearby light, which also served as a turnoff into the parking lot.

The Marina shopping district was a few blocks away, with numerous cafes, bars, and retail stores. That's where pedestrians would most likely be. Why a man would be walking around the yacht club parking lot during a private party seeking a cigarette was a really good question.

He supposed the trees and empty spaces leading into the Presidio might be a good place for a homeless person to blend into the landscape. On the other hand, most of the homeless population stayed in the more populated areas where there were people to panhandle, more places where they might be able to find food, water, and shelter.

He gave it another minute, then slowly walked back toward the club, his thoughts turning to Jim Beacham.

The Beachams had been longtime friends of Tori's family. Jim had been with Ben Hayden on that fateful fishing trip. He'd given the eulogy at his funeral. Jim was loyal to the Haydens and protective of Tori and Scott. Was it just a coincidence he'd been outside when Hawkins wanted to get a cigarette? Or had Hawkins approached Jim for another reason?

He couldn't imagine what that reason could be.

When he returned to the reception, the bride and groom were posing by the cake, ready to cut their first slice, the guests surrounding the small cake table.

He paused at the edge of the dance floor, wondering where Tori was in the crowd. He felt a wave of anxiety when he didn't immediately see her. He was so caught up in finding her that he didn't realize his mom had come over until she put a hand on his arm.

"Dylan? Everything all right?" she asked.

"Yes."

"Are you sure?"

He nodded, his gaze taking another trip around the room. He let out a breath when he saw Tori with Mitch and Joanie. She had her camera out, ready to take photos of the cake cutting.

"So it's like that," his mom said.

He turned his head and saw a knowing gleam in his mother's eyes. "Like what?"

"You're interested in Tori, aren't you?"

"She's Scott's sister."

"So..."

"It would be awkward. I've known her since she was a kid. We don't really even like each other. She's pushy and nosy, and she has a lot of opinions."

His mom laughed. "Well, that's the most you've told me

about a woman in years. It sounds like she's got you rattled, and that might be a good thing."

He frowned. "You just have love on the brain because we're at a wedding."

"And because you're my son, and I want you to be happy. And because it's been awhile." She paused. "I know Jenny did a number on your head, but the next woman won't be the same."

He didn't want to talk about Jenny or Tori. "I think we should get some cake. Looks like they're cutting the bottom tier."

"I'm going to pass on the cake. Your father is taking me to Mallorca this summer. I want to look good in a bathing suit."

"I haven't heard about that trip."

"It's for our thirty-fifth wedding anniversary in July. Your dad surprised me with the invitation last week. He even went so far as to buy airline tickets."

"Good for you. That will be fun."

"I think so. Anyway, I'm going to find your dad and call it a night. Come by the house soon. It's been awhile since we've caught up."

"I will," he promised.

"And give Tori a chance. She might surprise you."

As his mother walked away, he saw Jim Beacham sitting alone at a table. He was typing on his phone. Impulsively, he decided to join him, taking the chair next to him.

Jim's head jerked up, and he slipped his phone back into his pocket. "Did you check out the parking lot?"

"How did you know?"

"I figured you would. You and Tori seem to be tight these days."

"I just want to be sure she's not in any trouble."

"You should call the police," Jim said. "It sounds like Tori is in the middle of something dangerous."

"We're talking to a detective. They're looking for the man Tori thought she saw in the parking lot."

"Well, if you want me to talk to them, too, I will. I love Tori. I've always thought of her as a daughter. I've known her most of her life. If she's in trouble, I want to help, but what I don't understand is why she thinks there's some resemblance between this man and her father."

"I can't really explain it, either."

"Can I be straight with you, Dylan?"

"Of course."

"Tori and Scott—they've been looking for their dad for years. I think it's because they didn't see him after he died, but I did. He's dead. And the man in the parking lot was not his ghost."

Jim's certainty chased away the odd doubts he'd had. "You're right."

"I am right. Tori needs to let the police handle things and stop letting her imagination carry her away."

"I agree, but she's not the easiest person to convince."

Jim tipped his head in acknowledgment. "She takes after her father in that regard."

"Are you talking about me?" Tori asked, joining them at the table.

"I'm worried about you, Tori," Jim said. "What can I do to help?"

"Do you remember anything about the man you spoke to in the parking lot?"

"Not much. It was dark. He had a gruff voice, like someone who smoked a lot."

"Did he ask you anything about this party, what was happening inside the club, who was here…anything?"

"He just asked me for a smoke and a light. When you came out, he took off."

"Okay, thanks."

"I'm happy to talk to the police if you want. Maybe they can send a car out to look for this guy," Jim suggested.

Tori shook her head. "Thanks, but no. I promised Scott and my mom that there wouldn't be any more drama tonight." She turned to him. "We can talk to Max tomorrow."

He nodded. "Definitely."

"Well, let me know if you need me to do anything, including sleep on your couch," Jim said. "You know I will, Tori."

"Thank you, but that won't be necessary," she said. "Sorry if I upset you. I want you to enjoy the party."

"Well, then I think I'll go ask your mother to dance," he said with a small smile.

Tori took Jim's seat after he left, and he could see the strain in her eyes. She was putting on a brave face, but he knew she was still thinking about Hawkins.

"What else did Jim say to you?" she asked.

"He told me that you're not going to find your dad no matter how hard you look for him," he said bluntly.

Her eyes widened, and she didn't look too thrilled with his words. "So he thinks it's all in my mind?"

"Because your father is dead—yes. That's what he thinks. I'm sorry, Tori."

"I understand why Jim would think that. But whatever Neil Hawkins looks like, he's still showing up everywhere I am, and that needs an explanation. I don't know if he wants to talk to me or threaten me, but he definitely wants something."

"He's not going to get near enough to you to do either," he said. "As long as you stick close to me."

"You're going to be my bodyguard now? Last night, you couldn't wait to get away from me."

He frowned at the reminder. "This is not about that."

"Look, I appreciate that you've been helping me and looking out for me, and I hope we can check in with Max tomorrow, but I can watch out for myself."

"Why don't you stay with your mom tonight?"

"She'll think something is up."

"I'm pretty sure she already thinks something is up after the drama outside."

"Good point. But I'm not staying with her. I'm not ready to answer her questions, and I don't want to ruin this night. I'll be fine. I live in a safe building."

"If you don't want to stay with your mom, then I'm staying at your apartment."

Her eyebrow shot up. "What did you say?"

He almost regretted the impulsive suggestion, but it was too late, and he would feel better knowing she was safe. "I'll sleep on the couch."

"That sounds like an incredibly bad idea," she murmured.

"You don't have to worry about me, Tori."

A small, ironic smile curved her lips. "I'm surprised you're not worried about me."

His body tightened at that suggestive comment. *If she kissed him again, would he have the strength to stop?*

But, as he'd just said, this wasn't about that. "I think we can trust each other, can't we?"

"Tori," her mother interrupted, coming over. "Monica is going to throw the bouquet. We need you."

"Duty calls," she said. "You'll be up next for the garter."

"We're not done talking about this, Tori."

"For now we are," she said, getting up to join the other single women.

—————

As much as Tori did not want to have Dylan spend the night at her apartment, she also didn't want to be alone. Nor did she want to stay at her mother's house and raise more questions. She had to make a decision soon.

Dylan was talking to Paul, and her mother was saying goodbye to the Heddens, so she still had a minute, but probably not much more than that.

While she was thinking, she moved to the table where she'd left her wrap. As she picked it up off the back of her chair, Scott came over.

"Monica and I are about to make our grand exit," he said.

"Did you have a good time? Was it everything you wanted it to be?"

"Better. It was perfect."

"I'm so glad," she said, touched by the genuine happiness in his eyes. Scott had always looked out for her, especially after their father had died, and she'd been really lucky to have him as a big brother. A part of her wished she could tell him what was going on, because he was so level-headed and smart, but she couldn't burden him with anything now. "Have a good honeymoon."

"I intend to." He paused, glancing around, then turning back to her with a more serious gaze. "What was all that about in the parking lot?"

"We don't need to get into that now."

"It sounded like someone is following you."

"It was just my imagination. Nothing for you to worry about."

"I don't believe you, Tori. Just because I got married today doesn't mean you can't come to me with a problem. I know I laid down the law earlier, but that was to avoid any drama with Monica's parents. I don't want you to think I don't care about what's going on."

Scott had always felt so responsible for her and for everyone. "The only person you need to be responsible for is your wife. Don't give anything else another thought."

"She's right," Dylan interrupted, obviously overhearing her words. "You don't need to worry about anything, Scott. I'll help Tori with whatever she needs."

"I do appreciate that," Scott said, exchanging a glance with Dylan.

Tori wondered if these two would ever see her as a grown-up, but right now she just wanted Scott to go off a happy, untroubled man, so she let them have their "bro" moment.

Then she gave Scott a hug and followed him out to the lobby, where he joined up with Monica. The two families and remaining guests wished them well as they ran out to the limo for their ride to a local hotel. Tomorrow they would be heading to Hawaii for a week.

Once the bride and groom were off, she and Dylan

helped Ray finish putting the wedding presents into his car. Then she told her mother Dylan would be giving her a ride home, and she'd get her car from their house the next day. It seemed easier than going all the way out to the ocean and then back to her place, which was much closer to the yacht club.

Her mom seemed just as happy as Scott that Dylan was by her side. She pulled Tori aside for a quick moment, promising her they would have a longer chat very soon.

She knew that wouldn't be fun, but she had a short reprieve, and she would take it.

She felt pretty tired as she got into Dylan's car. It was after eleven, and she'd been going full speed since ten in the morning.

Dylan didn't have much to say on the way to her place. She couldn't help but note the number of times he checked his mirrors, but he didn't seem to see anything problematic. When they got to her building, she told Dylan he could park in the underground garage since her car was at her mom's house.

Once they got up to her apartment, Dylan made what was becoming his usual sweep of the place before giving her a nod. "All clear."

"Great." She set her clutch on the table and kicked off her high heels in relief. Then she walked into the kitchen, grabbed two bottles of water and brought one back to Dylan, who had already *gotten* rid of his coat and taken a seat on the couch.

She sat down next to him and took a sip of her water. "You're not going to be very comfortable on this couch."

"It's pretty soft," he said, patting the cushion. "I can sleep anywhere." He loosened his tie and pulled it off. "That's better."

She smiled. "You're not really a tie-wearing kind of guy, are you?"

"No, I am not. I much prefer casual clothes, but I was happy Scott only made us wear a suit and not a tuxedo."

"And I was happy not to have to wear a bridesmaid's dress. I've already been in three weddings, so my collection of unwearable dresses is beginning to grow."

"It's worse for the women," he agreed. "At least with a tux, I can just return it."

"Exactly. Have you been in any other weddings?"

"Two other ones—both fellow firefighters. I'm sure I'll be in my brother Ian's wedding, whenever that is."

"Funny that Ian would get married before you and Hunter. He was always so quiet and so smart, and nowhere near as into girls as the two of you."

"Ian is still an intellectual, but he fell for a gregarious, warm-hearted, elementary school teacher, who has put the biggest smile on his face that I've ever seen. She's from Ireland and believes in leprechauns and rainbows and all kinds of crazy legends, which is ironic since Ian stopped believing in Santa Claus before he went to Kindergarten."

"Ireland, huh? Is that where they met?"

"No, Grace is tied to the trip Ian made there with Emma and Burke. I'll have to tell you about it sometime. Emma found a little girl who needed a mother, and Ian met a professor—one of his idols—who asked Ian to take something to his estranged daughter Grace. He did, and, well, a lot of dangerous stuff went down, but in the end it all worked out."

"If I wasn't so tired, I'd ask for the longer version of that story."

"You should go to bed."

"I will in a minute." She sipped her water. "So Scott is married. Your best friend is no longer single. Is that going to cramp your style? You've lost your wingman."

"Scott hasn't been my wingman in a while. I'm happy for him."

"Me, too. I kind of wished I could freeze time today, make the moment last forever."

"There will be more good moments to come."

"That sounds optimistic from someone who doesn't seem

interested in the idea of marriage."

His expression turned wary. "Did I say that?"

"You said you hadn't been involved with anyone since Jenny and that ended years ago." She tilted her head. "What happened with her, Dylan?"

"I told you I don't want to talk about it."

"Scott once told me that Jenny did a real number on you. What did he mean?"

"It's not important."

"You're always so straightforward and direct—why so secretive about this?" She knew she was pressing, but she really wanted to know.

"Do you ever stop asking questions, Tori? You should have been a prosecutor. I can see people confessing just to get you to shut up."

"And you're stalling. Is it that big of a deal? Did she cheat on you?"

"No." He hesitated for a long minute, then said, "Jenny got really clingy over the years we were together. Her father had left her mother when she was a teenager, and she was really sensitive to me doing anything that didn't involve her, even if it was just basketball with the guys. When I became a firefighter, she hated the shifts, the fact that I'd be gone for nights at a time, and she was on her own."

He took a swig of his water, then continued. "Jenny became less and less independent the longer we were together. I was in charge of everything, and she looked at me with this sort of desperate reverence. It was like she built me up in her mind when I wasn't around. She kept telling me I was her hero, her knight in shining armor, that she couldn't live without me. She wouldn't do anything when I was at work except text me all day long. Then she started listening to the news and she even got a neighbor to lend her a radio that picked up our fire calls. She showed up at a couple of scenes, crying when I was inside the building, getting hysterical for no reason."

She couldn't imagine that would have gone over well.

"I told her she needed to get some help, talk to someone," he continued. "But she said she just needed me to love her. I realized that our relationship wasn't healthy, but when I tried to break up with her..." His voice trailed away. "I don't want to say too much about her private problems, but she had some mental health issues, and she became very depressed. She told me she couldn't live without me."

She was shocked and horrified by the story. She'd thought Jenny Meyer, one of the most popular girls to ever go to their high school, had had everything going for her. "I'm sorry, Dylan. I can't even believe it. She seemed so confident from what I knew of her."

"She had a lot of personal demons. It took me a long time to cut the ties."

"I can see why. You didn't want to be responsible for her doing something bad to herself. She didn't, did she?" she asked, suddenly worried about the ending of this story.

"No. I finally talked her into getting some help, and eventually we were able to break up, and she found a way to move forward. She actually got married last year. Hopefully, she's happy now, and she found the right person for her."

"Hopefully. I apologize. I didn't realize it was such a bad story when I asked. I thought it was going to be your typical we didn't get along kind of deal."

"I wish it had been that," he said heavily. "I don't know when Jenny stopped seeing me as just a guy and started seeing me as some kind of hero that she couldn't live without, but there was no way I was going to be able to live up to her expectations."

"It's hard to be at the top of a pedestal," she agreed.

"Have you been there?" he asked.

She smiled at that. "No, definitely not. No one can't live without me. Most people do just fine."

He grinned back at her. "I'm sure you've broken some hearts."

"I don't think so, but thanks for saying that."

As silence fell between them, the air seemed to get

hotter, thicker, and she started to think about the previous night when she'd cut through all the tension by kissing Dylan.

She really, really wanted to do it again, but she felt like the next time they kissed it had to be his idea.

So why wasn't he getting the idea?

"What?" he asked.

"Nothing. I'm tired. I'm going to go to bed. You really could go home, Dylan."

"I don't want to leave you alone."

"I'm behind locked doors. And you're not responsible for me." She was talking about more than just the possible threat lurking outside, and he knew it.

"I do want to keep you safe."

"Because you're loyal to Scott. I get it. But I'm not looking to you to save me."

"I know that, and my loyalty to your brother is not the only reason I'm here. I like you, Tori."

Her heart skipped a beat. "Since when?"

"Since always."

"No way. You did not like me when I was thirteen."

"Fine, since you came back. But I didn't dislike you before; I just didn't really know you."

"You didn't want to know me," she reminded him.

"You were a kid."

"I'm very aware of that."

"But I like you now," he said again. "And..."

She caught her breath at the sudden spark in his eyes. "And..."

"I'd like to kiss you."

"What's stopping you?"

"You'd want it to mean something," he said.

As much as she wanted to deny that, he was probably right. She'd kissed guys before without it meaning a damn thing, but this was Dylan. He'd always been in his own special category, and she didn't see that changing any time soon.

His gaze bored into hers, indecision in his eyes.

"Oh, what the hell!" He grabbed her by the arms and pulled her in for a kiss.

This time she was the one whose lips parted in surprise, who needed a second to grasp what was happening. But soon she was opening her mouth to his, savoring his taste, loving the rush of heat between them. He angled his head one way and then another, never giving her a chance to take a full breath.

Her senses were on fire, her breasts tingling, her body melting under the onslaught of desire.

When he pulled away, she stared at him in bemusement, her chest heaving with emotion, with want, as too many emotions ran through her body.

His light-blue eyes were as dark and as shadowy as they'd ever been. He ran a hand through his hair. "That was…"

"Yes," she said softly, meeting his gaze. "It was."

"I think you're right, Tori."

"About what?"

"I should go."

Now she wanted to ask him to stay, but he was already on his feet.

Maybe that was a good thing. She was still reeling, and they'd only kissed a little. He could knock her completely off balance, and despite her earlier bravado, she wasn't sure she was ready for that.

"Are you going to be okay?" he asked, with conflict in his gaze. "I want you to be safe."

"I'm safe and I'm better than okay," she said, standing up. "You were right, too, Dylan."

"About what?"

"I'm going to want it to mean something."

He gave a tight nod. "I can't give you what you want, Tori."

"I'm sure you can, but the real question is if you'd ever want to." She let that hang for a moment, and then said, "Good-night, Dylan."

He grabbed his coat as he headed for the door. He paused, his gaze firm as he looked back at her. "All this aside, Tori, I want you to call me if you have any problems. Actually, call 911 first, then call me. Don't hesitate. Don't think it's awkward. Even if it's a small sound, a bad feeling, let me know."

His words were scaring her a little, but she wasn't going to let him see that. "I will."

"And we'll talk tomorrow. I'm not abandoning you in the middle of this situation. I'm just giving us both a little space tonight."

"I get it. But this is my problem, not yours."

"I don't care. Until I know you're safe, we're not done."

Ten

Tori didn't get much sleep Saturday night. When she got up grumpy and still tired just after eight in the morning, she took a shower, dressed and then headed straight for the coffeemaker. While her coffee was brewing, her phone began to buzz.

Dylan's name flashed across the screen, and she felt annoyed at how happy that made her.

He'd been the subject of her dreams all night long, but along with the fantasies, there had been anger and frustration that he could make her so crazy. The only saving grace was that she'd obviously shaken him up, too. Dylan didn't run away from anything, but he'd bailed on her last night, and she knew it was because he was feeling the same mixed-up emotions running through her head. How they were ever going to get out of that place of turmoil, she had no idea.

They could be friends. But could they ever be more? *Should* they ever be more?

When she didn't answer, she saw a voicemail pop up. She was about to listen to it when her phone started ringing again.

Dylan would not be ignored.

Not wanting to scare him, she said, "Hello?"

"Why didn't you answer the first time? What's going on? Are you all right?"

"That's a lot of questions for first thing in the morning."

"You're rubbing off on me."

"I'm fine. I'm making coffee."

"Excellent. I hope there's enough for two."

"You're coming over?"

"I'm already here. Buzz me in. I brought breakfast."

She couldn't quite believe how cheerful and breezy he sounded, as if nothing tense or unsettling had gone down between them the night before. Well, she could play that game, too.

She buzzed him in, then waited for his knock before looking through her peephole and then unlocking the door and letting him in.

Dylan had a brown paper bag in his arms, and whatever he'd brought smelled delicious.

"Good morning," he said, looking more attractive than ever in jeans and a dark-blue T-shirt, his hair still damp from a recent shower, his skin glowing and emanating a deliciously sexy scent that was almost as good as the bacon that had to be in the bag he was holding.

She dug her hands into the pockets of her jeans, because she couldn't quite trust herself not to grab him and experience his kiss again in full living color, which would be much better than her dreams.

Clearing her throat," she said, "What did you bring?"

"Food from Viola's, my favorite breakfast place in the city," he said, walking over to her kitchen table. He pulled out cartons of food and began to open them. "I got both a veggie omelet and one with bacon, ham and mushrooms. I'm pretty sure you're not a vegetarian, unless something has changed."

"No, I still love meat."

"There are also pancakes, French toast, and a side of turkey bacon, just in case you want to be a little healthier."

"Wow. How many people are joining us?"

"I wasn't sure what you liked," he defended. "And I was hungry when I was ordering."

"How do you know I haven't eaten yet?"

"Have you?" he countered with a smile.

"No, and I don't have much in my refrigerator."

"Then this works, right?"

She let out a breath. "Yes, but Dylan—"

"After we eat," he said. "Then we can talk about whatever you want."

She'd take that reprieve. "All right. Do you want coffee? I also have orange juice."

"I'll stick with the juice this morning. I drink so much coffee at work, I like to take a break on my days off."

"It seems like you've had quite a few days off."

He nodded, as he sat down at the table. "I took a shift off for the wedding. I'm back at work tomorrow morning."

She went into the kitchen to pour juice and grab plates and silverware and then took everything to the table. She sat down across from him and surveyed the buffet he'd brought with a happy feeling running through her. "I love breakfast food. I don't know where to start."

"Which omelet do you want?"

"I don't know if I can choose."

He laughed. "I'm surprised. You're rarely indecisive. Why don't we split them?"

"Great idea," she said, cutting one of the omelets in two and taking half onto her plate. She also took the top pancake, and doused it with the accompanying syrup.

"So what's on tap for you today?" Dylan asked as they started eating.

"Well, I need to get my car from my mom's house at some point. I know she's going to have questions for me; I just have to figure out how much to tell her."

"Why not tell her everything?"

"Because it will worry her."

"It might worry her more if she thinks you're holding

back. And I suspect you got some of your interrogation skills from her."

Her mother was very good at getting confessions. "You're right about that. She could always see through a lie." She took another bite of her omelet, then said, "What about you? What are your plans?"

"Well, I'd like to make sure you're not getting into any trouble."

"Besides that," she said, rolling her eyes.

"I was going to finish up a few things on the 1971 Barracuda I'm restoring. It's at my parents' house. They're nice enough to let me use their garage since they have more street parking than I do."

"A Barracuda. That sounds sexy and fast."

He laughed. "It definitely is. It's also a convertible. And it's just about ready for a spin down the coast before I put it up for sale."

"Do you ever want to keep the cars you restore?"

"All the time. But I don't have anywhere to store them, and if I'm really honest, I enjoy the restoration more than just being the owner."

"I get that. I remember when you and Scott bought that old Chevy that you had to push into our driveway because it broke down two blocks away. Then it leaked oil all over everything. My mom had been tiptoeing around Scott, trying not to upset him because he was in so much pain after my dad died, but that day she just lost it with Scott. I'm sure the neighbors heard her yelling from a mile away." She smiled at the memory. "It was actually kind of a good thing. It was a release, like we were back to normal."

"Then I guess you should thank me."

"I wouldn't go that far," she returned. "So where is this Viola's? I have to go there. This food is delicious."

"It's a few blocks from me in the Marina."

"Is there an actual Viola?" she asked.

"There is. You'd probably think she's an older grandma type, but she's actually Asian, in her twenties, and a classically trained chef, who turned an old dive bar into the best breakfast place in the city."

"You know a lot about her."

"She's also friends with my cousin Burke's wife Maddie, who recently opened her own restaurant. Between the two of them, I eat very well."

"I bet. Do you cook at all for yourself?"

"Not too much. I have one dish I excel at—chili."

"Firehouse chili," she said with a smile. "How shocking."

"Hey, it is the best in the city. I have second shifts begging me to leave it behind for them."

"What's your secret?"

"I can't tell you that."

She smiled, liking how easy it was to talk to Dylan again. Maybe they were both putting up a front, but she wasn't going to tear it down. It was fun to get to know him better as the man he was now and not the boy she remembered.

"I'll drive you over to your mom's house," he added, as they finished breakfast. "While the two of you are catching up, I'll work on my car. When you're ready to leave, let me know, and I'll follow you back here or wherever else you want to go."

"I'll take the ride, but after that you can do your own thing. I don't need a babysitter."

"You might not want to be alone if that man shows up again."

"The thing is, that man hasn't ever approached me. He's just been where I am. If he wanted to hurt me, I think that would have happened already."

The humor in his eyes faded. "I wouldn't bank on that. Just because it hasn't happened doesn't mean it won't. Let's not forget about the warning note you received."

"I haven't forgotten, but in retrospect, it wasn't that bad. It's not like they said they were going to kill me. And I'm not really asking questions, because I don't know what to ask or who to ask."

"You are asking questions through Max and Emma."

"But he's not going to know that."

"I hope not."

She frowned at his somber tone. She wanted to argue, but he'd made good points, and the fact that Neil Hawkins had shown up at her brother's wedding was something to be concerned about. She didn't want to be foolish and downplay the seriousness of what might be happening around her, even if she couldn't completely understand it.

"I called Emma on my way over here," he said. "I told her that we thought Hawkins might have shown up at the reception. Max had to go in to work on another case, but she said she'd let him know."

"So they're up to speed."

"Hopefully, they can come back with some solid information or better yet, locate Neil Hawkins and bring him in for questioning."

"That would be the best scenario."

"In the meantime, you have to keep your guard up."

"I know that. But I'm not going to run scared. I have to live my life. I have to go to work tomorrow, and so do you. You can't watch over me every second."

"Let's take it one day at a time. And let's start with a ride to your mom's house."

"Fine, but you're not coming in. In fact, you can drop me off a few houses down. I don't need my mother to ask me why you and I are together so early in the morning."

"I'm okay with that," he said with some relief.

"I'm sure you are, because you know the first call my mom would make would be to your mother. And the last thing we need is our moms to get involved in what this is or isn't," she said.

He stared back at her as her words turned the conversation more personal.

"I know you're angry about last night, Tori," he began.

"I'm not angry."

"You're not?"

"Nope. I'm great. Are you great?"

He gave her a wary look. "I feel like that's a trick question."

She smiled. "I'm going to put my shoes on while you come up with an answer."

She didn't know if Dylan was still thinking about her question, but he was fairly silent on their drive across town, muttering something about how much traffic there was, even on Sundays. Other than that, he had nothing much to say.

As they got closer to their old neighborhood and her mom's house, she started thinking about what she was going to tell her mother, and she couldn't come up with a good, solid plan. She didn't want to lie to her mom. She also didn't want to worry her.

So what to do...what to do...

She tapped her fingers restlessly on her thighs as she gazed out the window. As the ocean came into view, she suddenly had an idea. It was a beautiful sunny May day, and the sea was shimmering in the sunlight.

"That Barracuda you were talking about," she said, glancing over at Dylan. "Is it ready for that spin down the coast?"

He glanced over at her. "You don't want to talk to your mother, do you?"

"Not yet. And I can't get my car at her house without stopping in. Even putting my problems aside, she'll want to gossip about the wedding. I just need a little time to get my head together, think about what I want to say. But if you don't want to—"

"I want to," he said, cutting her off.

"Great."

He turned right at the next corner and pulled up in front of his mother's house a moment later. He used his key to open the door, calling out as they walked into the home. There was no answer.

She was actually relieved that his parents weren't home. They'd probably have questions, too.

"They must be at church," Dylan said.

"Do they still do those big Sunday lunches?"

"Yes, they do. Today's lunch is at my Uncle Jack's house."

"Why aren't you there?"

"I make it once every two to three months. That's enough."

"You don't appreciate how great it is to live near your family."

"I appreciate it," he said. "And I see them quite often. I think my parents actually let me use the garage so I have to come over."

"I wouldn't put it past your mom," she said, as he led her through the kitchen and into the attached garage.

He flipped on a light switch. "Here she is—my latest baby."

She stared at the bright-orange convertible in amazement. "Your baby is very colorful."

He laughed. "It's the original color. Someone in the factory wanted to make a statement."

"They certainly did."

"Ready to take a ride? Or have you changed your mind now that you see the car?"

"I have not changed my mind. Let's do it. I feel like making my own statement today."

His expression turned at her words. "Maybe a convertible isn't the best idea."

"Oh, come on, Dylan. We'll be fine. No one followed us over here." She hoped she was speaking the truth, because she really wanted to take a ride with him. "And besides, this baby can outrun anything, can't it?"

"She is built for speed," he said, stroking the hood.

She laughed at his reverent gesture. "Let's see if she goes fast enough for me."

He opened the car door for her. "Have a seat and buckle

up." He slid behind the wheel, opened the garage door with a remote and backed out.

Within minutes, they were heading onto the Great Highway, a two-lane highway that ran along the ocean. It was a beautiful, sunny day, with only bright wispy white clouds to break up the blue of the sky. There wasn't much traffic out yet, either, so she felt like they had the road to themselves.

Her long hair blew wildly around her face and she wished she had a band to pull it into a ponytail, but she hadn't come at all prepared for this ride. Despite that small annoyance, it felt great to have the wind in her face, the salty taste of the sea on her lips, the sun beating down on her head. There had been so much tension lately, she just wanted to take a minute away from it all and not think about anything.

"Faster," she told him.

He smiled and put his foot down on the gas.

He was right. His baby was built for speed and so was she.

Dylan hadn't expected to drive so far, but with the beautiful Tori egging him on, he headed down the coast. Once they got south of San Francisco, he got onto Highway 1 and drove through the beach cities of Pacifica, Moss Beach, and El Granada, ending up in Half Moon Bay.

The ocean views, the happy woman by his side, the powerful car responding so well to his touch made this day one of the best he'd had in a very long time. He felt relaxed and re-energized, and despite the fact that Tori was wrestling with her long hair, she seemed to be feeling the same way.

All of their problems felt very far away at the moment. He'd kept an eye on traffic, watching for any suspicious cars, but they'd often had the road to themselves, so he didn't think anyone was on their tail, and he wasn't ready to turn around and go home.

He knew he'd been sending Tori mixed messages. It

wasn't something he normally did. If he wanted someone and they wanted him, then there was nothing to think about. But Tori wasn't just any woman. He couldn't risk hurting her. He also couldn't risk anyone else hurting her. So he had to stay close but far enough away at the same time. He didn't quite know how that was going to work, but he would give it his best shot.

"Pull over," she said, pointing to an upcoming sign for Pelican's Point.

He took the next right and drove down a one-lane road that led down to an ocean outlook with a small beach beyond.

Turning off the car, he glanced over at Tori, who was pulling strands of brown, silky hair off her face, her cheeks pink from the sun and the wind. Her dark-blue eyes sparkled very much like the sea in front of them, and her lips were curved in a wide, happy smile.

She'd definitely enjoyed the ride, and so had he.

"That was fun," she said, getting out of the car.

He followed her to the fence in front of them. She climbed over the rail and sat on the top, and he did the same.

"What a view," she added, glancing over at him. "It's a perfect day today."

He couldn't deny that. "It feels perfect."

"Your baby is a nice ride," she said with a teasing smile.

"I thought you'd like her."

"Can I drive back?"

He hesitated, which was ridiculous, because of course she could drive back. "Sure, if you really want to."

She laughed. "Wow, what a great response. Your enthusiasm is very underwhelming."

"I'm just usually the driver. And your hair gets in your eyes."

"I know. I wish I'd brought a band or a scarf, but it was worth it. I haven't been in a convertible in years. I actually haven't done much driving in a very long time. I lived in New York for eight years and then the last three in Boston. I'm used to subways, buses, trains, and taxis."

"I don't think I could ever get used to that. I like to have my own wheels."

"It does give you more control," she agreed.

"Why did you go so far away?" he asked curiously. "What was it about New York that drew you to the other side of the country?"

She thought for a moment. "I wanted a change. I wanted to live where there were seasons. I was also drawn to the fact that New York is the center of so many news organizations. I thought it would be a good place to learn. And..." Her voice drifted away.

"And?" he pressed.

"My dad lived there when he was in his twenties. He said the city inspired him to dream big, work hard." She shot him a quick look. "My dad keeps coming up. It feels ironic in a way."

"How so?" he asked curiously.

"You hardly say anything about your father, because he's alive, he's in your life. But my dad's abrupt departure from my life has actually given him a bigger presence now. It's strange how that worked out. Would I have made the same choices, gone across the country, followed him into the news if he'd lived, if he'd always been part of my life? I guess I'll never know."

"I think parents are a strong influence—alive or dead, good or bad. They're our parents, our blood. Maybe you would have made different choices, but that's not to say they would have been better or worse."

"That's true. And I don't feel like I've made bad choices; I just wonder sometimes."

"You wonder about everything all the time," he said lightly.

She smiled at him. "I was blessed with a curious mind. And don't change that to cursed," she warned.

"I wouldn't dream of it. You actually make me think I should ask more questions. It's easy to get complacent in life, especially when you live in the same town, work the same job, see the same people. You fall into patterns."

"Do you want to make any changes to those patterns?"

He hadn't thought he did, but since she'd arrived, he was starting to wonder if he was missing something—or someone—important. "I don't know," he muttered, glancing out at the sea.

"Or you know, and you don't want to tell me. You're very good at shutting people out with a smile or a laugh, as if you're not really doing it, but you are."

He turned his gaze back on her. "You think I shut you out?"

"Yes," she said, meeting his gaze head on. "I think I scare you."

He had to admit she was right about that. "Maybe you do."

"Really? I was kind of just guessing on that."

He laughed, loving how Tori could be so honest about everything. "You challenge me in ways I don't always appreciate."

"Maybe that's not scary—but good."

"Maybe."

"Don't you want to find out?"

"Right now, I just want to enjoy the moment. I have a feeling you don't do that very often, Tori. You're always five steps ahead in your mind, worrying, analyzing, questioning, overthinking…"

"Hey, don't get carried away," she protested. "In fact, we should stop talking and enjoy the moment." She closed her eyes and tilted her face toward the sun.

As he looked at her, he felt something inside him shift, as if a wall had come crashing down, a wall he might need later on, but he couldn't bring himself to worry about it now. So he watched her until her eyes opened and then he slid off the fence. They might be at the beach, but they were sliding into dangerous water, and he knew when to get out.

"Let's go back to the city," he said.

"So soon?"

"You have to get your car and talk to your mom."

"I thought we were living in the moment."

"We were. It's over now." If he didn't get them both back to the city and their everyday lives, he was going to kiss her again, and that couldn't happen.

She got off the fence with a slightly grumpy expression. "Fine, let's go back."

He held out the keys as a peace offering. "Do you want to drive?"

She smiled. "I know you want me to say no."

He didn't want to admit she was right. "I'm happy with whatever decision you make."

"Then you can drive," she said. "I'm going to relax and let the wind run through my hair, and at some point, I'm going to decide what I want to say to my mother."

Eleven

It was one o'clock when they got back to the city. Tori was sad to leave the drive behind, but she knew that she couldn't put off the rest of the day any longer. She had to talk to her mother, get her car, go home, and do some research into both her homeless article and the mysterious Neil Hawkins.

"I'll wait until you get inside," Dylan told her, as he pulled up a few houses down from her mom's house.

She didn't bother to argue. "Sounds good."

"I'd really like you to call me when you're leaving."

"I don't know how long I'll stay. It might be a few minutes or an hour or more."

"It doesn't matter. I can hang in my parents' garage until you're ready to go. If it's five minutes, then I'll just switch cars and come back."

"Fine. It will probably be at least an hour. I know my mother will want to talk about the wedding."

"Take your time. I'll be around when you're ready."

She got out of the car and walked quickly down the street to the house.

She rang the bell, and her mother answered a moment later, wearing white jeans and a soft plaid flannel shirt.

"Tori, I was wondering when you were going to show up. Did you sleep in today?"

"I did," she said, as she entered the house.

"What happened to your hair? You look like you've been in a wind tunnel."

"I had the window down. It's a beautiful day," she added, following her mom into the kitchen. "Did Scott and Monica get off to Hawaii this morning?"

"As far as I know. I haven't heard from them, but they should actually be in Maui by now. They had an early flight." She paused. "Do you want lunch?"

"No. I had a big breakfast, but I will take coffee if you have it."

"I just made a fresh pot."

"Where's Ray?"

"He's driving his brother to the airport."

"It was nice he came in for the wedding. It was great to see the extended family and your old friends."

"It was nice." Her mother set a mug of coffee in front of her and gave her a hard, pointed look. "Now that we've gotten the pleasantries out of the way, do you want to tell me what was going on last night outside the yacht club when you started yelling at Jim about some man he was talking to in the parking lot? Who is this man? And has he been following you? You have a lot of explaining to do, Tori. I don't know why you've left me in the dark."

"I realize that." She could see from the determination in her mother's eyes that she wasn't going to get away with any vague explanations. "I didn't want to bother you, Mom. You've had a lot on your mind with the wedding."

"I still need to know if my daughter is in danger. And you don't need to be concerned about my worries. I don't know why everyone thinks I'm so fragile. I'm not made of glass, Tori. If I was, I would have shattered a long time ago."

"I know that," she murmured, realizing she'd

shortchanged and judged her mother, much the way some people had done to her.

"Do you? Your father used to tell me there was nothing for me to worry about whenever I asked him a question he didn't want to answer. I don't know if he was hiding something or just wanted to protect me, but I didn't like when he said it, and I don't like when you say it. I know I've been distracted by the wedding, but that's over now, so talk."

"Okay. Last week I thought a man was watching me, and I believed he might be from a homeless encampment that I had visited while doing research for my news article. When he realized I had seen him, he took off. I followed him just to see where he was going. He went into a building, and as I got closer, there was an explosion."

"Oh, my God! The scratches on your face the other day. You didn't get them by getting tangled up in a rose bush."

"No. There was some flying glass." She deliberately omitted the part where she'd gone into the building.

Her mom stared back at her. "What happened to the man you were following?"

"It looks like he got out a back door and escaped the fire. Dylan was one of the firefighters who responded to the call."

"So that's why you and Dylan seem so close all of a sudden. That's why you were meeting him at Brady's, and that's why you kept talking to him last night when you thought Jim was meeting with this same man."

"Yes."

"So who was in the parking lot last night?"

"I don't know. It could have been the same man, but it was dark, and I didn't get a good look at him."

"You're downplaying it again. Let's say it was him. Why would he be there?"

"All I can think of is that he still wants to talk to me."

"How would he know where you were?"

"I don't know, Mom. That's the truth. He could be following me. Or he could have seen on social media that my brother was getting married. It wouldn't have been difficult to find out where the reception was being held. Or the man in the parking lot could have just wanted a cigarette."

Her mother's mouth tightened. "Is that it? All of it?"

"Not quite all of it. Someone left me a note on my car the day after the fire, suggesting I stop asking questions."

"I don't like this at all, Tori. We need to call the police."

"I've already spoken to the police. Dylan's cousin Emma is married to a detective. They're looking into everything. They're completely up to speed."

"Even on the man you saw last night?"

"Yes. Dylan spoke to Emma this morning." She paused. "I've run into this kind of thing before. As a journalist, I sometimes make people nervous."

"I understand. Your father got death threats once."

"I didn't know that," she said with surprise.

"He downplayed it, too. Luckily, the police found the person before they could carry out their threat. I really wish you weren't following in your father's footsteps. I know he'd be proud of you, but I worried about him, and I worry about you. You both like to shake things up."

"It's part of the job. I am careful, if that makes you feel any better. And Dylan has been watching out for me."

"Good. I'm glad you confided in him and that he has his family involved."

"Just don't mention anything to anyone else, especially his mother, okay?"

"I can keep a secret. I've kept many over the years."

"Oh, yeah?" she asked curiously. "Like what?"

"They wouldn't be secrets if I told you," her mother said with a small smile.

"Great answer," she said dryly. "So, getting back to the wedding? Any good gossip?"

"My sister said she saw one of the bridesmaids making out with one of the ushers. I think it was Ava and Paul."

"That would be my guess."

"So besides Dylan watching out for you, I thought the two of you looked good dancing together."

She held up a warning hand. "Don't go there, Mom."

"Why not?"

"Because it's not going to happen. Dylan sees me as Scott's little sister, and he would never jeopardize his friendship with Scott."

"Why would he have to lose Scott's friendship?"

She shrugged. "I don't know. I don't understand men."

"Well, I'm with you on that one. I've been married twice, and I'm still not an expert."

She pulled out her phone as it began to vibrate. "Speak of the devil."

"Is that Dylan?"

She nodded. "He says Emma called back and wants to talk to us."

"Have they found the man from the parking lot?"

"I don't know." She texted him back to come by the house. "I might leave my car here until later if that's okay. I'll ride with Dylan to Emma's house."

"Of course. It's not in the way, and we have plenty of street parking. You'll keep me posted?"

"Yes."

"And you promise to stay safe? I can't lose you, Tori. I just can't."

She saw the fear in her mom's eyes and almost regretted her earlier candor, but they'd always been honest with each other, even when it hurt. "You're not going to lose me."

Her mother let out another heavy breath. "Your father used to tell me that, too."

Dylan picked her up in front of her Mom's house. He'd switched back to his Mustang.

"Not worried your mom will see us together?" he asked, as she fastened her seat belt.

"No, I told her everything," she replied.

"Everything?" he said with surprise.

"Well, not about us kissing, but everything else: Neil Hawkins, the fire, the threatening note."

"That's a lot. What made you confess?"

"She heard too much last night when we were in the parking lot. She wanted the truth, and she reminded me that she'd been around during all of my father's dangerous investigations, so she wasn't going to break if I was honest with her. So I got honest."

"What was her response?"

"She'd like me to drop it, but she knows I won't, so she didn't press too much. What did Emma say?"

"Nothing. She just asked if we could come over. She said she had some new information, but she didn't want to get into it on the phone."

"That sounds promising," she said, hopeful they were going to get some sort of a break.

As they neared Emma's house, tension tightened her chest and quickened her breath. Her mind raced with the possibilities of what Emma and Max might have discovered. She really wanted some answers and if they'd found Neil Hawkins, that would be even better.

"Breathe," Dylan said, interrupting her thoughts.

She didn't know when he'd gotten so good at reading her mind. He'd always seemed pretty clueless when they were teenagers. But she did take a breath as instructed. "I'm just anxious about what we're going to learn. You have to be curious, too."

"I am, but I'm trying not to get too far ahead."

"You're much better at putting on the brakes than I am," she said, realizing a split second too late that he might think she was referring to the night before. But even if he did, it was the truth. He was better at going with logic than emotion. She'd always had to battle her heart over her head.

Dylan didn't seem inclined to comment, so they drove the rest of the way in silence.

Emma let them into her house with a friendly smile and waved them toward the couch, where Shannon was coloring in a sketch book on the coffee table.

"That's so pretty," Tori told the little girl, looking at her picture of a house and trees.

"It's a picture of my house in Ireland," Shannon said. "Where I used to live."

"I'd love to go there sometime."

"We're going to go after the baby is born," Shannon said, giving Emma a questioning look. "Right, Mommy?"

"We are," Emma agreed. "Why don't you take your coloring into your bedroom? We have to have some grown-up talk."

"Okay." Shannon obediently gathered her crayons and paper and went into her room.

"She's just adorable," Tori told Emma.

"She's almost too well-behaved," Emma said, as they settled onto the couch. "I think there's a part of her that worries we'll send her away if she's not good. I keep telling her that she's our little girl now, but I'm not sure it has completely set in."

"It will. Give it time," Dylan said.

"I'm trying. I'm not the most patient person. It's a blessing for me to have Shannon and now to be pregnant as well, but I do worry that Shannon won't feel like she's getting enough attention once the baby is here."

"Every kid with a sibling feels that way," Dylan interjected. "I had to watch five more kids get born after me, and you had at least a couple after you. We both survived."

"That's true," Emma said with a laugh. "And it was fun growing up with siblings. My sisters were my best friends. I'm glad Shannon will have that same experience."

"Let's not forget all the cousins she has now, too," Dylan added. "Your siblings are procreating at a rapid pace."

"I know. It's fun. A lot of the cousins will be close in age and hopefully great friends as they grow up. Anyway, I know you didn't come over to chat. Max is on his way home." She paused as the door opened. "Looks like he's here now."

"Sorry I'm late," Max said. "We're wrapping up another

case I've been working on for the past several months. I didn't
think we had any surveillance video from the neighborhood
around Brady's, but one of the shop owners came up with an
unexpected shot. Take a look at this."

Max handed her his phone. Max moved in closer to her,
watching the screen over her shoulder.

The black-and-white grainy image wasn't great, but once
she realized what she was looking at, she got excited. "That's
the front of my car."

"Keep watching," Max said.

A few seconds passed, and then a man came into the
frame. She couldn't see much of him as he was wearing a
heavy coat and a baseball cap on his head. He pulled up the
windshield wiper and slipped a piece of paper under it. Then
he turned toward the camera, and as he checked the street
before crossing, she caught a glimpse of his face. Shock ran
through her.

"Do you recognize him?" Max asked. "Is that the man
you were following?"

"I have to play it again." She pushed the button to repeat
the video, stopping on the frame. "Oh, no," she whispered.
Her heart thudded against her chest, and she felt a knot grow
in her throat. She turned to Dylan. "You know who that is,
don't you?"

He nodded grimly. "I think so. Why don't you say it?"

"Mitch Hedden—one of my father's best friends."

"That's what I thought," Dylan muttered.

She looked at Max and Emma. "This man is a longtime
friend of my family. I can't imagine why he would leave this
note on my car. I just saw him yesterday at my brother's
wedding. He didn't act odd in any way. He certainly didn't try
to warn me about anything. I don't understand." She stared
back down at the picture, trying to make sense of it.

"What does Mr. Hedden do for a living?" Max asked.

"He's a financial guy. He works in venture capital. I think
he's given my parents a lot of investment advice. He's been
married forever, has two children, some grandchildren. His

wife was a stay-at-home mom, active in the PTA. They're a super normal family." She realized she was rambling and Max and Emma were letting her have her reaction, but obviously they both had questions. "What else can I tell you?"

"Did he know you were going to Brady's?" Max asked.

She was about to say no, then realized that wasn't true. "Yes," she said with a nod. "I stopped at my mom's house before I went to meet Dylan at Brady's. She was having the Heddens and another friend over for dinner. They got there right before I left, and I said I couldn't stay because I was meeting Dylan at Brady's. But I didn't say anything about the fire or Neil Hawkins or what I was working on for the *Examiner*. It was literally a five-minute conversation."

"What about something personal?" Emma asked. "You said he's a family friend. Has he had any issues with your mom? Did she perhaps invest in something that didn't do well? Have you ever asked questions about any of his advice?"

"I don't think so—certainly not recently. I just don't understand. I really thought the man who'd left me the note was the mysterious Neil Hawkins."

"What about Neil Hawkins?" Dylan interrupted. "What have you found out about him?"

"Nothing," Max said. "The ID was a forgery. None of the information was valid."

"But the picture was real," she put in. "That's what he looked like."

"We ran the image through facial recognition, but we didn't get any hits," Max replied. "He's not in the system."

She let out a breath. "So he could be anyone, and he could be anywhere, including at the yacht club where my brother's reception was held."

Max nodded. "Emma told me about that. I was going to stop by the yacht club later and show the ID around, see if any of the employees saw him."

She had a feeling that wasn't going to yield any better results. "Another one of my father's friends—Jim Beacham—

spoke to the man. Jim said he'd be happy to talk to you. He told me he didn't recognize him, and the man just asked for a cigarette. But I know he was there for another reason, and it's tied to me." She wasn't sure of much, but she was certain about that. "I have to talk to Mitch. I need to confront him about what he did."

"Can you arrest him for this?" Dylan asked Max.

"No, but I can definitely talk to him. Right now, all we have him for is leaving a note, and one that isn't all that threatening." Max answered. "What we really want to know is why he did it and what else is going on. Getting his cooperation would be helpful."

"I can make that happen," she said. "I've known Mitch my entire life. I want him to look me in the eye and tell me why he left me a threatening note."

"That could be dangerous," Dylan put in. "We should let Max handle it."

"I'll get more out of him. He won't be able to clam up with me staring him down," she argued. "But I'm happy for you guys to go with me. I'm not averse to backup."

Max smiled and glanced at Emma. "She sounds like you."

Emma laughed. "Then you should know better than to argue. Why don't all three of you go?"

"Can we do it now?" she asked, getting to her feet. "I know it's Sunday, but I just don't want to wait."

"Then let's do it now," Max said. "But let's take two cars. I need to go down to the station afterwards."

"We really appreciate this, Max," Dylan said. "No one but you would have taken the time to track down that video."

"Not a problem," Max said with a brief smile. "And I had some help from a rookie police officer, who wanted to win some points from me."

"Whatever it takes," Dylan said.

"Exactly. But aside from that, you're a Callaway, Dylan. Emma takes family seriously, and so do I."

"I want you all to be careful," Emma said, as she walked

them to the door. "Especially you, Tori. Even if this man is a longtime family friend, you don't know why he did what he did, and until you do, don't underestimate him."

Joanie Hedden opened the door, surprise moving through her eyes. "Tori, hello. And Dylan, what are you doing here? Is something wrong?" Her gaze moved to Max and there must have been something about his official-looking suit that made her nervous. "It's not your mother, or Scott, is it?"

"No, nothing is wrong," Tori said quickly, seeing that Joanie's imagination was leaping ahead. "We just need to talk to Mitch about something. Is he here?"

"No, I'm sorry, but he and Jim left early this morning for a deep-sea fishing trip. They'll be gone until Wednesday or Thursday, depending on how the fish are biting."

Disappointment flooded through her at Joanie's words. She'd really wanted to get some answers.

"They didn't mention they were going fishing last night," Dylan put in. "Was the trip planned?"

"For a couple of days now," Joanie said, her gaze growing concerned. "What's this about? And who is your friend?"

"I'm sorry. This is Max Harrison," she said. "Dylan's cousin's husband."

"It's nice to meet you, Mrs. Hedden," Max said. "Tori tells me you're a long-time family friend."

"I've known her since she was born." Joanie cocked her head to the right as she gave them a speculative look. "What is this about? Is there something I can help you with?"

"We'll need to speak to your husband," Max said, sending Tori a pointed look.

He didn't want her to tell Joanie what was happening. She didn't know exactly why, but maybe he was afraid Joanie would warn her husband to stay away.

"Yes, I'm afraid this is a Mitch question," she said, going

along with him. She gave Joanie what she hoped was an easygoing smile. "It's about my dad and their fishing trips. It can wait until he gets back."

"You're thinking about your dad a lot lately, aren't you? Jim said you thought you saw a man who looked like him outside the reception last night." Joanie's eyes filled with sadness. "It's understandable that you'd miss him at such a big event."

"I did miss him," she admitted.

"Well, I can tell Mitch to call you when I hear from him. I'm sure he'll text me or check in at some point, although he enjoys being out of touch for days at a time. That's what he likes about fishing. He doesn't have to talk to anyone but fishermen and I'm pretty sure all they talk about is fish."

"That's fine. If he could get in touch when he gets back, that would be great."

"He definitely will."

"We'll let you get back to your day," she said.

"I was just cleaning, so nothing exciting. When Mitch goes fishing, I like to take some of his old clothes to charity. It's the only way his closet ever gets cleaned out."

"That doesn't sound too fun."

"I actually enjoy getting organized. You all take care."

As the front door closed, they walked back to their cars.

"That was a waste of time," she said with a sigh. "Do you think she told us the truth?"

"She seemed sincere," Max said. "I think you played it the right way."

"I just wish Mitch wasn't gone. I don't want to wait three or four days to get answers."

"I wonder if he is really gone," Dylan put in. "It seems very convenient that both he and Jim would disappear together."

"They go fishing all the time," she reminded him.

"Do they have their own boat?" Max asked.

She thought for a minute. "I'm not sure. Should I go back and ask Joanie?"

Max shook his head. "No. I can find out if he owns a boat and has it anchored anywhere around here. Let's not make Joanie any more suspicious. Right now, Mitch doesn't know he was caught on camera. I'd prefer to keep it that way."

"Okay, that makes sense," she said.

"I'm going to take off," Max said. "Call me if anything else comes up. Otherwise, I'll be in touch."

"Thanks again, Max."

As Max left, she got into Dylan's car. He started the engine, then paused.

"Where to?" he asked.

Her mind spun in a dozen different directions. "I don't know." As she glanced back at the house, she saw the curtain in the front room move. "I think Joanie is watching us." Her stomach churned at the thought that Joanie might be involved or know about the note. "I can't believe these people I've known my whole life might want to hurt me in some way."

"She's probably just curious about why we showed up to talk to Mitch and why Max was with us."

"I suppose."

"And maybe they're not trying to hurt you. Perhaps they're trying to protect you by scaring you away from something that could hurt you. Let's go somewhere to discuss it before Joanie comes out here with more questions."

"I still need to get my car, so let's go back to my mom's house."

"Do you want to fill her in on Mitch and the note?"

She thought about that. "I'm not sure. I wouldn't want to put her in the middle of things, but I was thinking that maybe I should talk to her more about Dad's family."

"Because you're still looking for the connection between Hawkins's face and your dad's?"

"Yes. And because the common denominator between Mitch and Jim is my dad. Maybe he had a sibling or a cousin who looked like him. I know my mom has photo albums from my dad's childhood up in the attic. She couldn't bring herself to get rid of his personal things. I would assume they're still there."

"That's a good idea. Maybe putting your dad's image on Neil Hawkins isn't about you missing your father. Maybe there is a resemblance, because there's a blood connection. It's a long shot, but worth taking."

She liked that he was on the same wavelength. "I thought you would say I was crazy."

"I don't like all your ideas, but some of them are interesting. I'd like to hear what your mom has to say. Mind inviting me in?"

"I might as well. She knows you texted me with information, and that you came to pick me up. But what am I going to do about Mitch? That's the information we got, and she's going to ask me what I learned."

"I think you were right when you said you didn't want to put her into the middle of things. She's tight with Joanie and Mitch and also with Jim. You don't want her rushing over to confront Joanie, maybe stirring things up in a bad way."

"I really don't," she agreed. "So what am I going to tell her?"

"You'll figure it out."

"That's not helpful," she said grumpily.

"I have confidence in you." He parked the car in front of her mom's house. "But you have about thirty seconds to figure it out."

Twelve

"You're back. What happened with Emma?" her mother asked, as she let them in the house.

"It was nothing," she lied. "They just wanted to ask me more about the guy I saw in the yacht club parking lot. Max is going to interview the employees, show them a photo of the guy I followed a few days ago, and see if anyone saw him around the club that night."

"Well, I'm glad someone is looking into it." She turned her gaze on Dylan. "And I'm glad you're helping her."

"Of course," Dylan said. "I'm happy to do whatever I can."

"So why are you back here now?" her mom asked.

"I can't seem to stop thinking about Dad," she said. "Dylan was asking me about him, his family and his background, and I realized I can barely remember his history."

Her mother frowned. "Oh, honey, that happens. It's been a long time. But I can tell you whatever you want to know." She glanced at her watch. "I just don't know that I can do that now. Ray wants to take me over to Sausalito for some shopping and an early dinner. We've been so busy with wedding plans the past several months we haven't spent much time together."

"That sounds like fun. We can talk another time. I was wondering if you still have Dad's photo albums from his childhood."

"Yes. They're in the attic. You know I can't throw anything away."

"Would you mind if Dylan and I look through them?"

"No, but is there something else going on?" her mom asked.

"I just need to see Dad's face again."

"You have photos of your father, Tori. I don't think you're telling me the whole story."

"Okay, fine," she said, seeing the sharp gleam in her mother's eyes. "I'm wondering if Dad had any relatives that looked like him—a cousin or an uncle or..."

"Or what?" her mom asked.

"Is it possible Dad had a sibling?"

"No. He was an only child."

"And there's no way his parents would have given a child up for adoption?"

"Well, I certainly never asked them that." She frowned. "This is about the man you saw. I can't imagine that he's related to your father."

"It could just be that he has similar features; that's why I want to look at more photos, but I also want to see if there's anyone in my grandparents' photos who bears a resemblance to Dad. There could have been a second cousin or someone."

"I suppose. Maybe I should stay and help you look."

"That's not necessary. Dylan is helping me."

"Someone has to keep her out of trouble," Dylan put in.

Her mom smiled. "That's what I used to say to Scott when I'd send the two of you out to look for her when she was a teenager."

"Why did anyone think I was in trouble? I was a good

girl," she said.

"But you were already an intrepid and determined reporter," her mother reminded her. "You followed the economics teacher to his house because you thought he was having an affair with a student. And you were wrong."

"I was wrong about that, but I did find out that he was selling pot on the side."

"I remember that," Dylan said. "Scott and I picked you up right before the police arrived, because one of the neighbors reported someone looking in the teacher's windows."

"We don't need to talk about the past," she said quickly, pausing as her stepfather came down the stairs.

"Tori—Dylan," Ray said in surprise. "I didn't realize you were coming over. Do you want to join us for an early dinner in Sausalito?"

"No, thanks," she said, hesitant to mention her father's photo albums in front of Ray.

Her mother apparently didn't feel the same. "Tori wants to look through her father's things in the attic."

He nodded, understanding in his eyes. "Missing your dad, huh?"

"A little," she said, feeling self-conscious. Ray had always tried to be a dad to her, and she liked him very much, but she'd never had the closeness with him that she'd had with her father.

"Just lock up when you leave," her mother said, grabbing her purse off the table. "Ready, Ray?"

"I am," he said.

"Have a good time," she told them.

After her mom and Ray left, she led Dylan up the stairs to the second floor and then pulled down a ladder at the end of the hall that took them into the attic.

"I haven't been up here in years," she said, turning on a light.

"It's musty," he said, walking over to crack a window.

"I don't think anyone ever comes up here." She looked

around, noting the stack of boxes in one corner, plastic cartons filled with old toys, schoolwork, art projects, all neatly labeled, including one that held Scott's model airplane kits.

"I remember these," Dylan said, moving over to that box and pulling out one of the already constructed airplanes. "Scott spent hours on these airplanes."

"My dad would, too. They loved building the planes."

"I used to think Scott would become a pilot, but instead he went into the law."

"My brother is practical. He thought a law degree would get him further than a pilot's license."

"I don't know about that. As a pilot, the whole world was there for him to see."

"It's funny that you both liked to put mechanical things together—Scott with the airplanes, you with the cars."

"True, but I built actual cars, not mini-planes. So I win."

"I didn't realize it was a competition."

He grinned back at her. "It was then." Dylan set the plane back in the box. "So where do you want to start, Tori?"

She let out a heavy sigh. "I don't really know."

His gaze sharpened on her. "Are you up for this, Tori? I know you're still reeling from seeing Mitch's face on the security camera."

"I have to be up for it. I have to keep going. I need to find answers."

"You might not like them."

"Anything is better than not knowing."

"I hope that's true," he murmured.

"I doubt there's anything earth-shattering up here. I really don't think my dad or his family had any big secrets." She paused as she realized how naïve that sounded. "On the other hand, I never thought Mitch would leave me a threatening note. So, what do I know?" She walked over to the bookshelves and pulled out an album. She handed it to Dylan, then grabbed the other one on the shelf and sat down on a rolled up carpet.

Dylan took a seat next to her, and they each opened their albums.

The first photo in her book was of her father as a baby. She recognized her grandparents from the picture that had sat on her living room mantel for most of her life.

There were a lot of photos of her father with his parents. They really looked like a family of three. There were some larger family shots, and there were other kids in those photos, but most of them were girls.

She paused on one photo of her dad at a birthday party. Her father appeared to be about ten, and there was a teenager of about fourteen standing next to him. "What do you think of this guy?"

Dylan leaned in closer to take a look. "He has similar features. Do you know who he is?"

"No clue. There are no names on any of these pictures. I probably should have had my mother go through them with us, although she might not know anyone, either. Have you found anything?"

"Not much. I've got your dad in his high school years. I didn't realize he was a baseball player. There are newspaper clippings of his home runs. He was quite good."

"When he was young, he wanted to be a professional ballplayer, but he said he wasn't good enough. I think he lived that dream again through Scott. They spent a lot of time on ballfields together."

Dylan nodded, his gaze reflective. "Scott was shattered after your father died. Those first few games that he had to play after the funeral were really hard on him. He'd get angry and frustrated when he didn't get a hit, which was not the way he usually reacted, but that year every strikeout made him feel like he was letting your dad down."

His words resonated within her, touching off old memories, some happy—many painful.

"Scott didn't want to play those games, but my mom told him it was something he could do to honor my dad's memory. So he played. Maybe in the end it helped him get through it."

"And you followed your dad into the news. He left legacies with both of you."

She appreciated the reminder. "He did encourage me to work on the school paper in the seventh grade. It was right before he died. I told him I was going to be a reporter like him. I'm glad he knew that, even if he didn't believe it." She quickly flipped through the rest of the pages in the album. "I don't think I'm going to be able to figure anything out from these photos. I can show my mom the one of the older kid and see if she knows who he is, but that's probably doubtful. She wasn't close to her in-laws. And if there was some big family secret, they wouldn't have told her."

"Unless your father told her."

"Unless that," she agreed. "But you would think she might have mentioned that to me at some point, especially since he's been dead for a long time. There's no reason to keep that kind of secret."

"There's always a reason to keep a secret. I found out something a year ago about my grandmother that shocked the hell out of me. She did some incredible things in her younger years that none of us knew anything about."

"Like what?"

"She ran an underground network for abused women, helping them escape and get to safety."

"That's amazing," she said, truly impressed. "How did she do that?"

"It was under the cover of a theater group she ran. She faced danger herself, too. She had to physically protect one of her friends. She was much more courageous than I ever imagined."

She saw wonder in Dylan's eyes and also a little regret. "What are you sad about?"

"That I didn't pay enough attention to her when she was completely healthy. She has Alzheimer's now. She's undergone some experimental treatments, which have given her more lucid days, but one day she will be gone, mentally and physically."

"Until she is, you use the time as best you can."

"I am trying to see her more often."

"I'm sure you're a good grandson." If there was one thing she knew about Dylan, it was that he was loyal.

"What's next?" he asked as he closed his album.

She looked at the filing cabinet against the opposite wall. "Let's look at my dad's files. I'm sure he just has notes from his news articles, maybe some personal bills, but there could be something in there about Mitch or Jim. Maybe we'll find out they were running some sort of scheme together that no one else knew about."

Dylan got up and went over to the cabinet. He took out the top drawer and brought it over to her. "You can start with this one. I'll get into the next one."

She pulled the drawer closer and looked through the folders. Most were neatly labeled and all appeared to be related to her father's work. The folders held a variety of papers, photos, handwritten notes, clippings, police and medical examiner reports. All the cases dated back at least twenty years, and nothing seemed particularly relevant. But as she looked through the articles, some of which had made his name as an investigative journalist, she felt both exhilaration and intense sadness. Her father had been brilliant, insightful, and very thorough. He was a man who saw the truth in the details. He was painstaking in his research. He didn't overlook even the most innocuous clue.

She needed to think more like her dad. Instead of trying to jump ahead and leap to a conclusion, she needed to assemble her clues and go through them with the same eye to detail.

Dylan liked to make fun of her for always asking questions, but that's what her father had done, too. She smiled as she read through a list of questions he'd compiled for an insurance fraud case. Apparently, she had more of her father in her than she'd thought.

"You're smiling," Dylan said, as he brought over another pile of files.

"Reading my dad's handwriting, following his thoughts in his notes, makes him feel alive again."

"I'm glad that's making you happy. A while ago, you had a different expression on your face."

"I think I've been trying to jump too far ahead when I should be building a ladder to get me there."

He gave her a quizzical look as he sat down next to her. "What does that mean?"

"My dad took things one step at a time. I've been jumping from one slippery rock to the next. I need to slow down and really think about what I know so far and what I need to figure out. Does that make sense?"

"Yes, but you're not the most patient person, Tori."

She made a little face at him, but he was right. "I could be better," she agreed. "I've just always felt like I have to know the answer as soon as I have the question. I'm impatient."

"It's not a bad thing. Your curiosity drives you. In your line of work, it's important to have that thirst for the truth."

"So you're complimenting me?" she asked with a raise of her brow.

"It seems that way," he said with a grin. "But here's an idea. If you're going to slow down— and I think that's a great idea, by the way—why don't we pack up these files and take them to your apartment? It's hot up here, and there's no way you're going to get through all of this before your mom comes back. And if we're still here when she returns from dinner, there are going to be more questions."

"Good point." She got up and grabbed an old suitcase. "This is empty. We can use this to transport the files."

"Perfect."

They loaded up the files in the suitcase. The few that didn't fit she carried down to her car and put them on the backseat.

"I'll follow you home," Dylan said.

"You really want to keep doing this with me?"

"I don't have to go to work until tomorrow. I'm yours

until then. But you may need to spring for some pizza, because breakfast was a long time ago."

"I can do that."

She was good at working independently, but none of her previous research had been so personal, and she didn't want her emotions to get in the way. Dylan brought a cool head, and she liked having someone she could trust by her side, because right now she felt like every step was taking her into quicksand.

Dylan did, however, bring other complications and taking him back to her apartment where they usually ended up getting closer than Dylan wanted might not be the best idea, but she didn't want to say good-bye to him yet.

He wasn't hers forever, but she'd take a few more hours.

Thirteen

--->>><<<---

As Dylan followed Tori across town, he wondered what the hell he was doing. He should be trying to get her away from investigating on her own and possibly getting into more trouble, but instead he was working right alongside her, spurring her on with his own ideas.

Since discovering that Mitch had left the note, his mind had been racing with possibilities, and now he was as invested as Tori in finding out the truth. He wanted to know what Mitch and Jim were involved in. He thought it had to be both of them. And they'd taken off because Tori was asking too many questions.

But how did they connect to Neil Hawkins and/or to the hotel fire and the murder of Robert Walker? Was it all one complicated scheme? Or were there two separate things going on? And how much danger was Tori in?

She wanted to believe she was in less danger now because Mitch had left the warning note, but was that true? He'd feel better if he knew who Hawkins was and whether or not he'd shot Robert Walker.

After watching Tori pull into her parking garage, he had to drive down the block to find a space. As he walked back to her building, he kept a sharp eye out for anyone sitting in a car or watching the building, but the street was empty.

Glancing at his watch, he realized it was almost six. It felt like a million years ago that they had driven down the coast, feeling happy and carefree. That feeling had certainly changed after seeing Mitch on the security camera footage. And now digging into Ben Hayden's photos and files had added another layer of weight to the day. He hoped that a few more hours of research would bring forth a new clue, because tomorrow he had to go to work, and he'd be at the firehouse for forty-eight hours. He really hated the idea of leaving Tori on her own.

Not that she'd let him follow her to work. She was a very independent person. He liked her strength, her opinions, her fierce drive to get to the truth.

He also liked the way she bit down on her bottom lip while she was pondering a problem, and how her eyes lit up when she smiled or came to some surprising conclusion, and how soft and sexy her mouth was when she kissed him.

That thought made the breath catch in his chest, and he actually stopped walking for a second, wondering again what the hell he was doing.

It had been hard enough to walk away the first time, and even more difficult the second time, but what about the third? Would there be a third kiss—a third choice to end things or take them further? His body was screaming *yes* while his brain was yelling *no*.

He forced himself to move again. Tonight wasn't a date. He was helping her find answers.

Most importantly, he was watching over her, making sure she didn't get into trouble, the way Scott had wanted him to do. He was being a good friend, a big brother…he needed to remember that.

She buzzed him into her apartment and when he got inside, he realized she'd already managed to drag the suitcase and the loose files upstairs. Some of those files were now spread across her kitchen table, while the suitcase had been placed on the floor and opened with the lid propped up against the wall.

"I would have helped you bring those up," he said.

"I didn't need you for that," she returned. "Do you want something to drink?"

"Coffee would be good."

"I'm already making a pot. It feels like forever since we had breakfast here this morning."

"A lot has happened in a few hours," he agreed.

"Shall I order pizza? There's a good place a few blocks away that delivers."

"Sounds perfect. And I like anything that goes on a pizza, so order what you want."

"You're easy. At least when it comes to pizza."

He wasn't quite sure what she meant by that but decided it was more prudent to leave it alone.

His phone buzzed. "Max," he said, putting the phone on speaker.

"Is Tori still with you?"

"She is. I have you on speaker."

"Great. I just wanted to let you know that Mitch Hedden's fishing boat is still in its slip at the Bayside Marina, and according to the owner of Open Water Fishing Excursions, neither Mitch nor Jim is on any of their trips. In fact, the owner said he knew Mitch and hadn't seen him around the marina in a few weeks."

"So Mitch is still in the city," he said, uneasiness running through him at that thought.

"I don't know where he is, but I doubt he's at sea," Max said. "I'm going to see if we can find him."

"Thanks for keeping us posted," Tori said.

"Let me know if you hear from him or anyone else."

"We will," he promised, then ended the call.

"Well, that's new—I don't know if it's good or bad," she said. "Do you think Joanie lied to us or Mitch lied to Joanie?"

"I think he lied to her."

Tori's eyes lit up. "Wait a second. At the yacht club, when Joanie asked me to find Mitch I overheard him on the phone. He said, 'I can't keep lying to her.' Maybe he was talking about Joanie? For a second, I thought maybe he was having an affair, but perhaps it was about something else."

"Who knows? But I don't think he would have left Joanie behind if he thought someone could get her to talk, so I think he's keeping secrets."

"But why disappear at all? We were with him last night. He was dancing and talking like normal. What happened between now and then?"

"The man in the parking lot."

"Right." She let out a breath. "Okay, so now we need to figure out where they're hiding."

"You never see a dead end, do you?"

"A puzzle is like a maze—you hit one end, and you back up and make a different turn and try again. If you're asking me if I ever quit—not so far. And certainly not when it's personal, which this has become."

He found himself admiring her steadfast determination. "Got it. But Max has more resources than we do, so he might be able to find them faster."

"I hope he does, but I can still think about where they might be. I spent a lot of time with them over the years. I know where they vacationed, places they used to go in the city. I bet there's a clue in my head somewhere; I just have to find it. Anyway, I'll order the pizza and then we can get started."

He sat down at the kitchen table while Tori placed their order, thinking about her words. When she got off the phone and sat across from him, he said, "Let's talk about the day of your dad's death."

"Why?" she asked warily.

"Because it ties to Mitch and Jim. And because you reminded me awhile ago that the information could be in the details. What do you know about that weekend besides the fact that they went fishing, ran into a storm, and your dad died?"

"I don't know that I have many more details," she said slowly. "I was twelve when it happened, and after I heard my father had died, I didn't hear much else."

"Think, Tori," he said, sensing she probably knew more than she thought.

"Okay, give me a second."

He waited as she breathed in and out and suddenly realized he'd just asked her to relive what was probably the worst night of her life. "I know it's painful. If you don't want to do this, then—"

"No, I do," she interrupted. "I'm just gathering my thoughts. Let's see—they left on a Wednesday. I remember that because it was the winter concert, and I was playing the cello that night. My dad hadn't heard me play in a while, because he was working a lot. I was excited for him to be there. But that morning he came into my bedroom before I went to school and said he was going to have to miss it."

She paused, her brow wrinkling as she retrieved her memories. "He said that Jim had gotten laid off from his job, and he was really upset about it, so Mitch and my father wanted to take him out on the sea, get him away from his problems. He said he hoped I understood how much he valued his friends."

"You must have been disappointed that he wasn't going to be at your concert."

"I was. I got really angry with him. I said he shouldn't miss my concert, and he told me that if he didn't have a really good reason, he would be there. I didn't care about Jim's job loss, but my dad just said that someday I'd understand that he was a very loyal person. He asked me to play my solo for him before I went to school so he could hear it. At first, I said no, but he was very persuasive, so I played for him. He told me I was amazing, and that he was really proud of me and that I should never forget that." Her eyes blurred with tears. "That's the last time we spoke. I guess I should be glad that we had that moment."

"What happened next?"

"I went to school, and I guess he went to meet Mitch and Jim."

"When did you hear there was a problem on the trip?"

"Friday afternoon. I came home from school, and the front door was wide open. I heard my mom crying. I walked into the kitchen, and Joanie was there. So was Elaine, Jim's wife. I think there were some other people around; it felt like the room was crowded, but all I could see was the devastation on my mom's face."

"Where was Scott?" he asked quietly.

"Baseball practice. Someone went and got him. I remember him coming into my room later. We didn't talk. We just sat on the floor by my bed." Her chest heaved with emotion. "I didn't believe it. I couldn't grasp the truth of what everyone was saying. My mom came in at some point and hugged us. I don't think any of us slept that night."

"Maybe we should stop," he said, hating to see the pain in her gaze.

"I'm okay. It was a long time ago."

"But now it feels fresh again."

"Yes," she admitted. "But if it helps me figure anything out, then I should keep going."

"Were there any other details given about the actual accident? How were they rescued?"

"They sent out a call for help when the storm first hit. Mitch said they thought they could ride out the waves, but a huge monster wave crashed on the deck and the boat filled with water. Mitch and Jim were on the deck, but my dad was downstairs. He got trapped down there, and by the time the storm was over, and they were able to pull him out, he was dead." She drew in a breath. "Another fishing boat found them and rescued them. Mitch's boat sank to the bottom of the sea."

"That's enough," he said, seeing her wipe away a tear.

"I'm fine. I just haven't thought about it in a long time.

Jim was crying at the funeral. He told my mom it was all his fault, that he should have forced my dad to come up on the deck. I don't know if that was just survivor's guilt or if he meant something else by it. But it seemed like Mitch and Jim were destroyed by his death. They watched out for us after that. They were at every other concert I ever played. Ironic, huh?"

He nodded.

"Three years later, my mom met Ray. They went out for about a year, and then he moved in and my life changed again. I like him, don't get me wrong, but it was different having him there. It felt like his house. I was glad to leave for college. It wasn't home anymore." She cleared her throat. "So that's the story. Did I say anything that helped?"

"I don't want to mess up your head, but did it feel in retrospect that your father was saying goodbye to you that morning?"

She stared back at him, her eyes widening. "You think he knew he was going to die?"

"Maybe there was something about that fishing trip that was more dangerous than any of you knew. You said Mitch oversaw some of the family's investments. Maybe there was trouble with the finances."

"If there was, no one said anything. I don't remember my mom mentioning any financial trouble, but I was young."

"Forget I said anything."

"No, hang on. You're right. In retrospect, his words that morning now seem a little prophetic."

"He told you that he wanted you to know how proud he was of you. Was that the kind of thing he would normally say?"

"I don't know. But how could he know he might not make it back? If he thought Mitch and Jim were dangerous, why would he go with them?"

"Maybe he didn't know where the danger was coming from."

"You're suggesting that they killed him."

"They were the only witnesses to his death. What did the medical examiner's report say? Did it back up drowning as cause of death?"

"I think so. I don't know that I ever saw it, but no police came around. No one acted like his death was suspicious."

The apartment buzzer went off, and they both jumped.

"That has to be the pizza," she said.

"I'll go down and get it. Lock the door after me and don't open it again until I say it's me. In fact, don't open it unless I say Scott."

"Why do we need a code word?"

"Just covering the bases."

After he left, he heard the bolt slide into place. Then he went down to get the pizza, really hoping he wouldn't find anyone but the delivery guy.

Fourteen

Tori leaned against the door, her heart beating way too fast as she waited for Dylan to come back. She felt shaky and unsettled, and those feelings hadn't just come from reliving the day of her father's death, but from the ridiculously crazy idea that his death hadn't been an accident.

She had nothing to back up that theory, and neither did Dylan. If there had been anything suspicious about her dad's death, someone would have investigated.

She should probably ask her mother if there had been any questions asked. She certainly hadn't been aware of any discussions like that. She remembered planning the funeral, picking out photos to make a poster of her father's life, the stream of people bringing food by the house, the heavy pall in the air when she walked by her parents' bedroom.

She remembered that her mom had slept on the couch for almost two weeks, unable to go back into the room she shared with her husband. And she remembered her father's two best friends always being around, bringing her treats, telling her how much her dad had loved her.

It was unthinkable that Mitch and Jim could have had anything to do with his death. They had to be on the wrong track.

A knock came at the door, followed by Dylan's voice. "It's me, Tori. Scott says let me in."

She undid the bolt, happy to see him alone with a large pizza box in his hands. "Glad you made it back."

"Me, too."

She followed him over to the table and put some of the file folders on the floor to make room for the food. Then she went into the kitchen, got some plates and napkins and brought them back to the table. "What do you want to drink? I'm thinking about opening a bottle of red wine."

"I'll share that with you," he said.

She poured two glasses, then sat down across from him. While he'd opened the box, he hadn't touched the pizza.

"It looks good," she said.

"It does. I'm just not that hungry anymore," he said.

"Me, either. Maybe in a minute," she said, sipping her wine.

"Look, Tori, I shouldn't have suggested that your father's death was anything but an accident."

"I don't think you're right about that, but I think it was smart to put it out there. We can't overlook any possibilities. I know I'm going to have to talk to my mom about some of this. I was too young to know what was going on back then. Scott might remember more than me, but I don't know if he was paying attention to anything but the fact that our father was gone."

"That makes complete sense. And we can put that theory aside for now."

She saw the guilt in his eyes. "Don't beat yourself up, Dylan. It's nice to not be the only one with somewhat out-there ideas."

He smiled. "I'm supposed to be the one keeping your feet on the ground not joining you on the ledge."

"I won't tell anyone." She glanced at the pizza laden with

vegetables, and her stomach rumbled. "Okay, I think I can eat now." She slid a large slice onto her plate. Dylan quickly followed.

"Let's talk about something normal," she suggested, as they ate. "Tell me about your coworkers. Are they all young? Are they all men?"

"We have an all-male firefighting crew but there are several female paramedics. We have two firefighters in their forties; the rest are about my age."

"You said you work with your cousin Burke—what about your brother?"

"Hunter works at a different house. So does Colton, Burke's younger brother."

"So there are Callaways all over the city," she murmured.

"Pretty much."

She finished her slice and grabbed a second one. "Tell me some firehouse stories. I bet you have a lot."

"I can think of a few."

"I'm all ears."

As they ate their way through the pizza, Dylan told her some funny stories about some of their wilder calls that had nothing to do with fire. She was actually surprised at how many things they did that didn't involve flames but rather people stuck in unusual places.

It was clear that Dylan loved his job and that he had a real fondness for the people he worked with.

When they finished their pizza, they took their wine over to the couch, silently agreeing to put off their research for a while.

She had a lot to think about already and she wasn't quite ready for more. Plus, it was just fun to talk to Dylan, to hear about his life, to discuss mutual friends and teachers and neighborhood kids they'd both known. She couldn't remember the last time she'd talked to anyone from her past. It felt good to share the memories.

When they came to a pause in conversation about an hour later, she realized she was still hungry. "What do you think about some ice cream?"

"Do you have ice cream?" he asked doubtfully. "I've seen inside your fridge, and there's not much in it."

She smiled. "I can't deny that, but I do have ice cream. It's my guilty pleasure, and it's always stocked in the freezer."

"What flavor?"

"This week it's mocha almond fudge."

"Sold."

She went into the kitchen and pulled the ice cream container out of the fridge. "Want it on a cone?"

"You have cones, too?" he asked, coming into the kitchen behind her.

"Of course. Sugar or plain?"

"I'm going all in. I'll take the sugar cone."

She made him a cone and handed it to him. "Ice cream always makes things better."

"I would say you're an easy girl to please, but I think that's only where ice cream is concerned."

She rolled her eyes at his teasing comment. "I'm not that difficult."

"That's usually what difficult people say."

"Well, it's not like you're a pushover, Dylan. You've always gone after what you want, and I know you have strong opinions. How are we so different?"

"I guess we're not. But there's no way I ask as many questions as you do."

"I would have agreed with you until today, but now you have as many questions as I do, if not more." They sat down at the kitchen table again to eat their ice cream. Her first lick was perfect. "Heaven," she murmured. "I think this is my new favorite flavor."

"What was it before?"

"I had a love affair with pecan praline for a while and before that it was mint chip. I had a brief fling with pistachio almond, but it was a little too nutty for me."

"Imagine that," he said dryly. "So while you don't have an ex-boyfriend, you do have some exes in the ice cream department."

"I guess you could say that," she said, amused by the idea. "Some of them are exciting at first—the perfect new adventure—but then there's a lingering aftertaste. Like bubble gum ice cream. It sounded like it might be fun but it definitely wasn't. Who knew ice cream could be a metaphor for love?"

"Certainly not me. But then being around you, Tori, is usually an eye-opening experience."

"I'm sure you don't mean that as a compliment, but I'm going to take it that way," she said, finishing her cone, and licking the last drops of cream off her fingers.

Dylan's gaze darkened as she did that, and suddenly the air between them grew tense.

He popped the last bite of his cone into his mouth, leaving a slight ice cream moustache over his upper lip. A wave of reckless desire ran through her as she fought the impulse to lean over and lick his lip clean.

She drew in a deep breath. She'd obviously had too much wine and too much ice cream. They'd both gone to her head. Or maybe it was Dylan who had gone to her head.

She'd been able to keep her attraction to him at bay with all the surprises that had come their way today, but now the feelings were rushing back in full force.

Dylan abruptly got to his feet. "It's not going to happen, Tori," he said firmly.

She stood up to face him, feeling a little sad when he wiped the ice cream off his mouth. But she also felt angry that Dylan thought he was in charge.

"Why not?" she challenged, knowing she was playing a dangerous game, but she didn't care.

"You and your damn questions," he muttered. "Why can't you just take no for an answer?"

She didn't know how they'd gone so fast from easy and playful to angry and tense, but the air was crackling between them.

There were so many things in her life right now that were

nebulous and unclear, but what she felt for Dylan was not in doubt. She'd never been in a position to do something about it before, but now...

"Maybe I can't take no for an answer, because I can see the conflict in your eyes," she said. "You're attracted to me."

"Doesn't matter. I am not going to mess around with my best friend's sister."

"This isn't about Scott. It's about you and me. You need to stop using him as an excuse."

"He's not an excuse. He's a friend. And he would not want this to happen."

"I don't know if that's true, but even if it is, I don't care. Like I said, this is about us. You and Scott can have your friendship. This won't affect that."

"It sure as hell would," he retorted, planting his hands on his hips. "It's a rule. You don't sleep with your friend's sister."

"Since when do you follow the rules? What's the real reason you're fighting so hard to stay away from me? And don't say Scott again."

He stared back at her, anger sparking out of his light-blue eyes. "Fine, you want another reason?"

"I really do."

"I don't want a relationship—especially not with you."

"What does that mean?" she snapped, his words stabbing her in the heart. "*Especially not with me?*"

"You had a crush on me years ago."

"I did not," she denied, although that might have been partially true.

"Yes, you did. And it's still there. You see me as some kind of hero, and I've been down that road, and it doesn't end well."

"Now you're talking about Jenny."

His lips tightened. "I couldn't sustain Jenny's adoration. She put me on a pedestal and then found out I wasn't perfect."

"Well, that won't happen with me, because I already know you're not perfect. You're judgmental, and you have too many opinions about other people's lives. Plus, you like to run, and I hate people who run, because they usually want me to run with them."

"Well, I don't want you to run with me," he countered.

"Good."

"Great," he snapped back. "But it wasn't just Jenny who looked at me like I was bigger than life. I've had that same experience on the job, too. A few months ago, I broke my long-standing rule and dated someone I rescued from a car accident."

"So you admit to breaking the rules."

"That's not the point, Tori. I thought we could get past the fact that I had saved her life, but we couldn't. I was her knight in shining armor until she realized I worked a lot and didn't want to spend every second with her. She wanted the man of her dreams, just like Jenny did. I can't be your personal hero, Tori. I can't be the guy you dreamed about when you were fourteen."

She finally realized that there was more in play besides his loyalty to Scott. For all his fearlessness, Dylan was afraid of love, of expectations, of commitment. But she wasn't like those other women.

"I've known you a long time, Dylan, longer than you've been running into burning buildings. You say you don't want to be a hero, but look at what you've been doing the last few days. You've been watching over me, making sure I'm safe, spending your spare time looking through a dusty old attic at photo albums of people you don't even know."

"I'm doing that for Scott."

It might have started out that way, but she didn't believe that was his only reason anymore. She knew when a man was interested in her, even if he didn't want to be.

"Once I know you're safe and we solve the puzzle, then I'll be on my way," he added. "And I don't intend to leave anyone with regrets."

She knew she should just accept what he was saying, but she was tired of being told no by someone who clearly wanted to say yes. "You want me, Dylan," she said, hoping she really wasn't misreading the situation. "Can't you be honest?"

"It's not about that."

"It's *all* about that. I don't need a hero. I don't need you to save me. I don't need you to promise you'll be here tomorrow."

"Yes, you do."

"No, I don't. But I'm really attracted to you, and I want to do something about it. My God, Dylan, the air is sizzling between us right now. I know you can feel it, too. You're an expert on fire, after all."

"I put fires out. I don't start them," he said shortly.

"Well, I think we should put this one out together, and we should do it really slow," she said, dropping her voice down a notch as she inched closer to him.

He tensed, but he didn't move away. "Is this some sort of a game, Tori? You want to prove something?"

"It's not a game. I'm being completely honest right now. I'm putting myself on the line by telling you what I want, and that's you. Sex won't change anything between us if we don't let it."

"You're going to regret this," he warned.

Maybe she would, but she was willing to take the risk.

"You only regret the things you don't do," she said.

"That's not true. I've regretted a lot of things I've done."

She let out a sigh. "If you don't want me, Dylan, then go. I'm safe. You don't have to worry about me. We can talk tomorrow. We can pretend this never happened. We can go back to being friends or whatever you want to call it."

He didn't reply, and she could see the turmoil in his expression. He was fighting as hard as he could.

"But if you stay," she continued. "Then we see where this goes. No second thoughts. No bailing out after one kiss. It's your choice, but those are the terms." She held her breath as he took his time answering.

"I really don't want to hurt you, Tori. You say you won't care, but I know you. You're a girl who always cares."

"I'm a woman," she corrected. "And whether or not I care isn't your problem."

"You say that now—"

"I promise I won't hold you to anything. It's just a night, Dylan. But I'm done trying to convince you. If you want to go, go." She turned away, but he grabbed her hand and pulled her back to face him.

After a long, tense look, he said, "I'm staying."

Her heart thudded against her chest. "Then I'm glad." She licked her lips, not sure what to do next. She hadn't thought much beyond the fight to get him to admit he wanted her, too. "Aren't you going to kiss me?"

A smile played around the curve of his lips. "You're running things, Tori. Show me what you want."

"Really?"

"No second thoughts, remember?"

"I'm not having second thoughts, just thinking about where I want to start." She stepped forward and planted her hands on either side of his face, his beautiful, masculine face that had filled her dreams so many nights. She could hardly believe this was actually happening. Every nerve ending tingled with anticipation.

But as she licked her lips, doubts ran through her. Were they going to ruin things between them? Was she going to break up a longtime friendship between her brother and Dylan? Was she being selfish? Was she being naïve to think they could make love and not have it mean anything?

This wasn't just any guy; this was Dylan.

"You're not asking any questions," he said quietly, "but I can see them spinning through your eyes."

"I often overthink things," she admitted. "But I'm not going to do that with you. I have no more questions."

She had no answers, either, but she was putting all that on the backburner. She ran her thumbs over the shadowy beard on his face, loving the masculine feel of his skin, then she pressed onto her toes and kissed him.

He let her take the lead, and while there was a part of her

that wanted to go fast, another part of her wanted to go slow, to savor the taste of his mouth, the slide of her tongue against his teeth, the lingering hint of fudge on his lips.

She angled her head one way, then the other. He groaned deep in his throat and slid his hands down her waist to her hips, pulling her up against his chest.

Feeling that hard body against hers drove all thoughts of going slow right out of her head. She wrapped her arms around his neck, pressing her breasts against his chest as desire shot through her.

Another long, deep kiss sent her head spinning, and as his hands crept under her shirt, his fingers running over the bare skin of her back, her legs went weak.

She wanted more—so much more. She pushed him back, but only so she could pull off her top, revealing a barely there lacy bra.

"Nice," he said. "Keep going."

"Your turn," she countered.

He obliged by pulling off his T-shirt, and she swallowed hard at the sight of his body. She'd known he had muscles, but he was ripped, and she loved the way the dark hair on his chest ran down into a vee, disappearing under his jeans— jeans that were showing a distinct bulge.

Her mouth watered. She wanted to touch him, taste him, explore every inch of him. "Keep going," she said, repeating his words.

"You first," he replied.

"We're really going to see each other naked?" She couldn't quite believe it.

"Unless you've already changed—"

"I haven't," she said quickly. She drew in a breath, feeling a little shy in front of Dylan, but need overcame her reluctance. She unhooked her bra and let it fall off her shoulders. Heat ran through her as his gaze dropped to her full breasts. And then his hands were on her, his thumbs teasing her nipples into hard points of desire as his mouth covered hers.

As desire built within her, she reached for the button on his jeans. He backed her up against the wall, trapping her in a haven of heat. As he ran his mouth down her neck, her heart started beating so fast she could barely breathe. She'd never felt so overwhelmed by need, so desperate to rip off the rest of her clothes and Dylan's, too. She cupped his ass, pulling him against her.

He muttered something and lifted his head, his eyes glittering with passion. "We should slow down."

"I was thinking just the opposite," she said breathlessly. "Like we should get rid of your pants."

"I like your idea better."

She undid the button on his jeans and slid down the zipper. As she pushed down his jeans and briefs, she gave in to the temptation to touch his delicious male hardness. She was so caught up in him, that she barely realized Dylan was getting her out of her jeans, too.

Finally, there was nothing more between them. She gasped with pleasure as Dylan's fingers teased the slick heat between her legs.

He suddenly swore and pulled away.

"What?" she asked in confusion.

"I don't have anything with me. Protection."

"Oh. I do. In the bedroom."

His eyes lit up at that piece of news. "Then take me to bed, Tori," he told her, letting her know she was still calling the shots, only it really didn't feel that way. She was so mindless with desire she could barely think.

Somehow they stumbled their way into the bedroom, pausing here and there to tease each other with promising kisses and caresses. She opened the drawer next to her bed and pulled out a condom, but Dylan wasn't interested in putting it on just yet.

He pulled her down onto the mattress and explored her body with torturous delight until she couldn't stand it anymore. She wanted to repay all the favors, but now Dylan was putting on the condom, and soon he was filling the aching heat within her. They moved together in perfect sync, each sliding movement bringing greater pleasure and then they were in a free fall, clinging to each other as they came slowly back to earth.

As she gasped for breath, she looked into Dylan's light-blue eyes, not just seeing him, but feeling him—all the way down to her soul.

She was in big trouble. Her earlier words came back to haunt her.

Sex wouldn't change anything, she'd told him.

Yeah, right...

"You okay?" Dylan asked, stroking Tori's back as she snuggled up against him, her head on his shoulder, her arm resting on his abdomen, her naked body tangled up with his.

He was trying not to think about the shocked look in her eyes a few minutes ago. It seemed as if she'd just come to some surprising revelation, and he didn't think that was a good thing. He probably shouldn't have asked a question he didn't really want an answer to, but he needed to know where things stood.

"Better than okay," she reassured him. "You?"

"Better than better than okay."

She lifted her head and smiled. "Always so competitive. You have to be first."

"So do you," he said with a grin.

"True. In that case, I'm better than better than better than okay."

"Okay, we need to stop. This could go on forever."

"Or at least until we do what we just did again." She licked her lips. "I mean, if you want to do it again." A flicker of uncertainty danced through her eyes, which surprised him.

"You know I do. Give me five minutes."

"Really?"

"Maybe ten."

"What do you have in mind for round two?"

"All kinds of things," he replied, letting his finger run down the side of her beautiful face. Her cheeks were pink, and her hair fell in soft, dark, silky clouds around her bare shoulders.

"I thought I was the one with the big imagination," she said.

"You're rubbing off on me."

"In a good way?"

He nodded, liking how easy it was to be with Tori. Whether they were talking or fighting or making love, there was a connection between them that was stronger than anything he'd ever felt before.

She could definitely get under his skin, make him a little crazy with her impulsive curiosity, reckless stubbornness, and her endless questions, but she could also make him crazy with the way she kissed, the way she explored his body with the enthusiasm and passion she brought to every aspect of her life. When Tori committed to something, she went all the way in. She gave a hundred and fifty percent. And she went after what she wanted, with no thought of backing down or quitting.

The word *committed* stuck in his throat, and the thought of her going after him made him swallow hard. He'd been fighting his attraction to her since he'd seen her at the fire. But obviously, he hadn't fought hard enough, and look where they'd ended up.

But this was supposed to be one night of fun, nothing more. She'd made a strong case for that, and he'd chosen to believe her, because his need for her had overwhelmed his usually logical brain. But knowing Tori, he didn't see it really going down that way.

"Your eyes darken when you get serious," she told him. "And your lips draw into a hard line," she added, sliding her thumb across his bottom lip.

He caught her hand and kissed her thumb, thinking that she could read him more than he liked.

"What are you thinking about?" she asked.

"Whether I should be on the top or the bottom next time," he lied.

"Are those our only choices?" she said with a smile.

He grinned back at her, warmed by her open, candid, joyful smile. Tori lived life. She didn't hold back. She put herself on the line. That made her vulnerable, and he didn't want her to get hurt.

"Tori—"

"Uh-oh, I don't like the sound of that."

"I just said your name."

"It was the way you said it, like you were about to deliver bad news. Is it not going to be ten minutes? Do you need a half hour? You *are* over thirty."

"Hey," he said, knowing she was trying to avoid a serious conversation and appreciating her for that, because if this got too serious, he was going to ruin the rest of the night. Since they'd come this far, they might as well go until morning. He couldn't take back what had already happened. They'd have to deal with that reality when the sun came up. But until then...

He moved quickly, tossing her onto her back. She squealed with delight, and as her hand cupped him, she said, "Oh, my, looks like you don't need those minutes after all."

"Not with you around, I don't," he said before kissing her smart, sexy mouth and losing himself in her arms.

They might be headed for a fall, but it was going to be a hell of a ride.

Fifteen

Tori woke up at six on Monday morning, exhausted and achy, but deliciously satisfied. Glancing over at Dylan's bare chest, tousled hair, and perfectly chiseled male face made her suddenly hungry for him again. She still couldn't quite believe she'd slept with Dylan Callaway. She smiled at how silly that sounded, even in her own head. But her teenaged self had never imagined this could actually happen.

Being with Dylan had been better than her most amazing fantasy. But what next?

She knew Dylan had been asking himself the same question a few hours ago, but she'd managed to derail that train of thought by making love to him. She hadn't wanted to give up the night for the reality that had now arrived. There was sun coming through the windows. She had to go to work today and so did Dylan.

After she used the bathroom, she put on a robe and went out to make some coffee, deciding to let Dylan sleep for a few more minutes. He'd said he had to be to work at nine, so he had some time. After pouring herself a mug and making some toast, she grabbed a pile of files out of the suitcase and sat down at the table. She'd dropped the ball on the investigation last night. But she would get back to it today.

The first few files didn't appear to be too important. One was labeled random book ideas, and as she skimmed through it, she saw that her father had put down some ideas for a nonfiction book. She hadn't realized he'd thought about writing a book. It made sense, though. It would have given him more space to devote to a big story on any subject that interested him.

The next few files were more work-related articles. Reading through his notes, she realized that he'd often made a game plan, labeling players he needed to talk to, defining possible motivations, and sometimes making a counter-argument against himself. He really did leave no stone unturned, and he certainly didn't shy away from talking to important people.

She'd thought she'd known a lot about his work, but she'd known very little. She sipped her coffee, then grabbed some more files from the suitcase. The first file wasn't labeled, which was odd.

Inside, was an opened envelope that contained a newspaper clipping. Her gaze narrowed as she looked at the photo of a suburban house with the headline: *Family of four dies from carbon monoxide poisoning.*

As she read through the article, a name jumped out at her—Henry Lowell. She knew that name. He'd been friends with her father.

In the news story, Henry was referred to as a reporter for KTVC News in San Jose. He'd died along with his wife, a teacher, and their two daughters, who were both under the age of seven. What a terrible tragedy! *Why hadn't she heard about his death? Why hadn't they talked about it at home?*

She zeroed in on the date of the clipping and realized that Henry had died two days before her dad had left on the fishing trip. Her stomach began to churn. Was it a coincidence that they had died so close together? But Henry's family had been taken out by a carbon monoxide leak and her father had died thousands of miles away.

She picked up the envelope that had contained the clipping. Her dad's name and home address were typed on the center of the envelope, and the postmark was San Francisco, the date the day that the article had appeared in the paper. *If her father had requested the clipping, wouldn't it have come from San Jose? And why would he send for the clipping? On the flip side, if he hadn't requested it, why would someone send it to him?*

She pressed a hand to her temple, her head beginning to throb. She really wished she could come up with some answers instead of more questions.

"Tori?"

She flinched as Dylan's voice startled her. She'd been so caught up in the latest puzzle that she'd almost forgotten she wasn't alone.

Turning to face him, she caught her breath for a different reason. Dylan approached her wearing nothing but a low slung towel. He'd obviously taken a shower, his dark hair damp, and droplets of water still clinging to his extremely sexy and powerful body.

"What's going on?" he asked. "Did you find something?"

"Uh..." She had to think for a second. "Yes—maybe."

A glint of humor appeared in his eyes. "You don't sound very definitive."

"You're distracting me with that very small towel," she admitted.

"You want me to take it off?"

"Yes—no," she said, realizing she was coming off as a dithering idiot. "Why do you have to look so damn good?"

"I was going to ask you the same question," he said, leaning over to give her a quick kiss. "But since we both have to go to work shortly, why don't I get dressed and you can tell me what you found?"

"Okay." She looked back at the clipping, trying not to notice the wet towel that dropped to the floor as Dylan grabbed his clothes off the couch and put them on. "Someone sent my father a clipping about the death of a TV reporter that happened a few days before my dad died."

"What?" He moved next to her as he pulled his shirt over his head.

She handed him the clipping. "It's possible my dad requested the clip from the newspaper, but he never did that before, so…"

"Did you know this Henry Lowell?"

"I met him a few times. He was friendly with my father."

Dylan looked up from the article with troubled eyes. "The timing of his death is disturbing."

"It looks like an accident. His whole family died, not just him."

"And days after that, your father goes on a fishing trip and doesn't come back."

His words echoed her earlier thoughts. "I know." She got to her feet and walked over to the window, glancing out at the street below. The city was just waking up. People were leaving for work. It was a normal day. But inside, she felt like the day was anything but normal.

Dylan came up behind her, slipping his arms around her waist. She leaned back against him.

"You think Henry and his family were killed, don't you?" she asked.

"It's a possibility."

"The same possibility as my father's death not being an accident." She turned in his arms, needing to face him. "Are we crazy?"

"There is another scenario."

"What would that be? Please give me another idea, because I'm not liking the last two."

He gave her a long look. "Maybe I shouldn't. This is all just speculation. We should be dealing in facts, not theories."

"There are no facts; that's why we're speculating. Come on, Dylan, tell me your latest brainstorm."

"You're not going to like it."

"Tell me anyway."

He hesitated one more second, then said, "I actually had this thought last night when you told me about your last conversation with your dad, which sounded like a good-bye. Now, seeing this news story about a reporter who died just before your dad makes me ask myself: What if your father got scared after Henry died? What if he thought it wasn't an accident? What if...he didn't actually die?"

She sucked in a quick breath, his words rolling through her like a tidal wave. "That's...I don't know what that is."

"I knew I shouldn't have said anything."

"But you did."

"I'm sorry."

She stared back at him, seeing the regret in his eyes. "No, don't apologize. We have to consider everything. So, you're saying my father faked his death?" She could hardly believe she'd said that out loud.

"With the help of his best friends."

"And he stayed dead for seventeen years?"

"If he had a reason to hide that long..." Dylan paused. "That clipping could have been sent to him as a warning. He knew he had to disappear. You said the trip happened suddenly."

"Because Jim lost his job, or at least that's what I was told."

"We can check it out. In the meantime, let's consider that your dad and Henry were working on a story that was dangerous. What if your father was afraid that his family would end up the same way as Henry's family?"

She swallowed hard. "But why would he disappear without us? Why would he leave us without protection?"

"Maybe you didn't need protection if he was dead."

She ran her fingers through her hair, thinking about his words. "It's wild but it kind of makes sense. Or do I just want it to be true because then my father might still be alive?" She jumped to the next conclusion. "Maybe Neil Hawkins isn't a relative. Maybe he *is* my father."

"Maybe, although you didn't think the photo looked exactly like him. And I would trust your gut."

She thought back to the moment when she'd first seen the man calling himself Neil Hawkins. He'd been across the street, at least fifty yards away. She had felt an odd tingle run through her. It was that weird feeling that made her get up and follow the man. There had been something familiar about him...

But the photo hadn't been conclusive. There were similarities, yes, but she hadn't felt like Hawkins was for sure her father, and wouldn't she know her own father? Wouldn't she be absolutely free of doubt if they were the same man?

"I don't know what to think," she muttered.

"We can go back to the idea that your dad has a relative you don't know about. Maybe he helped your father disappear. Maybe Mitch and Jim know about him."

"But they're nowhere to be found." She paced around the room. "Okay, I don't know where this is going to go, but you've brought up some new ideas to follow. If my dad was working on a story that might have gotten him killed or forced him to fake his death or took the life of his friend, then I need to figure out what that story was."

"It could be in these files. What about your father's computer? What happened to that?"

"He had it with him on the boat. It was allegedly lost at sea."

"All right. What paper was your dad working for when he died?"

"The *Herald,* but it got bought out by the *Journal* the year after my dad died."

"Do you remember the names of anyone your father worked with?"

"I'd have to think about it. Wait—I do know one guy— he's a reporter at the Examiner with me—Jeff Crocker. He said he was fresh out of college and worked with my dad for a few months before he died. I'm sure he could give me other names."

"That's great."

"I'll ask him as soon as I get to work." She paused, struck by a terrifying thought. "Do you think my mom or Scott could be in danger? I thought this was only about me, but maybe it's not."

"I think you have the most to worry about, Tori. You're the one doing the digging."

That didn't make her feel better. While she was the one asking questions and perhaps a more obvious target, she couldn't forget that Henry Lowell's entire family had died with him.

"Maybe I should talk to Ray about getting Mom out of town for a few days. Her birthday is coming up in two weeks. I wonder if I could put together a spa getaway and tell Ray the only days I could get are this week. Scott won't be back until the weekend, so he's set for now."

"If that will work, I don't think it's a bad idea to get your mom out of town, but that brings us back to you. I think I should call in sick today. And so should you."

"No," she said, shaking her head. "We need to act normally. We need to look like we know nothing."

He frowned. "I understand that, but Tori, I'm not going to be available once I'm on shift, not unless it's a real emergency."

"I understand that. I'll be careful. But I need to go to work. I need to speak to Jeff, and I have meetings this morning that I can't miss. And I can also do some digging into Henry Lowell's death."

"I still don't like the idea of leaving you alone for even a second." He took her hands in his. "Promise me one thing."

"What's that?"

"You'll at least take a cab or a car to work. I don't want you just walking around the streets. And no following anyone. In fact, if you get any clues or go anywhere, text me what you're doing. Even if I can't answer, I'll feel better knowing what you're up to."

"I can do that, but you need to concentrate on your job

and not worry about me."

"I can do both," he said firmly. "So where's my promise?"

She gave him a grateful smile. "I promise. And thanks for being here, Dylan. For everything."

"You're more than welcome."

"I'd love to make you breakfast, but..."

He grinned. "I know. All you have is ice cream."

"I've had it for breakfast before."

"I'll bet you have." He squeezed her fingers, then let go. "I'm going to take off now, but we'll keep in touch."

"So often you'll find me annoying again," she said with a smile.

"Again? When did I say you stopped being annoying?" he teased.

"I think it was last night when you were shouting my name and thanking God I was born."

He laughed. "I don't remember that, either." He leaned over and gave her a long, slow kiss that went from playful to sensual in about ten seconds. He tore himself away. "You stay safe, Tori. I mean it."

"I will. And you do the same."

He nodded and headed to the door. She locked it behind him and then got ready for work.

Tori's day flew by in a flash. She had a bunch of emails to respond to as well as a meeting at a nonprofit charity that was working with several real-estate developers in the hopes of providing some low-income housing. As she'd promised Dylan, she took cabs or cars everywhere she went, careful to keep an eye on her surroundings, but nothing seemed out of the ordinary.

She'd tried to find Jeff to speak to him about her father, but he had meetings out of the office, and by late afternoon, she had yet to catch up with him. It was just as well, she needed to spend time on her work assignments and save the personal mystery for after work.

Jeff came into her cubicle a little past five and sat down in the chair next to her desk. "Connie said you were looking for me earlier."

"Yes. You've been busy today."

"Mondays always seem to be like that. Would you like to get a drink after work? A few of us are going around the corner to Allen's."

"Thanks, but I have a lot of notes to get through tonight."

"Well, if you change your mind, you know where we'll be. So, what did you want to talk to me about?"

"You said you worked at the Herald with my father. Do you have any idea what he was working on right before he died?"

"That was a long time ago, Tori."

"I know. I was just hoping it was something big enough for you to remember?"

He shook his head. "Sorry, I have no idea. We weren't exactly on the same level. I spent a lot of time fact checking over reporting back then. Why do you ask?"

"I found some of his old files, and it got me thinking about what his last story might have been. Was there anyone else at the *Herald* who might have worked more closely with my dad that you could point me to?"

"Sure. Let's see. Lindsay Parker would be one. She was a staff writer, but I think she helped your dad with research. She got out of news a few years ago and married a rich financier named Todd Vaxman about ten years ago. She had a daughter and opened up a boutique on Union Street for expensive baby clothes."

She jotted down the name on a pad on her desk. "That's good. Anyone else?"

"I don't know. I'd have to dig up an old copy of the paper and look at the staff. Once the *Herald* was bought, I left and so did a lot of other people. What's this really about, Tori?" he asked, giving her a speculative look.

"Just what I said. You commented the other day that I might not know my father as well as I think. This is part of me getting to know him."

"Well, don't let it take up too much of your time. We've got a full load of current stories to cover this week."

"Those are always my priority."

"Good to hear."

After Jeff left, she stared at her computer screen for several minutes, but she couldn't get back into her article.

She opened a new search window on her computer and typed in designer baby clothes in the Marina. The first hit was for a store called Baby Boss, owned by Lindsay Vaxman. Lindsay might not actually work at the boutique, but hopefully she could find someone who could put her in contact with Lindsay.

She closed her laptop, put it in her tote bag and then left the office. Most people were already gone, probably to have drinks at Allen's. She knew she needed to make a better effort to mingle with her coworkers, but that would have to wait, too.

When she got out to the sidewalk, she flagged down a cab. The marina was only a few miles away, but with rush-hour traffic, it took her about twenty minutes. It was ten minutes to six when she arrived, thankfully just before closing.

As she entered the boutique, a woman was just completing a purchase at the register. A very young clerk packed up a bag of clothes for her.

She wandered toward the back of the store and was standing by the last rack of clothes when a tall, red-haired woman with green eyes and pale, freckled skin came out of the back room. She appeared to be in her early forties.

"Hello," she said. "Are you by any chance Lindsay Vaxman?"

The woman stopped abruptly, giving her a surprised look. "Yes, can I help you?"

"I hope so. I'm Tori Hayden. My father was Ben Hayden.

I don't know if you remember him, but he was a reporter for the *Herald*."

"Of course I remember Ben," she said, relaxing at Tori's question. "He was insightful, relentless, and charming all at the same time. It was a tragedy that he died so young." She paused. "I remember you from the funeral—you and your brother and your mom. I felt so bad for you."

"It was hard," she agreed, swallowing a knot of emotion. "I'm a reporter now, too. I work for the *Examiner*."

"Well, isn't that something? Your dad would be proud."

"I hope so."

"What can I do for you?"

"I'm trying to find out what my father was working on when he died. My current editor, Jeff Crocker, told me that you used to do some of his research for him."

"I did for a short time, but then your dad decided he wanted to work on everything himself. I thought he had something big brewing, because he got really secretive, but to be honest, I don't know what it was." She paused. "Why do you want to know?"

She couldn't tell the truth, because she didn't know what that was, so she decided to spin her answer. "I'm considering writing a book about him: his life, his work, the big stories he worked on."

"Well, that would probably be interesting. Your father wasn't afraid to go after anyone."

"What do you mean?"

"Most of his articles had to do with greed and the corruption of power. That often involved some heavy hitters in the city."

"Do you remember any in particular?"

"Mayor Oscar Martinez wasn't a big fan. I know they had a heated argument about something."

"But you don't know what?"

"I wish I did. There is one person who can probably tell you more than I can—my former editor, Hal Thatcher. He was the editor-in-chief of the *Herald*. If your dad spoke to anyone, he talked to Hal."

"Do you happen to know where I could find him?"

"I know he lives on a boat in the Sausalito Harbor—if that helps."

"It does. Thanks so much."

"No problem. I remember how nice it was when I got an actual lead to follow."

"Do you miss reporting?" she asked curiously.

"Not even a little bit," Lindsay replied. "It was not nearly as glamorous as I imagined, and I learned quickly that making people talk when they didn't want to doesn't make you the most popular person in town, and I liked to be popular. I wasn't comfortable with having doors slammed in my face, and the pay wasn't great, either."

"No one does it to get rich, that's for sure," she agreed. "But I was never popular, so I'm used to slamming doors."

"I hope you find what you're looking for. It would be nice to see your father's work get some additional exposure. He worked hard to fight injustice. More people should do that." She tilted her head to the side, giving Tori a thoughtful look. "I always wondered if your dad's death was an accident, but no one else seemed suspicious. I figured there were other people who knew him a lot better than I did, so if there was something to find, they'd go looking for it. But no one ever did—until maybe now. Is that why you're really asking?"

"Partly," she admitted.

"Well, I'm hoping you don't find anything, and that it was truly just a tragic accident."

"So do I," she said heavily, although there was a tiny part of her that wondered if there had been an accident at all.

Sixteen

―――→>≫≪<←――

Dylan walked outside the firehouse to call Tori. It was after seven and they'd just finished dinner after a fairly uneventful day, which was fine with him, since he hadn't gotten a lot of sleep the night before. But he certainly had no regrets about that. In fact, he had no regrets about anything, which he probably should have. He suspected that time would illuminate a truckload of complications that he and Tori had created by taking their relationship to a very intimate level, but at the moment he just didn't care.

He was too caught up in her to feel anything but frustration that they weren't together. He'd never had a problem leaving a woman to go to work...until today.

And it wasn't just that he was concerned she was in danger; he simply missed her—her smile, her wit, her curiosity, her smile, her beautiful eyes... He sucked in a breath as his body tightened at the memories running through his mind. Then he lifted his phone and punched in her number.

"Hi," she said somewhat breathlessly.

"Where are you? Are you all right?" he asked.

"I'm fine. I just got in the apartment."

"Were you at work?"

"I was, but then I got a lead on a woman who used to work with my dad—Lindsay Vaxman. She's out of the news business and she didn't have much information to impart, but she did tell me that my father went after big hitters with no fear and had problems with Mayor Oscar Martinez."

"About what?"

"She didn't know. But Lindsay also gave me the name of my father's former editor, who lives on a boat somewhere in the Sausalito Harbor. I'm going to see if I can find him tomorrow. I was going to do it tonight, but it was getting dark, and I didn't know which boat was his."

"I'm glad you didn't go tonight. If you can wait until I get off tomorrow at five, I'll go with you."

"That should work. I'm going to concentrate on going through the rest of my dad's files tonight. Then I can put those out of my mind."

He was happy that she was staying put for the evening. "Did you have any problems today?"

"Nope. I didn't see anyone watching me or following me, and I was careful."

"I'm glad to hear that."

"How was your day?"

"A couple of motor vehicle accidents, a car fire, a man stuck in an elevator—nothing too exciting."

"That's a good thing, right?"

"It is," he agreed.

Silence fell between them. There were a lot of things he wanted to say to her, and a lot of things he knew he shouldn't say to her.

"Are you still there?" she asked.

"I am. Sorry. I wish I could help you tonight."

"It's probably better that you're not here. If you come over, I might get distracted."

He smiled at that. "You've been distracting me all day.

Distance doesn't seem to lessen that."

"Really? I've been on your mind?"

"You have."

"And in a good way, right?"

"Very good." He knew he should hang up, but he was having a hard time breaking the connection between them. And then the alarm went off.

"Sounds like a call," Tori said.

"Yes. I have to go."

"Be careful, Dylan."

"You, too." He ended the call and went back to work.

The fire was in a pawn shop, and when they arrived on the scene, there were a half dozen people out on the sidewalk.

"Anyone still inside?" he asked, as he jumped off the truck.

"No. I was the last one out," a tattooed guy of about fifty said to him. "I was just about to lock the front door when something exploded in the back room. Maybe the furnace or something. I came out the front and saw flames coming off the roof."

"All right, everyone move back," he told the other bystanders, as Burke barked out orders to the rest of the crew.

It took them thirty minutes to knock down the fire, and the intensity of it reminded him of the fire Tori had narrowly escaped from. He checked out the back room, curious as to how the fire had begun. While the store manager had suggested the heater was a problem, from the burn pattern it appeared that the fire had started near the opposite wall.

He heard footsteps behind him and turned as Gary Kruger came into the room.

"What have we got?" Kruger asked.

"Not sure. The manager heard an explosion. He thought it was the heater, but it doesn't appear that way to me."

"I'll take a look."

"Will you let me know if you see any similarities between this fire and the one at the hotel last week?"

"I'll let you know when the report is done," Kruger

replied, a terse note in his voice. "That's standard procedure— even if your last name is Callaway."

He didn't respond to that taunt. He'd heard it before, but every time he heard it, it pissed him off. He'd never traded on his name for anything. But he didn't need to get in a pissing match with Kruger.

He made his way back outside. The manager was pacing in front of the store.

"Was it the heater?" he asked.

"The investigator will determine that."

The man ran a hand through his hair. "I can't believe this happened. Martin is going to be furious."

"Who's Martin?"

"My landlord."

"What's his last name?"

"Fleming. You going to call him? I really don't want to tell him about this. He's going to blame it on me, even though I swear I don't know what happened."

He put a hand on the man's shoulder, seeing the agitation in his eyes. "It's not your fault."

"Can you tell Martin that? He thinks I drink on the job, but I am sober, man."

"Trust me, he'll be notified and informed of the investigator's findings."

"All right."

"Take it easy." He walked back to the truck and joined the rest of his crew. After putting away their equipment, they returned to the station.

As they were making their way inside, Burke motioned him toward his office. "Talk to me for a minute," he said.

He followed his cousin inside. "What's going on?"

"You tell me. I saw Emma last night. She said she and Max are looking into the hotel fire and that you're spending a lot of time with Tori Hayden. Emma thinks Tori might be in some trouble, which means you might be in some trouble."

"I'm fine. Tori—I don't know. It's complicated."

Burke's steady blue gaze raked over his face. "All right.

You don't have to explain, but tell me this—do you think the fire today was connected to the hotel fire?"

"I have no proof, but in my gut, I do believe that. I'd like to know what Kruger comes up with, but I doubt he's going to tell me. He made a point of telling me my last name wasn't going to get me any favors."

"I'll see what I can find out."

"I appreciate the help."

"Any time."

Burke leaned forward, his gaze thoughtful. "So...you and Tori Hayden? Something going on there?"

"There might be," he conceded.

"How's Scott going to feel about that?"

"I don't think he'll love it."

"Is she worth losing your best friend?"

"I hope it doesn't come to that, but...she might be."

—▸▸◂◂—

Tori left work at five thirty on Tuesday to meet Dylan downstairs, and she couldn't believe how excited she felt at the prospect of seeing him again. It had only been a day and a half since she'd seen him, but it felt like much longer. When she reached the street, she saw the very sexy Dylan leaning against his blue Mustang, waiting for her.

For a split second, the image took her back to middle school, when she used to walk across to the high school at three so Dylan and Scott could give her a ride home from school. Every day, they'd been waiting by Dylan or Scott's car with a crowd of girls around them, and they had never, ever been happy to see her.

But today a smile split across Dylan's face when their eyes met, and all the little doubts she'd had about taking their relationship too far vanished in that instant.

"Hi," he said, a husky note in his voice. "Ready to go track down your father's former editor?"

She was more ready to go back to her apartment and

tumble into bed with him.

Something must have flashed through her eyes, because Dylan's gaze dropped to her mouth, and she thought he might kiss her. Instead, he stepped back and opened the car door. "Later," he murmured.

She raised a brow, her heart beating way too fast at that one word. "Later what?"

He looked into her eyes. "Whatever you want, Tori."

"I thought it was a one-night stand, Dylan."

"Maybe we'll have to take it to two..." he drawled. "But first, we have work to do—don't we?"

"Yes," she said, drawing in a breath. "We do. I found an address for Hal Thatcher."

"Let's go."

She got into the car and said, "He lives on a houseboat in the Sausalito marina. He retired when the *Journal* bought the *Herald*, which happened four months after my father died," she added.

"Is that significant?" he asked, as he pulled into traffic.

"I don't know. It seems like the *Herald* was completely swallowed up. Only two reporters from the *Herald* went on to work at the *Journal*."

"That often happens in mergers."

"I suppose."

"Did you find anything else in the files?"

Guilt ran through her at his question. "I really wanted to read through everything, but last night I just couldn't keep my eyes open," she said. "I fell asleep at the kitchen table before nine and then dragged myself off to bed when I woke up an hour later. I brought some files in my bag to look at during lunch, but one of the writers was out sick, and I had to step in and do some interviews for her that had already been set up. I feel badly that I didn't get through all the files. I really wanted to."

He gave her a sympathetic smile. "Don't beat yourself up. You can finish them off later."

"How was your shift?" She thought he looked a little

tired, too.

"Not bad. We went to a fire last night that had a similar explosive beginning as the one at the hotel."

"Where was it?" she asked, surprised by his words.

"A pawn shop, about three blocks away from the hotel."

"Was anyone hurt?"

"No. Luckily the manager was locking up the front door when there was an explosion in the back. He was outside when we arrived."

"Well, I'm glad no one else died," she said slowly, wondering if the fires were connected.

"Me, too. The same investigator—Gary Kruger—is working on the case. We'll see if he comes up with a link."

"It would be really interesting if there was a connection. And a little scary, too," she added. "Maybe there are more fires to come."

His profile hardened at her words but all he said was, "I hope not."

"I feel even more guilty now that I fell asleep on the job last night."

"I don't think your father's old files would have had any clue that would have prevented the pawn shop fire. If your dad was investigating something dangerous, he wouldn't have left critical information lying around. He was too smart for that."

"You're probably right. If he had anything, it was on his computer or in his head."

"We can still hope that his former editor knew what he was working on."

"That is what I'm hoping," she agreed.

As they crossed over the Golden Gate Bridge on their way to Sausalito, the waterfront city across the bay, she tried to get re-energized by the view. She'd told Dylan that she didn't quit, that when she ran into obstacles, she just backed up and tried another way, but she was feeling a little tired of running around in circles with no clear direction or solid leads.

But looking out at the water, the colorful sailboats enjoying the warm weather and the late afternoon breezes made her feel more optimistic. This wasn't the end. They had a lot left to do. She just had to keep her head down and stay focused and somehow she'd find the answers she needed.

As they came off the bridge, they headed down the hill into Sausalito. The city was beautiful and charming with a mix of upscale mansions clinging to steep hillsides, as well as modest apartments for the younger generation who commuted into San Francisco. And then there were the houseboats, where an eclectic community of artists, boaters, and people who just wanted to feel a little more away from it all lived.

They parked and headed toward the docks. The boats ranged from weathered and barely holding it together to fancy and modern. Some owners had put up flower boxes around their boats, making an almost traditional yard around their homes. Others had painted the sides of their boats with murals or vibrant colors. She'd read up a little on the community while trying to find Hal's address and knew that the owners were passionate lovers of what they called their floating homes.

Hal's home was modest, no colorful artwork, and no frills, but there were comfortable chairs on the deck, and it appeared to be well maintained. She went up the steps, calling out, "Hello? Anyone home?"

A moment later, a man came out of the front door. He was in his sixties or early seventies, with white hair, tan, weathered skin and some extra pounds around the middle, but his dark-brown eyes were sharp and questioning.

"What can I do for you?" he asked.

"I'm Tori Hayden," she said, watching to see if her name would ring a bell, and it clearly did.

He straightened, his eyes widening in surprise. "Ben's little girl?"

"Not so little anymore, but yes. And you're Hal Thatcher?"

"I am. Last time I saw you was at the funeral. How are

you? How's your mom?"

"We're both well—my brother, too."

"Right. Your brother played baseball. I heard a lot about those games."

"I'm sure you did. This is Dylan Callaway."

"Nice to meet you," Hal said, shaking Dylan's hand. "What can I do for you, Tori?"

"I have some questions about my dad."

"All right. Why don't you come inside?" he said, leading them into the house.

She was actually surprised at how much the boat felt like a house. If there wasn't a gentle rocking motion under her feet, she could almost forget they were on the water. The sitting room was small, but there was a love seat and a comfortable arm chair, so they were all able to sit down.

"What do you want to know?" Hal asked.

She took a breath and then dove in. "Do you remember what my father was working on before he died?"

Hal gave her a long, thoughtful look, but he didn't give away much in his gaze. Finally, he said, "Yes. He was trying to find a serial arsonist."

Her gut clenched at his words, and as she glanced over at Dylan, she saw the same startled light in his eyes.

"A serial arsonist?" she echoed.

"San Francisco was going up in flames with suspicious fires all over the city. The fire department was stretched thin, trying to keep up with them. It was clear that there was a very enthusiastic fire starter at work. But your father didn't think it was just your normal run-of-the-mill thrill-seeking arsonist; he thought there was a bigger scheme."

"What kind of a scheme?" she asked.

"He didn't share all of his thoughts with me, but I know that he believed the fires were about money."

"Insurance money," Dylan muttered.

Hal nodded. "That—and more. Ben had a gut feeling that there was a powerful person or group behind the fires. He told me he had some good leads and that I should be prepared to get the lawyers on board, because he was going to be dropping some big names, and it wasn't going to be what I might think."

"That sounds mysterious," she said with a frown. "Did he tell you the names of the people he was investigating?"

"No," Hal said, giving a firm shake of his head. "Ben kept everything close to the vest. I was surprised he told me that much. He never told a story until he felt it was ready to be shared with the world. He didn't want to go off half-cocked and then not be able to back up his ideas. He liked to have all his facts before he put them into an article. I appreciated that. It saved the paper from lawsuits. Unfortunately, Ben never finished the story, and I never even saw a draft."

"Did anyone pursue the story after he died?" she asked. "It seems like a big news event that someone would have wanted in on."

"I asked Lindsay to look into it. She'd worked with Ben and had some insight into how he thought and who he might have spoken to, but she never came up with anything concrete. She told me there was nothing on his desktop computer about the fires, and we knew his laptop computer was probably at the bottom of the sea. Not that I really thought there would be anything on the computers. Whatever notes he'd made he'd probably done by hand. Anyway, the fires died down in the next few weeks, so all the news organizations stopped covering them. Several months later, the *Herald* got bought up by the *Journal*, and the office was basically decimated. I decided to retire and write some books, do some sailing, and get out of the vicious and demanding news cycle. I was ready for a break." He paused. "Can I ask why you're so interested in what your father was working on? It's been a long time."

"I'm a reporter now for the *Bay Area Examiner*, and I'm thinking about writing a book about my dad's life," she said, sticking with the story that had worked with Lindsay. "But I realize that I don't know enough about his work. I have some of his old files at my house, but his computer was lost when he died."

"You should be able to get clippings of most everything he wrote."

"I'm more interested in his notes, how he got to where he was going."

Hal crossed his arms. "That's a good explanation, but it's not the whole story, is it? You're suddenly wondering if your dad's death wasn't an accident."

She was taken aback by his words. "Should I be wondering that?" she countered. "That's a bold statement to make."

"And yet you're not really surprised I made it. We had a break-in at the paper the day of your father's funeral. No one was in the office. We were all paying our respects. Nothing much was taken, but our IT guy told me that someone hacked into the system, into your father's files, as well as others."

"Did you report that to the police?" she asked.

"I did, but nothing came of it. There wasn't anything in the files about the fires. And there was no suspicion regarding your father's death. It was witnessed by his best friends. Since it didn't appear that your family had any concerns, I dropped it. I told myself that it was just a coincidence, that your dad always had a big story he was just about ready to break, that this one was no different than any of the others. He was always going after big fish. Assuming that one of those fish had something to do with his death was a big stretch in the absence of any evidence whatsoever."

She didn't like that he'd given up so easily, but would she have done any differently? All he'd had was conjecture, and it was difficult to go against the fact that Mitch and Jim had told the same story about what happened on that boat. The men had been friends for twenty years. No one doubted their version of events.

"You said the fires stopped after Ben died," Dylan interjected.

"Yes. I think there was one small suspicious fire that made me wonder about the story again, but that was it."

"Did anything else happen besides the hack?" she asked. "Any other odd conversations or people looking for anything after my dad died?"

Hal thought for a moment. "I did talk to the fire investigator. He'd had a few conversations with Ben about the arson fires and wondered if Ben had left any notes that might be pertinent to the investigations, but as I mentioned before, there wasn't anything."

"Do you remember the name of the investigator?" Dylan asked.

"Sure do. It was Wallace Kruger. We worked with him quite a bit that summer."

"Kruger?" she echoed, looking at Dylan. "He's the guy working on the hotel fire."

"No," Dylan said. "That's Gary Kruger, Wallace's son."

"Oh." So it wasn't the same man, but it was his son. It still felt like an unexpected connection that might be significant.

"That's about all I can tell you," Hal said. "Do you have any more questions?"

She usually had a dozen ready to go at all times, but at the moment she couldn't think of anything. "Not right now. But can I keep in touch?"

"Sure. I'm here most days."

"Thanks," she said, as they all stood up.

"You're more than welcome," Hal said. "I respected your father more than just about anyone on the planet. He was one of the best journalists I ever worked with. He left some big shoes to fill. I hope you know that."

"I'm not trying to fill them, just hoping to do good work myself," she said, as they walked back up to the deck.

"I'm sure you will. Have a good night."

She and Dylan didn't speak until they got into the car, then she said, "It's weird, isn't it? The arson fires? The Kruger connection? The computer hack? Or am I reaching? If I am, you need to pull me down to earth, Dylan, because I am getting some wild ideas in my head."

He gave her a small smile. "I don't think you're reaching, but before you jump off a cliff, let's talk it out."

"Instead of us talking to each other, maybe we should talk to Gary Kruger."

"He is not interested in talking to me. I spoke to him at the pawn shop fire yesterday and he made it clear he was doing his job and I should stick to doing mine."

"It's weird that his father was the investigator seventeen years ago."

He nodded. "I'd forgotten that his dad was in the department. Gary gives me crap for being a Callaway, but he followed in his father's footsteps, too."

"There's a lot of that going around," she said.

He nodded. "There is. Let me talk to Emma about it. She'll know how we can work with Kruger or go around him to get what information we need."

"Maybe she can also go back seventeen years and find out whether there was any evidence linking anyone to the fires my dad was looking into."

"That's an excellent idea." He pulled out his phone and put in Emma's number. "Voicemail," he said, when she didn't answer. He waited a moment, then left a message. "Emma, it's Dylan. We have some information on fires that happened seventeen years ago. There might be a connection to what's going on now. Call me when you have a chance." He set his phone down. "She'll call us back."

"I know. I just hate waiting."

"We have a lot to discuss. That will make the waiting go faster, and I'm thinking we should have our conversation over dinner. I'm hungry. What about you?"

"My stomach is churning. But I don't know if that's anxiety or hunger."

"I think some crab cakes and some wine might take care of both," he said lightly.

"Let's give it a shot."

Seventeen

Dylan had never seen Tori so quiet. Over crab cakes and wild salmon, her expressions changed quite a bit, but few words came out of her mouth. She was working a lot of things out in her head, which was also different. She usually liked to talk things out.

"Okay, what's going on in your brain?" he asked, as she let out the third sigh in a row.

"What?"

"You are somewhere far away. Care to invite me along?" he asked.

"You wouldn't like the trip. I feel like I'm in a pinball machine."

He smiled. "I think I know where you're going with that, but let's see."

Her eyes sparkled at his words, which made him feel a lot better. Tori was definitely resilient. She always bounced back. She had good survival skills, probably some of which she'd learned after her father died. But mostly it was just not in her personality to stay down on the mat too long. She was always up on her feet and ready to fight again.

"I'm like that silver ball in the machine bouncing from one thing to the next," she explained. "I think I'm heading in one direction, and then I hit a wall and find myself upside down and spinning in a different direction."

"I like pinball. I'm good at it, too."

"You think you're good at every game," she said dryly. "Remember when we used to go to the Village Host? You and Scott would play the arcade games for an hour straight. You were obsessed."

"We were high scorers on a couple of those machines."

"Ah, the glory days. You were good because you spent about a thousand dollars in quarters to play the machines."

"I cannot deny that we didn't run through a lot of cash. But it was fun."

"Those were certainly simpler days," she said with another sigh.

"Were they?" he challenged. "Growing up is its own pinball game. Lots of wrong turns and brick walls to run into while you're figuring things out."

"I'm surprised you would say that. Your path to adulthood seemed pretty straightforward. I don't remember you having an awkward phase with braces, glasses, acne, and a tendency to say the wrong thing all the time."

"You weren't that bad. And we all had insecurities in high school. It's part of growing up."

"I suppose, but some people seem to skip the worst parts of adolescence whereas I usually hit them head on."

"Maybe that's why you're so strong."

"Maybe."

"So where are we in our pinball game?"

"Okay," she said, gathering herself together. "Let's see. We have the arson connection—the fires my dad was researching, the hotel fire I was caught up in, and the one from yesterday. All of those fires link back to an investigator with the last name of Kruger."

"That's not that unusual. The fire department is filled

with legacy firefighters and investigators. And arson is an ongoing problem."

"Which might have spiked back when my father was investigating and is spiking again now, for some reason we don't know."

"Okay, I agree with that. What else do we have?"

"The computer search at the *Herald* after my dad's death."

"And there was the disappearing laptop after the boat trip," he added. "But if someone was looking for something after your father died, I wonder why they didn't go after the files that are now in your possession, and were, I presume, in your mom's house this entire time."

"That's a good question," she said, her teeth worrying her bottom lip as she considered his comment. "I should have thought of that."

He smiled at her annoyance. "You usually think of all the questions. Maybe there are just too many in your head."

"So, let's come up with some answers…"

"All right. Let's consider that someone did look through the files in your mom's house," he said.

She met his gaze with a knowing gleam in her eyes. "Someone who didn't have to break in, because he was there all the time."

"Mitch or Jim."

"Or both. They were always around." She tapped her fingers restlessly on the table top. "Mitch is a money guy. He worked in banking, accounting, and venture capital, and he's well-connected in the city. He has a lot of wealthy clients and friends. Could he have somehow been involved with whoever my dad was trying to take down?" Shadows filled her eyes revealing anger, pain, fear… "I can't believe what I'm thinking, Dylan."

Because she couldn't seem to say it out loud, he did. "You're thinking that Mitch set your father up."

"I don't want to believe that. But he could have taken the laptop, gotten rid of my dad, searched my mom's house, pretended to be devastated, and kept an eye on us just to be sure my mom didn't know anything."

"That would be a huge betrayal," he said quietly.

"Bigger than huge. And it's not just betrayal; it's murder. How can I think that about Mitch? He's been a second father to me."

"Let's consider another alternative. Your father finds out that his friend Henry Lowell and his family have been killed. He's afraid he's next. So Mitch and Jim help your father disappear because he's in trouble."

"And they keep the secret for seventeen years?" she asked doubtfully.

"To protect you and your family—yes."

"Where would my dad have been all these years? Why wouldn't he have come out of hiding at some point?"

"The danger lingered, or he did something he couldn't take back. Maybe your father crossed some sort of line. If he came out of hiding, he could go to jail."

"I can't see my father committing a crime. He was a hero, Dylan. He fought for the little people. He was all about truth and justice."

"He could have had to do something wrong in the pursuit of that. Or maybe he was being framed or blackmailed and had to disappear," he suggested.

She didn't look happy with any of his comments.

"I know you're trying to help, Dylan, but it's so impossible for me to believe in any of those ideas."

"Well, you don't have to believe. We're just talking." He picked up his water glass and finished it off. "Do you want dessert? Ice cream?"

She shook her head. "Maybe later. I still have some at home. It's time to get back to work. I'm starting to think there's nothing in the files at my house, but I might as well finish reading through them to be sure."

"I agree. We need to start crossing some things off the list. I'll help."

"You must be tired after your long shift."

He was tired, and if he had any sense, he would drop her off and go home. But where Tori was concerned, he didn't seem to have any sense at all.

—⇒⇐—

Two hours later, his weariness was catching up to him, and he noticed Tori yawning more than a few times in a row, but they were almost done with the files, and he really wanted to finish them off, so there would be no loose ends.

Tori rolled her head around on her neck as she set a folder on the kitchen table and picked up another one.

"Time for ice cream?" he asked.

She smiled. "You read my mind."

"I'll get you a cone. One or two scoops?"

"It's definitely a two-scoop night."

He went into the small kitchen and pulled the carton out of the freezer. He made her a cone and took it out to her. "I think you'll have to go shopping tomorrow. There's enough for a cone for me, but otherwise you're out of your most vital food group."

She took the cone from his hand and gave him a smile. "I'll definitely have to find time for a trip to the market."

He went back into the kitchen and made a cone for himself, then returned to the table.

As he ate his ice cream, his gaze settled on Tori. Her hair was mussed. She had a tendency to run her fingers through her hair or tuck strands behind one ear when she was thinking. There were dark shadows under her eyes. He had a feeling she hadn't been sleeping well, and he wished he was responsible for her lack of sleep and not this damned case she was caught up in.

As her tongue snaked out to catch a drip of ice cream, his body hardened. She really had a great mouth, and she could definitely use it for more than questions, as he'd found out the other night.

This wasn't the time to let his thoughts go in that

direction, but he couldn't seem to stop himself. He was completely caught up in Tori—in ways that were both terrifying and exciting. He didn't know where the two of them were going, but that was part of the thrill.

Tori challenged him in ways that other women had not. She pushed him with her questions. She saw through his defenses. She knew things about him that very few people knew. He felt more like himself with her than he'd ever felt with anyone.

But...and, of course, there was a *but*...he wasn't quite sure what to do about his unexpected and ridiculously strong attraction to a woman he should be treating as a little sister. That had gone out the window Sunday night when Tori's persuasive mouth had made it impossible to keep his hands off her.

It was supposed to be one night of fun—no strings, no promises, no regrets. Only problem was he wanted another night—maybe tonight and tomorrow and the night after that...

"Wait a second," Tori said suddenly, swallowing the last bit of her ice cream cone.

"What?" he asked, seeing her gaze on the file in front of her.

"I might have something."

She pulled out a piece of paper and put it on the table between them. It looked like a flow chart with words and arrows.

"Look," she said. "Wallace Kruger's name is at the top."

He ran his gaze down the chart, which had arrows leading from Kruger to four other boxes labeled respectively: Henderson, Castleborough, St. John's Manor, and Randolph. Underneath was another row with more names: Oscar Martinez, John Litton and Neil Lundgren.

"What do you think it means?" Tori asked impatiently.

"St. John's Manor could be a building. In fact, the first four boxes could be people or buildings or streets."

"Or fire locations," she suggested.

"Possibly."

"Kruger was the fire investigator that my dad spoke to. We know Martinez was the mayor the year my father died. The Lundgrens are big real-estate developers."

"The Littons are, too," he said.

"I wonder if we just found our big fishes." She grabbed her computer out of her bag and opened it up. She quickly typed in a name, then said, "John Litton founded Litton Capital, a corporation invested in real estate, commercial construction, venture capital and numerous other businesses. Some of his bigger holdings over the years have included the Viceroy hotel, the Delancey Inn, and the Italian Social Club. He died about eight years ago. His son Eric and his daughter Sheila now run the company. There's a grandson in the mix, too."

"What about Lundgren?"

"Let me pull him up. I know that Peter Lundgren is a developer. He was actually at one of the meetings I recently attended with representatives from the various housing agencies." She paused. "Okay, I've got a bio on him. Neil Lundgren was Peter's father. The Lundgrens own quite a few historical buildings in the city, including many of the oldest Victorians, or painted ladies as they're called."

"So the Littons and Lundgrens probably know each other. They seem to move in the same circles," he said.

"Yes. Neil Lundgren died eight months ago. He's survived by his wife Constance and three sons: Peter, Donald and Tyler. It looks like Donald is a doctor and Tyler works with Peter on the real-estate end." She looked up from her computer. "We need to find out if any of the buildings torched seventeen years ago can be tied to these families."

"And whether or not insurance claims were filed," he added. "If we can figure out who might have been profiting from the fires, we'll know who your father was looking into and who would have been most afraid of his questions."

"I agree."

"Look up St. John's Manor," he said.

"Okay." She took a moment, then said, "St. John's Manor was a six-story, turn-of-the-century apartment building that survived two major earthquakes and was home to many in San Francisco's art community. It was burned down seventeen years ago." She raised her gaze to meet his. "Our hunch was right. These names are probably arson sites."

He pulled out his phone. "I'm going to try Emma again." The phone rang a few times and then Emma picked up.

"Hi, Dylan. Sorry I didn't call you back. I had a late doctor's appointment."

"I hope everything is all right."

"I'm fine. I just wish doctors didn't make you wait an hour to have a five-minute checkup," she grumbled. "So you have some information for me to check out?"

"Yes, and by the way, you're on speaker with me and Tori."

"Great. Hi Tori."

"Hi," Tori said. "Sorry to bother you."

"No problem. What's up?"

"We think that Tori's father was investigating a string of arson fires in the city seventeen years ago," he said. "We have some names for you to check on. I don't know if they're buildings or streets, but I have four."

"Okay, hang on one second. Let me grab a notepad. All right, what are the names?"

"St. John's Manor, Henderson, Castleborough, and Randolph," he said. "We think Wallace Kruger was involved in those investigations."

"Where are you getting this information?" Emma asked.

"From my dad's old files," Tori put in. "He also mentions Neil Lundgren and John Litton, but I don't know what the context is."

"Lundgren and Litton," Emma repeated. "I know those names. They're important San Francisco families. What's their connection?"

"We don't know yet," he said. "They could have owned the buildings in question or be connected in some other way."

Dylan frowned as he heard someone talking to Emma. "Is that Max?"

"Yes," Emma said, only to be cut off by her husband.

"Dylan, Tori," Max said. "Why did you bring up Lundgren to Emma?"

"His name is mentioned in my dad's notes, along with another man, John Litton," Tori replied. "We believe my dad was investigating a serial arsonist right before he died. We don't know how Lundgren and Litton would be tied to that, but their names are on the same piece of paper as information relating to several fires."

"That's interesting," Max said. "We've been digging into Robert Walker's background. He was the victim of the hotel fire. He worked for Neil Lundgren as a super at one of his apartment buildings until he was laid off about a year ago."

Dylan exchanged a quick glance with Tori, then said, "So there's a tie between the possible fire starter and the Lundgrens?"

"Yes. But there's also a tie to Litton Capital. One of their subsidiary companies is called Galaxy Ventures, and they hold the deed to the residential hotel. The owner of Galaxy, Vince Davenport, filed an insurance claim yesterday. Galaxy and Davenport are located in Los Angeles, so we've only been able to speak to Mr. Davenport by phone. He's been friendly and helpful but has been unable to provide any leads to who might have wanted to burn the building down. He suggested it was squatters using space heaters, but, of course, that's not what happened."

"We responded to the scene of a similar fire last night," he put in. "It was a pawn shop. Looked like a similar explosive start to the fire. Gary Kruger is investigating. I asked him to keep me in the loop, but he made it clear the loop was closed to me. Do you think you could talk to him, Emma?"

"He already told me to stay out of his investigation into the hotel fire, so I'm not sure I'll get anywhere," she replied. "But I can try. Gary's father Wallace was one of the best investigators who ever worked for the department. I think Gary is working hard to live up to his father's name. He wants to make sure any achievement is purely his own." She paused. "But I should be able to dig into the older files without causing him any discomfort. I can do that tomorrow."

"That would be great," he said.

"You two have been busy," Emma added.

"Mostly asking questions instead of finding answers," Tori said. "We really appreciate your help in all this."

"No problem," Max said. "I'm also still looking into Mr. Hedden's whereabouts. He hasn't used his cell phone or his credit card since Saturday night. That might not be unusual if he is on a boat at sea, or it could be that he's laying low. At any rate, let's all stay in touch. And don't do too much on your own. You're pulling up a lot of rocks, and who knows what's coming out from underneath?"

"We're being careful," Dylan said. "Thanks again." He ended the call and let out a breath. "Lots more to think about."

Tori nodded. "We're circling around something important, but I still don't know how close we are. I'm really glad we have Max and Emma working on this from different angles. It helps to have their expertise and their resources."

"Big families come in handy for resources," he said.

"And Callaways are very helpful to each other."

"We're a tight group," he admitted. "My grandparents always made sure we understood that family is everything."

Her expression turned more somber. "It is everything," she said heavily. She got to her feet and walked over to the window.

She did that a lot, as if she were looking for some answer on the streets below.

He stood up and moved in behind her, wrapping his arms around her waist. She leaned back against him.

After a moment, she said. "What am I doing right now, Dylan?"

"That feels like a loaded question," he said lightly.

"Am I trying to prove my father was killed? Or am I trying to find a miracle scenario where my dad turns out to be alive?"

"Does it have to be one or the other?"

"Doesn't it?" she asked, turning to face him. "I'm having a hard time believing the original story—that my dad went fishing with friends and ran into an unexpected storm."

"And yet that could still be the truth."

"Then why would Mitch and Jim suddenly go missing? Why would Jim be talking to Neil Hawkins?"

"I don't know. But we'll figure it out."

"I'd like to believe that."

"You can. We're getting new leads all the time."

"I guess. By the way, I got my mom out of town. I called her this morning and told her I'd booked her and Ray into a Napa spa for three nights, my treat. I wanted them to have a chance to reconnect after the last few months. I told her that I'd already talked to Ray and he was thrilled. Then I called Ray and told him about the plan and that I'd already spoken to my mom and she was thrilled."

He smiled. "Quite the manipulator."

"Neither one wanted to disappoint the other, so they're out of town until Friday. I don't know if we'll be able to figure anything out before then, but I feel better knowing she's tucked away somewhere safe."

"It's a good plan."

She slid her arms around his waist. "I hope so. My head is spinning right now."

"You need to take a break and let some information settle in."

"I think you're right. I'm feeling a little scattered and not sure which of my ideas are good ones and which are bad."

"I can help you with that."

She smiled. "You tend to think most of my ideas are bad, Dylan."

"Not all the time. You had a lot of good ideas the other night."

Her gaze darkened. "You're veering into dangerous territory."

He knew he was, but he couldn't stop himself. "So what if I am?"

"You'll be pushing back our end date..."

"So what if I do?" he murmured.

"You said you only wanted one night. We already had that."

"I didn't actually say that; you just made that assumption."

"And I was wrong?"

"Let's just say that it's up for negotiation."

She gave him a sexy smile. "How do you want to negotiate?"

"Well, I think we should start in the bedroom."

"By getting naked?"

"Yes. And that's a *good* idea, by the way, in case you were wondering." He put his arms around her and gave her a kiss, then another and another. He wondered if he would ever get enough of her. *One night, two nights, three nights...would any number of days actually be enough?*

The question went unanswered, because desire was driving away all conscious thought. He didn't want to think anymore; he only wanted to feel. And what he wanted to feel was her naked, soft, sexy body under his.

They stripped off their clothes on the way to the bedroom and then he got her exactly the way he wanted her.

Eighteen

It was after midnight, and she should be asleep. She was certainly tired. Making love to Dylan had left her happy and exhausted. But she didn't want to close her eyes, didn't want to drift away, didn't want to lose the connection between them.

"What are you thinking about?" he asked, as they lay on their sides facing each other.

She tucked her hands under her face as she looked at him. His face was lit up by the moonlight streaming through her windows, and she had the feeling she could look at him forever and never tire of the sight of his handsome, well-defined, masculine face and light-blue eyes that shimmered and changed colors when he was excited or angry—two emotions she seemed able to bring up in him quite often—sometimes at the same time.

"Tori?" he quizzed.

"Nothing much," she said. "I like looking at you. I was kind of hoping you'd fall asleep, so you wouldn't see me watching you."

"I was hoping the same thing."

"You were not."

"Do you know that you're amazing?" he asked.

"Actually, I do. It just takes some people a long time to realize that about me," she said pointedly.

"It wouldn't have taken me this long if you hadn't left town for ten years."

"Oh, I don't know about that," she said.

"I do. You were a teenager the last time I saw you. It was Christmas, I think. You were home from college."

"Yes. I'm surprised you remember that. I was nineteen, so you were about twenty-three. You came over on Christmas Eve to see Scott, and you brought Jenny with you."

He grimaced at the reminder. "Yes, I did. She wasn't happy about it. She wanted to go to a party with her friends, but I hadn't seen Scott in a while, and I wanted to catch up." He paused. "You were already changing then, but I wasn't quite ready to see it."

"Well, compared to your bombshell girlfriend, I hadn't changed that much. I had gotten rid of the glasses and the braces, but I still didn't know what to say to you."

"I intimidated you?" he asked, surprise in his voice. "I never knew that. You always seemed happy to talk back to me."

"When we were in a group or with Scott, but sometimes, when it was just the two of us, which wasn't that often, I felt tongue-tied. Most of the time I could hide my crush on you, because you were with Scott, and usually you guys were annoyed with me for some reason or another. Or you were both acting all big brotherly because you thought I was doing something I shouldn't be doing. Never mind the fact that you two were way worse than me."

"We probably were doing much worse things. But Scott and I were both older brothers. We had sisters. We didn't want them to run into guys like us." He paused. "Which is why Scott is not going to be thrilled when he finds out about us."

"He'll get over it. And it's not his business."

"He's very protective of you."

"I know. He watched over me even before my dad died, but after that he was very concerned about every move I made. It got to be a little much at times. I remember my mom telling him once that she was the parent, not him, and that she was the one who could tell me what to do." She smiled to herself. "He didn't like that at all. I think he needed to take care of me and my mom, because it filled the empty space in his heart."

"What about you?" Dylan asked, running his fingers down her arm. "How did you handle all that pain?"

"I ate a lot of ice cream."

"So you weren't just coming to the ice cream shop to stalk me?"

She made a face at him. "No, well, maybe, but seeing you and getting a cone at the same time always gave me a lift."

"I wish I'd been more sensitive back then."

"You were a teenage boy; they're not generally known for their sensitivity."

"True."

"I turned my grief into a determination to be just like my dad. That's why I got so caught up in the reporting. Now, I wonder if..."

"If what?" he asked curiously.

"If I did it for the wrong reasons."

"Why would you say that? You love being a reporter. Whether you started out following in your father's footsteps or not doesn't change that."

"But what if he wasn't the man I thought he was?"

Dylan considered her question for a long moment. "Then you'll figure out how to deal with it."

"You make it sound easy."

"I don't think it would be easy at all, but ultimately you have to find a way to break your father down into the different roles that he played. He was a dad—and a good one, right?"

"He was great. He was busy, but he always made time for us. He was a sounding board. He was wise and warm and funny. He had the greatest laugh, too. It was loud and contagious. You just couldn't not laugh with him."

"I remember that laugh. Your relationship with him is true, Tori. You lived it. Whatever was happening in his work life, with his friends, with your mom—that was separate. Whatever he was doing or not doing on the job doesn't change the connection you had with him."

"You're far more insightful than I ever realized."

He grinned. "That sounds like an insult masked as a compliment."

"I didn't mean it that way. I guess we both judged each other a little harshly in the past."

"And we both probably deserved it."

"Maybe. I like talking to you, Dylan."

"I like talking to you." He ran his hand down to her bare hip. "I like *other* things, too."

"Are we ever going to go to sleep?" she asked with a smile.

"Not just yet," he said with a warm, husky laugh, and then his breath washed over her face as he kissed her lips in a tender assault that quickly grew more passionate.

She sighed with pleasure. She liked doing *other* things with him, too.

———

Tori spent most of Wednesday working on her homeless article. She was still trying to find the new angles Stacey had requested, but she wasn't getting too far. And when Jeff came by around four to ask her if she had a draft done yet, she didn't have a good answer.

"Still working on it," she told him.

"Are you?" he asked. "You seem distracted, Tori. Are you still looking into that hotel fire?"

"Not really," she lied. "I just don't think the information

I've collected on the homeless article is good enough yet. Stacey wants something groundbreaking, and I don't have it."

"What do you have?" he asked, sitting down by her desk.

"A lot of corporate-speak from developers, spin from local politicians, and idealistic hope without practical ideas from nonprofits. The truth is no one knows what to do, and there's so much red tape that even some decent ideas just don't get executed."

"You're working too far on the outside. You need to make this personal. Your story will resonate better if people care."

"I know that, but I haven't found too many homeless people willing to talk, either."

"Keep trying. Your story is out in the streets. It's not in public housing meetings."

"You're right. I will get back out there."

"Good." He stood up. "Is there anything else going on? Did you ever talk to Lindsay about your father's last story?"

"I did, and I managed to track down Hal Thatcher, too."

"Good old Hal. What's he up to?"

"He's living on a houseboat and enjoying being retired. He's written some books."

"Not a bad life. Were they able to help you?"

"A little. They said my dad was working on a series of suspicious fires."

"Oh, right," he said, a light coming into his eyes. "I forgot about that. He was looking for a serial arsonist, I think."

"Yes, but he died before he could find him."

"The arsonist must have moved on. It seemed like the fires died away." Jeff paused, a new gleam in his eyes. "You think they're starting up again, don't you? That's why you're so interested in the hotel fire."

"Maybe. But honestly, I have no idea."

"Have you talked to the fire investigator again?"

"No, he's not being forthcoming at all. He just says it's an ongoing investigation."

"That kind of answer never stopped your father."

"You're right. I need to keep pushing."

"Let me know if I can help—on either story."

"You already have helped me on the homeless article. You reminded me that the best stories are personal. I need to get back out on the street."

"I think that's where you'll find your answers."

As Jeff left, she turned back to her computer and read through her notes on her article. She definitely did not have a good angle. Maybe she would stop by a homeless shelter on her way home or on her way in to work tomorrow. Talking to more people who were living the life she needed to write about might give her some fresh ideas.

In the meantime...

She saved her file notes, then opened up her search engine, turning her attention back to her personal mystery. She'd researched St. John's Manor the night before, but what about the other names on the list? She hadn't heard back from Emma yet, so she'd see what she could find online.

Pulling her dad's chart out of her bag, she set it on her desk and typed in Castleborough. She soon discovered that there was a low-income housing development named Castleborough that was located in the south of Market area and had been built in the sixties. Late one night in 1999, a fire broke out in the basement and the building burned down. Twenty-three people were displaced, and two people died in the fire.

She skimmed through several more news reports on the incident. There were mentions of suspicious persons and arson, but she couldn't find any information on whether or not anyone had been charged with starting the fire.

She moved on to the next words on her father's chart, Henderson and Randolph. Adding the word *fire* to that search brought more good results. An apartment building on Henderson Avenue had burned down two months after Castleborough. The Randolph Street fire took down a convenience store, also under suspicious circumstances, and had occurred six weeks before Castleborough. So all four fires had occurred within five months. And the dates correlated with the months right before her father died. These had to be the fires he was looking into.

For the next hour, she read through more articles on fire and arson, looking for something that connected the fires and finally found it.

Neil Lundgren was the owner of the Henderson Avenue apartment building. He'd received insurance money for the fire and hired a construction firm, JL Design, to build a new structure. But that's when things got interesting, because JL Design was a subsidiary of Litton Capital.

Lundgren and Litton had been mentioned together in her dad's notes. And now they were tied to at least one fire. Actually, they were tied to more than one fire, because Max had told her that the owner of the residential hotel was Galaxy Ventures, a subsidiary of Litton Capital.

She tapped her fingers on her desk as she considered what she'd learned.

What if people were making money two different ways for the same problem?

They could be responsible for torching a building, but keeping their hands clean enough to get the insurance money, and then one or the other would get awarded the contract to build a new structure. Was the money going around in a circle?

Could they possibly be burning down each other's buildings so the crime couldn't be traced to them, but then making money on the back side?

If that were true, how did they decide which building to burn? The condemned residential hotel probably hadn't had much insurance on it. And what about the pawn shop? The neighborhood of the last two fires was run-down, begging to be redeveloped. In fact, there had been discussion at the housing meeting she'd attended about whether that neighborhood could be targeted for a new low-income housing development.

A chill crept down her spine. There could be city contracts on the line. Getting rid of those blighted structures would open up new financial opportunities.

She pulled up a map on her computer. She knew what street the hotel that she'd gone into was on. And after searching for pawn shops in the area, she had a good feeling she knew where the second fire had occurred. They were only a few blocks apart.

She opened up another search window and went to the city records database. She put in the address for the pawn shop and within minutes pulled up the deed. The owner was Viceroy Ventures. They had acquired the building three years earlier from Lundgren Real Estate Development. Another shiver shot down her spine.

Nibbling on her bottom lip, she spent the next thirty minutes trying to figure out what else Galaxy, Viceroy, Litton, and Lundgren owned, especially around the neighborhood of the previous two fires. The fires her dad had investigated had all been within three to five miles of each other, too. Was a similar pattern developing?

Litton owned another building around the corner from the pawn shop that housed a printer on the first floor and a marketing agency upstairs. More checking revealed that the print shop was actually closed. She tried calling the number for the marketing agency, but it went to voicemail. If the businesses were closed down, was the building empty?

She printed out a map of the neighborhood, circling the residential hotel, the pawn shop, and the third building she'd just found. Could it be a potential target?

She needed to figure out if there were any other buildings owned by any of the four companies that she'd linked together so far. Although, the scam might involve even more people. This could be just the tip of a very big iceberg.

Grabbing her phone, she called Dylan. They'd touched base around lunchtime, and she knew he'd gone to help his uncle on a construction job. But hopefully after work they could get together and go over what she'd come up with.

He answered on the first ring. "Hi, Tori."

"I have a theory," she said. "Do you have a minute?"

"Yes. I'm actually on my way to meet Emma. She said Kruger left early so she's going to go into his office and see if she can find anything that she doesn't have access to on the computer."

"That's great."

"Where are you?"

"Still at work. Do you want me to tell you my theory now?"

"Absolutely," he said.

"Okay, it's going to sound crazy, but hear me out. There was a movie awhile back where two strangers conspire to kill each other's wives. They figure since there's no known connection between them, and no known motive for either to kill the other person, that it's the perfect crime."

"I remember the movie. What does it have to do with anything?"

"Just think about how smart it would be to hide one crime by getting someone less obviously suspicious to commit it. What if Lundgren hired Robert Walker to burn down the residential hotel owned by Galaxy Ventures, but he did it for someone else?"

"You have to be talking about Litton Capital?"

"I am," she said, happy he was keeping up with her. "I found out that Litton and Lundgren have worked on numerous projects together. One of the fires my dad was looking into took place in Lundgren's building. His insurance company paid off, and he hired a subsidiary company of Litton Capital to rebuild it."

"That's interesting."

"So going back to the hotel fire. What if Galaxy collects the insurance money, which goes into Litton's pockets? He hires one of Lundgren's companies to construct a new building. Maybe he even hires them to sell the building."

"So it goes in a circle," Dylan said.

"Exactly. The owner of the building would always be the

first suspect in an arson case, but this way that person's hands are so clean that insurance has to pay out. When they collect the money, the other guys get rich on the back end."

"That makes sense to me."

"Good, because I also learned that the pawn shop that you went to the other day is owned by a company called Viceroy Ventures and the acquired from Lundgren three years earlier. I know it's going to take some time to figure this out, and I have to be as meticulous and thorough as my dad was in order to get concrete proof, but I think I'm on to something, Dylan." She couldn't hide the excitement in her voice.

"I think you might be, too," he said. "I'll run all this by Emma. And then I'll come and meet you. When are you leaving work?"

"I'm going to head home in a few minutes."

"You're taking a taxi, right?"

"Of course, but it's been quiet the last few days. Really, nothing has happened since we saw Hawkins at the reception on Saturday night."

"I still want you to be careful. I'll come by your place after I talk to Emma."

"I'll see you then."

After she hung up the phone, she shut down her computer, stashed it in her bag along with the map she'd printed out and the other notes she'd made, and left for home.

She took a taxi to her building and went upstairs to her apartment without running into anyone. She washed up, changed her top, and fixed her makeup, then walked into the kitchen to grab a bottle of water out of the fridge. Seeing her empty shelves, she thought it might be a good idea to order in some food. Or maybe she'd just wait for Dylan.

As if on cue, her phone rang, and Dylan's number flashed across the screen.

"That was fast," she said. "Are you already done with Emma?"

"Emma was attacked," he said tersely.

"What?" she asked, shocked by his words.

"A security guard found her in the stairwell. She was hit from behind and she fell down some stairs. She's on her way to the hospital."

"Oh my God! Did you see her?"

"Yeah, but she was going in and out of consciousness," he said heavily.

She could feel his fear through the phone. "She's going to be all right."

"This is my fault. I got her involved."

She suddenly realized what he was saying. Emma had been knocked out because she'd gone up to Kruger's office to look for information on the fires. "What about Kruger? Where is he?"

"I don't know. The police are here. I told them that she was looking for information that he had on a fire investigation. They're going to try to find him. The offices were empty when it happened. Everyone had gone home. I'm not sure why Emma was in the stairwell. If someone grabbed her and pushed her inside, or if she'd decided to take the stairs for some other reason."

"What about Max?"

"The police called him. I haven't spoken to him, but he's meeting her at the hospital."

"He must be terrified."

"I can't even imagine." He drew in a breath. "What if she's hurt really bad, Tori? What if she loses the baby? She's been so happy. She just got Shannon. That kid needs a mother."

"Then she has to be all right," she said, trying to infuse as much confidence into her voice as she could.

"I have to make some calls to my family, and then I'm going to the hospital."

"Of course. I'd like to join you, unless you'd rather I didn't."

"No, I'd like you to come, Tori. I need you," he said on a husky note. "If you don't mind."

"Of course I don't mind." She was thrilled he would let

her be there for him.

"St. Mary's on Fulton Street."

"I'll see you soon. Keep the faith, Dylan."

"I can't do anything else."

She set her phone down on her kitchen table, feeling the same guilt Dylan was experiencing. If they hadn't brought their problems to Emma, if they hadn't involved her in the case, she'd be home with her husband and her child and her baby-to-be.

Who on earth would attack a pregnant woman?

Would Gary Kruger really do such a thing? They were coworkers. They'd traveled the same path from firefighting to arson investigation. They both had followed in the footsteps of parents who had set the bar high for them.

Maybe that didn't matter. If Kruger had something that could get him into real trouble, he might not have cared who he hurt to get away with it. She really needed to finish connecting the dots. But right now she had to get to Dylan. The fact that he'd admitted to needing her made her heart ache. She just wished she could fix this for him.

Grabbing her bag, she left her apartment. She was just about to shut the door when she felt a presence to her right.

Before she could see who it was, she was tackled from behind.

Strong, beefy arms pulled her against an iron chest. Her bag was ripped off her shoulder. Something dark and thick came over her head. She kicked out her legs and threw her fists at anything she could reach, but she couldn't get out of the man's grip.

She was blinded by the material covering her eyes, and air was getting harder to find. Gasping, she tried to scream, but even she could barely hear her voice.

She was thrown over someone's shoulder and being upside down made her even dizzier. She had the terrifying feeling she was losing consciousness. She had to get away now. She wouldn't have a chance later. But her struggling did nothing, and when her head smashed against something hard, fireworks exploded in front of her eyes.

Moments later, she was tossed onto her back and felt a sharp, stabbing pain in her back from some sort of metal.

A door slammed. She was in a trunk and the car was moving. *Where the hell were they taking her?*

Nineteen

—➤➤◄◄—

When Dylan got to the ER waiting room at St. Mary's Hospital, he was told that Emma had been taken up to Labor and Delivery on the fourth floor. His heart pounded at the implications of that piece of information. She must have gone into labor. But it was too early. She wasn't even on maternity leave yet. *And what about her head injury? How would that factor into anything?*

When he got to the fourth floor, he looked around for Max but was told he was in with his wife and there wasn't any news yet.

He paced around the small waiting room for almost five minutes and then he heard his Uncle Jack's booming voice at the nurse's station, so he walked into the hall.

Jack Callaway had pepper gray hair and blue eyes and was a big stocky man with a big presence. His wife Lynda was blonde with a softer, quieter personality, but there was no doubt she could be as determined and stubborn as any other Callaway.

Lynda saw him and hurried over. "Dylan, what's

happened? Do you know anything?"

"Not much," he said shortly, wishing he had better news for Emma's mother. "She was hit over the head, and it looks like she fell or was shoved down the stairs."

"I can't believe this is happening." Lynda put a hand to her mouth as if she might be sick. "This was at her work? It's a government building. Isn't there security?"

"Max will get to the bottom of it," he said, hoping that would reassure her.

"Where is Max?"

"He's with Emma."

Lynda let out a breath. "Okay, good. What about Shannon?"

"Sorry, I don't know."

"She must be at daycare. I need to call them." As Lynda took out her phone, it vibrated. "Nicole? You got my message?" She paused. "Oh, thank goodness. I was worried about Shannon. You stay with the kids. I'll let you know what's happening." She bit down her lip. "Yes, we're all going to be strong, because Emma is fierce, and she's a fighter."

Lynda blinked back tears as she put her phone into her purse. "Nicole is taking care of Shannon, and she's calling the rest of the family."

"I already told Burke," he said. "And my parents are on their way."

Jack came over and put his arm around his wife. "She's hanging in there. She has a concussion, and she's gone into early labor, but the doctors are doing everything they can to make sure that both Emma and her baby are going to be fine."

"I can't believe this, Jack," Lynda said with a confused shake of her head. "Everything was going so well for Emma. She had all those miscarriages, and she didn't think she could have her own child, and then she got Shannon and found out she was pregnant at the same time. It was a miracle. It was amazing. She can't lose her baby, and I—I can't lose her."

"You won't lose her," Jack said firmly. "Emma will never quit. We all know that."

"That's what I'm hoping."

Jack turned to him. "Do you know what's going on? The police told me you were there."

"I got there after she was hurt. She was looking into some suspicious fires that Gary Kruger was handling."

"Wait, this is about a fire investigation?" Jack demanded.

His uncle wasn't just Emma's father; he was also second in charge of the SFFD. "Yes," he said. "Emma was helping me look into a fire at a residential hotel last week as well as some other suspicious fires, most of which were handled either by Gary Kruger or his father Wallace."

"What are you saying?" Jack asked. "Kruger is the one who hurt Emma?"

"I don't know, but the police need to find him. He was being extremely secretive about his work, and Emma was attacked near his office."

"I'm going to make some calls." Jack turned to Lynda. "You'll be okay?"

"Of course. You do whatever you need to do to find out who did this to Emma."

As Lynda finished speaking, more Callaways poured off the elevator: Burke and his wife Maddie, and Emma's younger brothers Sean and Colton. His parents followed along with Ian and his girlfriend Grace. He was surprised to see them.

Explanations followed, but everyone seemed to share the same sense of bewilderment and fear.

"When did you get into town?" he asked Ian, pulling his brother aside.

"Grace had an interview this morning, so we drove down last night. We were at the house when you called Dad," Ian replied. "I can't believe this has happened to Emma." He saw the worry in Ian's eyes, and he knew that Ian and Emma had gotten close during a trip to Ireland the previous summer.

"She's tough. She'll make it." Turning to Grace, he added, "It's good to see you again."

The red-haired Grace smiled back at him with a

concerned gaze. "You, too, Dylan. I wish these weren't the circumstances."

"Me, too. So how did the job interview go?"

"Very well. I really liked the school. If I get the job, we'll be officially living in San Francisco this summer."

"That's great news."

Ian was lucky to have found a woman willing to relocate her life because it was more important for Ian's work to be in San Francisco than for Grace to be in Tahoe. But he also knew that Ian was so madly in love with Grace that he would have found a way to make Tahoe work if he'd had to. He'd been commuting back and forth since Christmas, spending every second he could with Grace, and Dylan had never seen his brother so happy.

He felt an odd ping of jealousy. He'd chosen to stay single, to stay out of committed relationships. Now he wondered why. Because it seemed like he might be missing out on something wonderful.

The waiting room got busier as Emma's brother Drew and his wife Ria showed up, followed by Shayla, whose presence brought a hush to the room. Shayla was a doctor and while she didn't work at St. Mary's apparently she knew enough people there to get better information.

"They're delivering the baby by cesarean section," Shayla said somberly. "Emma has suffered a concussion. She also has a broken arm and some cracked ribs."

"What about the baby?" Lynda asked. "Emma wasn't due for another seven weeks."

"It's early, so we'll have to see what challenges are ahead," Shayla said. "But there's a good chance they'll both be fine."

Seeing the shadows in Shayla's eyes, Dylan wondered if that was true, or if Shayla was trying to put a good spin on it, but for now, he wanted to believe in a good outcome.

As Shayla went to check on Emma's progress, small groups broke out, and quiet chatter filled the room. He suddenly realized that Tori hadn't shown up yet, and he wondered why.

Glancing at his watch, he realized it had been almost an hour since he'd spoken to her.

He moved into the hall and toward a vending machine area as he called her phone. It rang eight times and then her voicemail picked up. His gut tightened, his instincts going on alert. He wasn't one to panic, but with everything that was going on, he really wanted her to pick up her phone.

He left a message asking her to call him. Then he texted her as a backup. He waited five minutes, then went back to the waiting room. He made small talk with his family for another fifteen minutes, then tried Tori again. There was still no answer and his gut was screaming at him that something was wrong.

She'd told him she would meet him at the hospital. There was no way it would take her an hour and a half to do that, and he didn't think she'd do something else without texting him back.

Burke came over to him, giving him a hard look. "What's going on?"

"Tori was heading over here an hour ago, and now she's not answering her phone. I need to find her." He hesitated. "I hate to leave, but—"

"Go. Find Tori. There's nothing you can do here. And call me if you need help."

"I'll let you know," he said, slipping out the door before anyone else could ask where he was going.

———

After being pulled out of the trunk, Tori was tossed over someone's shoulder.

He smelled like beer and cigarettes, and as she struggled, he ordered her to be still or he'd knock her out. With some sort of sack tied around her neck preventing her from seeing or getting much air, and an iron grip around her body, she decided to save her energy and stop moving.

Doors opened and closed. She felt like they went down some stairs. She strained her ears, trying to figure out where she was, who might have her. The man carrying her was strong, and she didn't have the feeling she would recognize him even if she could see him. Certainly, his voice hadn't sounded familiar.

A moment later, he tossed her onto the floor like a big bag of flour. She yelped as her hip hit something hard, and her head bounced backward against what was probably the floor.

Footsteps moved away from her. A door slammed. She reached for the tie around her neck. Her fingers trembled as she tried to undo the knot. Her pulse was racing. She expected someone to stop her at any moment.

But it felt like she was alone. It was very, very quiet. She didn't know how long that would last. This might be her only chance.

The knot was hard to budge and she almost cried in frustration, but she had so little air, she was afraid to use up what she might have left by sobbing into the fabric.

Finally, after minutes that felt like hours, she undid the knot which loosened the fabric, and she was able to pull it off her head.

She gulped in deep breaths of air as her gaze darted around the room. She had to blink several times to adjust her eyes to the night shadows.

She thought she might be in a basement. There were wooden stairs leading up to a door. Next to that were two big water heaters. There were empty crates tossed along one wall.

As her gaze ran around the room, she saw small windows near the ceiling that brought some light into the room, maybe from an outside streetlight. It was definitely getting dark outside now.

The floor she was on was concrete—chipped and dirty. There were some boxes across the room, but she didn't know if anything was inside.

She crawled onto her knees and then made it to her feet.

She felt shaky and unstable, but she gathered her strength together. She needed to find a way out.

Moving across the room, she hoped to find some sort of weapon in the boxes, but the containers were empty. She tossed them aside. She wanted to scream in frustration, but would that make things worse?

A dozen questions ran through her mind.

Why was she here? Who had kidnapped her? How had they gotten into her apartment building? What did they want?

She could hear Dylan's voice in her head telling her to start thinking of answers instead of questions. She needed to problem solve. It didn't really matter who had brought her here or why. She just had to get out. She walked over to the crates, wondering if she could break them apart, use a jagged piece of wood as a weapon.

Her brain whirred with possibilities. Maybe she could crouch behind the stairs, find a way to get the jump on her kidnapper.

She wondered why they hadn't bound her hands, hadn't tied her to something. Maybe there really was no way out.

She walked up the steps and tried the door. It didn't budge even a hair when she tried to twist the handle.

Moving back down the stairs, she grabbed a crate and smashed it against the cement floor. It broke apart in big pieces. It also made a great deal of noise. She held her breath for a long minute, wondering if someone would come back to see what she was doing, but nothing happened.

She took one of the pieces of wood and hit it against the ground again, trying to sharpen it into a point. It kind of worked, but she didn't have a lot of confidence that she could take down anyone with it.

She sat back on the floor and blew out a breath, trying to keep the fear at bay so she could keep thinking, stay focused on being strong and ready to defend herself. But inside she was terrified and wanted to burst into tears.

Don't give in, she told herself.

She could do this. She wasn't dead yet. Maybe there was

a reason for that.

But what could they possibly want? She wasn't rich. Her mom had no money to speak of. And if this was about what she'd been investigating, then they probably wanted to shut her down, and the best way to do that was to get rid of her.

More fear ran through her.

Footsteps suddenly sounded overhead.

They were coming back.

She grabbed the piece of wood and jumped to her feet, holding her makeshift weapon behind her back. She moved closer to the stairs, hoping they wouldn't see her in the shadowy light.

The door opened. Her heart jumped into her chest.

A figure crossed the threshold. The man who had brought her down here?

But the man stumbled as someone shoved him from behind. He fell halfway down the stairs as the door slammed behind him.

For a split second, she thought it might be Dylan. He'd come after her, but he'd gotten caught, and they'd thrown him down here with her.

Then she saw the heavy coat, the baggy clothes, the graying hair, and she was suddenly terrified for another reason.

This was the man she had followed, the man she had seen outside Scott's wedding, the man who looked like her father.

"Who are you?" she asked, moving around to the bottom of the stairs, putting herself back in the light.

He straightened, lifting his head, his gaze finally meeting hers.

Oh, God! His face. His eyes. He was older, and he had changed, but he was also the same...

Twenty

—➤➤◄◄◄—

"No. It can't be you," she said, shaking her head. Her mind was playing tricks on her. She'd been starved for oxygen. It was dark. This man was Neil Hawkins...or someone else...but he was not her father. He couldn't be.

He took a step down the stairs. "Tori," he said, a plea in his eyes.

She immediately backed up, shaking her head. "You're dead," she said flatly. "It's not you. It can't be you."

"It is me, Tori."

His voice brought a huge knot into her throat. Burning tears assaulted her eyes, but she wiped them away with one hand and raised the stick in her other hand, still not ready to believe what was right in front of her.

"I'm not going to hurt you, baby."

"I am not your baby. I don't even know who you are."

"I'm your father."

"You can't be. My father died. We buried him in a cemetery. He has a gravestone. We had a funeral. We grieved for him." She was shouting by the time she got to the end.

Every word had made his face go another shade of pale. His dark-blue eyes, so much like her own, stared back at her. "I'm sorry, Tori."

"What does that even mean?" she asked in bewilderment.

"I had to fake my death to protect you and your mother and Scott. They were going to kill you. They were going to kill all of us. There was no other way out."

"There had to be."

"There wasn't," he said flatly.

He moved down the stairs. He was still taller than her but only by about six inches now. And his face had aged. There were lines under his eyes and around his mouth. His hair was gray. He looked so much older than he had the last time she'd seen him.

"I—I don't understand," she said, taking another step back so there was at least two feet between them.

"I know you don't. I have a lot to explain."

"Yes, you do."

"You say you don't believe it's me, but is that really true? I thought maybe you had guessed after you saw me outside the wedding. You asked Jim questions about me."

"Yes, I did ask Jim, and he lied to my face."

"Jim was protecting me."

"Like Mitch?"

"Yes," he said heavily.

"So they both knew you were alive all these years?"

"They helped me fake my death."

"Well, of course they did. They had to. They were with you. Did you even go on a fishing trip down to the Caribbean?"

"We did. Everything was exactly as Mitch and Jim described, except the part where I died."

She looked at him in disbelief. "I can't believe it. How could either of them look us in the face and tell us so many lies? How could they hold me when I cried over you? How could they have hurt Mom the way they did?" She thought back to the first few terrible days, so many random moments becoming much more important now. "That's why Mitch told Mom he didn't want her to see your body, that it would be better if you were cremated before they brought you back. She was so off balance and devastated, she didn't fight it. Was there anything in the urn we buried?"

"Ashes from a fire."

"And the death certificate?"

"Paid for."

"Well, you thought of everything." She paused, another question coming into her head. "Did Joanie and Elaine know?"

He gave a negative shake of his head. "No, we were afraid they'd tell your mother."

"What a huge secret to keep," she muttered. "I still can't believe Mitch and Jim could have acted so normally around us for so many years. They came to all my events. They saw how much I missed you, but they never veered from the story."

His eyes turned bleak. "They couldn't. They knew the stakes were too high. I asked them to look after you, Tori."

"But that was *your* job."

Her words struck a blow, and pain flashed through his eyes.

"I had no choice," he said.

"There's always a choice." It seemed unimaginable that he could be alive. "For seventeen years you've stayed in hiding, and there wasn't a time before now that you could show your face to me?"

"No. The men who were after me were still alive. I couldn't bet your life on the fact that they wouldn't still act if they realized I hadn't died."

She was suddenly reminded of where their reunion was taking place. "Do they know now? Where are we? Someone grabbed me outside my apartment. They put a bag over my head, and they put me in the trunk of a car. But we didn't drive for very long."

"We're in a building on Grant Street."

She sucked in a quick breath, knowing exactly where they were. "Where there used to be a print shop."

He raised an eyebrow in surprise. "How did you know that?"

"Because I've been looking into suspicious fires in the city after I almost got blown up in a residential hotel last week—the same hotel you went into but somehow escaped." Her gaze narrowed. "Did you shoot Robert Walker?"

"Yes," he said without apology. "I didn't know that was his name at the time. The building was supposed to be empty. He came at me with a gun, and I managed to get it away from him. I shot him, but I couldn't stop him from setting off the explosive. I barely made it out."

"Me, too."

He drew in a shaky breath. "I didn't know you were in the building, Tori, not until the next day. I thought you might have seen me watching you, but I never guessed you'd tail me to the building. Why would you do that? Especially if you didn't recognize me?"

"There was something about the way you looked at me, and I was doing a story on the homeless population and thought maybe you'd seen me at the encampment and had thought about trying to approach me but had second thoughts."

"You should never have followed a stranger into an empty building. Are you crazy?"

"Now you're the one who's angry?" she asked in amazement.

"You're right. This is all my fault."

"Damn straight it is. So who are the bad guys? Who threatened to kill the family? Who's the reason we're both locked in this room? If I'm going to die, I would like to know what I'm dying for."

"We're not going to die."

She would have believed him, if she hadn't seen the lie in his eyes. "We're not? Is someone coming to save us? Mitch and Jim, maybe?"

His lips tightened. "No, they're out of town. I sent them away. You were getting suspicious, and they didn't think they could lie to you anymore. I was hoping you'd let the police and fire department figure out who set the fire in the hotel and that you'd run into enough brick walls with your other questions that you'd give up."

"I don't quit because of a few obstacles, and if you'd stuck around for more of my life, you might know that about me," she said, hurt and rage racing through her.

"I know more than you think. I wasn't in your life, Tori, but I watched you from afar. I've seen what you've accomplished. I've read your work. You're an incredible writer—a far better journalist than I could ever be."

"That's not true. And I don't believe you've read my work." She wanted to believe it, but there was too much pain coloring her thinking right now.

"I have. I can name every article. I had to leave you, Tori. But I couldn't not know what you were doing. I followed you on social media. I went to your graduations— high school and college. I watched your brother's baseball games. I was in the back of the church when he got married."

"I didn't see you there," she whispered, so many emotions running through her.

"I had on a wig, glasses, and a cap on my head. I came into the church as the ceremony started and left through the side door when it ended. I knew it was a risk, but I couldn't not be there when my son was getting married. Every year we've been apart has been more difficult than the last."

She gave him a long look, trying to judge if he was a really good liar or if he was telling the truth. As a child, she'd never considered that he could or would lie to her, but faking his death had changed all that.

"Where have you been all these years?" she asked.

"Roaming around the country, changing my name, my address, keeping out of sight for the most part, staying away from San Francisco except for special events."

"Like Scott's baseball games?"

"I only went to the play-offs."

"He knew you were there. He used to tell me he felt your presence. I was a little jealous of that, because I never felt you watching me."

"I was watching you, too. There were so many times I wanted to reach out to you, but I couldn't. Every time I thought about it, I remembered not just the threats I'd gotten, but what they'd already done."

"Like killing Henry Lowell's family?"

Shock widened his eyes. "You know about that?"

"I've been going through your old files this week. I saw the clipping someone sent you."

"I didn't realize I left it in the house. I should have been more careful about cleaning everything out, but things were moving fast back then. I didn't have a lot of time to tie up loose ends. I figured once I was dead, they'd leave you alone. And they did."

"After they searched your office files to make sure there was no one still working on the story," she said.

"Who told you that?"

"Hal Thatcher."

"You tracked down Hal?"

"Through Lindsay Vaxman. She's the one who gave me Hal's name. I didn't know you were alive, but I started to think maybe you'd been killed, that the fishing trip hadn't ended in accidental death. I even wonder if Mitch had killed you. I had to know what you'd been working on before you died."

"Why would you think that Mitch killed me?" he asked in surprise.

"Because Mitch was caught on a security camera leaving a warning note on my car."

"He was caught on camera?" her father echoed.

"Yes, he was."

"I can't believe it."

"That's what you can't believe?" she demanded.

"Sorry."

"So if Mitch and Jim are innocent, who was going to kill us seventeen years ago, and is it the same person who has locked us in this basement?" she asked. "I've pieced some of it together already. I know there's some kind of insurance and real-estate scheme going on."

"There is—a large, very profitable, and long-running scam, Tori. It started seventeen years ago. The biggest, richest, and most powerful men in this city were burning down buildings, collecting insurance, then winning bids for new construction and new sales opportunities on the back end. They hid their tracks through layers of corporations and by keeping their hands clean. They also had help from industry and political leaders, who were paid well for their trouble."

"Who was in charge?"

"The ringleader was Neil Lundgren. He was the one who created the circle of associates, who each had a job to do. Seventeen years ago, Lundgren inherited a large portfolio of real-estate in the city from his father, but many of the buildings were in run-down neighborhoods. The real-estate market wasn't hot back then. He couldn't sell them, and it would cost too much tear down and rebuild everything. Lundgren was friends with John Litton, a member of another prominent family, who had a similar problem. So they came up with a plan."

"They would torch the blighted buildings for each other, get the insurance money, and then rebuild," she said.

Admiration filled his eyes. "Exactly."

"Who else was involved?"

"The mayor—Oscar Martinez. Lundgren and Martinez went to school together, and Lundgren donated a great deal of money to Martinez's campaign. Martinez would give Lundgren a heads-up on potential government building projects. Some were worth millions of dollars and some required redevelopment in the neighborhoods where Lundgren and Litton owned properties."

"They also had a partner in the fire department, didn't

they?"

"Wallace Kruger. He had a gambling addiction and a lot of money problems."

"So they paid him to cover up the suspicious fires?"

"Yes. There were others involved, too. Litton had a brother in construction. He did a lot of work for them, too. They also made up dummy companies that no one could trace back to them."

"Okay, I think I've got it. They each used the other to keep their hands clean for the insurance payout, which then gave them money to rebuild and reinvest."

"And sometimes sell for quadruple the price of what the building would have been worth before the fire. The mayor liked the scam, because in an odd way they were cleaning up the city."

"How did you find out about it?"

"Henry Lowell. Henry had gone to school with Lundgren and Martinez. Over too much wine one night, Martinez told him he was worried about Lundgren's power and said something about selling his soul to the devil they both knew. Henry needed someone to start asking questions who wasn't as close to them as he was, so he brought me in." Her father's expression turned grim. "But Lundgren had spies everywhere. Someone betrayed me."

"Okay, back up. Everything you just told me happened a long time ago. You stayed dead and far away from here to protect us and to stay safe. What changed? Why did you come back? Why were you in that hotel?"

"I came back because the fires started up again. The scheme ended after Henry was killed and I disappeared. I think it got too hot for them, so they laid low. I watched the news over the next several years, looking for the pattern of fires to start up again. I thought I could somehow figure it out and find evidence from afar. I still wanted to put them away. But it was quiet for a long time. Martinez left politics after his term ended. Wallace Kruger retired from the fire department, so those allies were gone. Eight years ago, John Litton died of cancer. And then last year, Neil Lundgren passed away from a heart attack."

"If all the players were out of the game, how did it start up again?"

"Peter Lundgren—Neil's son," her father replied. "He took over his father's company after Neil's death, and I'm guessing he got some of the band back together, including Litton's son Eric, only this time it was the next generation. I was watching the news one day, and I heard about a fire in the south of Market area, an empty warehouse in a rough neighborhood, and it gave me a bad feeling. I did some digging and found out the company was owned by Lundgren. That's when I came back to San Francisco."

"To finally write the story you wanted to write seventeen years ago?"

"And to stop them. Another fire in a small house in the middle of a commercial zone confirmed my theory that the game was back on. I tried to work it on my own for a couple of months, but I didn't have enough resources or access to information, so I reached out to someone for help."

His words surprised her. "Who?"

"A man I'd worked with briefly at the *Herald*. He was a young, hotshot reporter back then, and he reminded me of myself. I thought I could get him on board with the lure of a potentially huge story, and I was right."

Her stomach flipped over. "Are you talking about Jeff Crocker?"

"Yes. You're incredibly astute, Tori."

"No. It's just that the pieces of the puzzle are finally falling into place. Is that why they hired me? Because you reached out to Jeff?"

"No, I had nothing to do with that. In fact, I was shocked when I heard. I wondered if Jeff was playing some game, but he assured me that his boss hired you, that you'd sent in a resume on your own and said that you wanted to move back to the city."

"Well, that's true."

"He told me that he would keep my secret and that he'd keep an eye on you. He said he would let me know if he thought you were in danger."

She didn't know what to make of that, but she decided to leave it alone for the moment. "All right. So how did Jeff help you?"

"Last week, he told me that he'd come across a building in his research that looked like the perfect target—the abandoned residential hotel. It had just been condemned. I did some research and discovered it was owned by Galaxy Ventures, which I knew was connected to Litton Capital. Jeff told me it was going to be knocked down the next day. If something was going to happen it would be before that. So I went over there."

"And ran into Robert Walker."

"Yes. I learned later that night that Walker was dead. I figured no one else would know I was there. I didn't realize you'd followed me until the next day when I made contact with Jeff. He told me what happened."

"Why didn't you come to me then? You knew where I lived, where I worked."

"Mitch and I talked it over, and we decided to wait until after the wedding, so Mitch put the warning note on your car, thinking it would buy us some time. I didn't think you were in danger. You were asking questions as a reporter, but Jeff assured me you weren't close to figuring anything out. I believed him."

She saw the flash of anger in his eyes and suddenly knew where it had come from. All of her conversations with Jeff in the last few days ran through her head: the questions he'd asked her, the information he'd fed her on how to find out what her father was working on. It suddenly all made sense. "Jeff was playing you, wasn't he?"

"Yes. Unfortunately, I didn't figure that out until a few minutes ago," her father said heavily. "Jeff told me to meet him here, that he had finally gotten the evidence that would nail Lundgren to the wall, but when I arrived, I was jumped by a big guy I didn't recognize. He shoved me through that door, and when I saw you, I knew I'd been duped. I'm sorry, Tori. I should have stayed dead. I shouldn't have tried again to take them down a second time. They beat me once. And they beat me again."

She paced around the room, needing to move so that she could release some of the adrenaline running through her body. Then she paused, listening for sounds from overhead.

"Why is it so quiet? What's the plan?" She looked into her father's eyes, and she knew the answer without needing to hear him say the words. "Of course. I wondered why they didn't tie me up. They didn't need to. There's no way out of here, and there's no one else in this building, is there?"

He shook his head. "I don't think so."

"There's going to be an explosion, but this time we're not getting out." Her mouth trembled as the truth hit her hard. "Does anyone know you're here? Did you tell Mitch or Jim?"

"No. We agreed not to communicate."

"Then we have to find a way out of here on our own."

He looked around the room. "There's nothing down here." His gaze fell on the stick still in her hand. "Were you going to stab someone with that?"

"I wasn't going to give in easily."

He smiled. "That's my girl."

"I have not been your girl in a long time." As she finished speaking, she heard footsteps overhead, and she froze. When she took her next breath, she smelled gas. Someone was pouring gasoline.

All it would take was a match...

Her stomach heaved at the thought of what was coming next.

Her dad reached out his hand to her. She hesitated, but then she took it. It felt right and wrong to hold on to him, but she couldn't seem to let go. The tremendous love she'd once felt for him overwhelmed her. When she was a kid, she'd looked to him to protect her. But he couldn't save her from this.

"You have to know how much I love you, Tori," he said. "You and Scott and your mom—you were my life. I never married anyone else. I never had other kids. You were the only family I ever wanted. I wish your mother and Scott could know that."

"We can't just give up," she said defiantly. "Maybe we can break those windows, let some air in. Maybe the fire department will get here in time."

"Maybe they will..." he said, squeezing her hand. "It's going to be okay, baby."

She'd always believed him when he'd told her that as a child, and she really wanted to let the words reassure her now, but she wasn't a little girl anymore, and she didn't know if either of them were going to make it out alive.

She tried to tell herself it was good she'd had the chance to see him one more time, but knowing what her mom and Scott would go through when they found out the truth made her heart hurt. There would be so much pain, so much confusion.

Dylan would try to explain things to them. He'd be the only person who could really put the pieces together. But thinking about Dylan brought more tears to her eyes. She'd been trying to play it light and easy with him so she wouldn't spook him, wouldn't make him think she wanted more than he had to give. Now, she wished she'd been more honest. Now, she wished she'd told him she loved him.

After following a pizza delivery guy into Tori's building, Dylan found her bag lying outside her apartment door. He grabbed her purse and seeing that her door was ajar, he pushed it open, calling out her name.

There was no answer.

He jogged into the bedroom and checked the bathroom, but Tori wasn't there, and he knew there was no way she would have left her purse on the floor in the hallway. He dug

BARBARA FREETHY

254

through it.

Her phone was inside, flashing with the texts he'd sent. So were her keys.

She hadn't left the building under her own steam. Someone had taken her.

He felt sick to his stomach. He should have told her he'd come and get her and take her to the hospital. He'd been so worried about Emma he'd dropped the ball when it came to Tori.

He wanted to call Max, but he was at Emma's bedside. Calling 911 would bring officers here, but he'd have to wait for them to arrive, and what were they going to find when they got here? Nothing.

He looked around the room again. Her apartment was in the exact same condition as when he'd left that morning. The night they'd spent together seemed like a million years ago now.

Since there was no sign of a struggle, it was clear that Tori had been taken from the hallway. He was a little surprised her purse had been left behind, but he doubted she'd gone willingly.

Terror ran through him at the image of Tori fighting for her life.

He forced himself to breathe, refusing to let fear overwhelm him. He had to stay calm, focused, and work the problem.

Running a hand through his hair, he paced around the room, going over what little he knew.

First Emma was attacked while looking for information in Kruger's office. In his gut, he believed that Kruger had shoved Emma down the stairs. Whether he meant to hurt her or just get her out of the way, he didn't know, but Kruger was the best suspect, because he had access to Emma's building, which the general public did not.

Kruger didn't seem like the person most likely to have grabbed Tori, although he did know where she lived, because he'd gotten her personal information as a witness.

Still…it didn't quite ring true.

Kruger had probably taken off after attacking Emma. He'd know he couldn't get away with it. There were security cameras in the building. He'd probably left the city as fast as he could.

So who else…

Mitch? He was allegedly out of town.

The mysterious Neil Hawkins? But he'd had opportunities to grab Tori long before this. Still he couldn't discount him.

Or was it one of the guys involved in the real-estate insurance scam they were trying to unravel? Lundgren or Litton or God knows who else?

His gaze moved back to her bag. He pulled out her computer, and as he did so, two pieces of paper fell out. One was a handwritten chart. Like her father, Tori had tried to make sense of the clues by laying them out. There wasn't much they hadn't talked about the night before.

He flipped to the next paper. Tori had printed out a map of the city and on it she'd circled several buildings. He knew two of those buildings: the hotel and the pawn shop. But the third one was new. It was a printing company. Tori had written next to it: *Out of business. Owner Litton Capital.*

He knew what that meant. The building was a perfect target for a suspicious fire. No people to worry about.

Unless…

He suddenly knew where Tori was. What better way to get rid of her?

He almost threw up at that thought.

Tori was fine. She had to be. He couldn't lose her.

So he would find her. He would save her. He would be her hero.

There was no other option.

He ran out of her apartment and down the street to his car. The building wasn't too far away, but despite the short distance, it took him ten minutes to get through the traffic.

He thought about calling 911, but he wasn't completely

sure she would be there when he arrived.

After a lot of swerving and swearing, he finally made it through the traffic, turning down an alley and parking by a dumpster. He ran down the narrow alley, seeing a sign for Value Printers.

He was almost to the entrance when a blast rocked the air, and he was blown backward.

He landed hard on his ass as plaster and glass rained down on top of him. His ears rang from the explosion. Disoriented, he tried to get up, then fell back down again. But the heat of the blast, the now crackling flames, drove him to his feet. He had to get to Tori.

He looked around for his phone to call 911, but while it had once been in his hand, it was long gone. At the end of the alley, he saw people stopping to look. Someone would call for help. He needed to get inside.

He ran into burning buildings every day on the job, but this was different. Tori might be inside. *Could she have possibly survived the explosion?*

The front door had been blown off, so it was easy to get into the building, but the fire was blazing and the smell of gasoline was incredibly strong. He took a step forward, dodging quickly to avoid a falling, flaming beam of wood.

The downstairs was in rubble, and the stairs going up to the second floor were engulfed in flames.

His heart pounded against his chest, as he moved forward, calling out for her in the brutally hot, smoky darkness.

"Tori," he yelled. "Where are you?"

His chest began to burn as the smoke thickened. He pulled his shirt up over his mouth and nose and got low to the floor. The last thing he needed was to go down from smoke inhalation before he could find her.

He took a few more steps, seeing a solid door to the right. He ran toward it, putting his hand on the handle, but he couldn't open it. The lock had been broken off.

"Tori," he yelled again.

"Dylan?" a faint voice said.

His heart flipped over. *She was alive!*

Anger and desperation sent him two steps back, then he launched himself forward, kicking his way through the door. He ran down the stairs and Tori fell into his arms.

"You're okay," he said, holding her tight.

"My dad," she said. "Help me."

"What?" he asked, confused by her words.

She moved toward a pile of rubble. "I can't get him out. He's pinned, and he's not moving anymore. I don't know if he's still breathing."

"Your father?" he asked in shock.

"I'll tell you later. Help me."

Fire was racing toward them, coming through the shattered ceiling that had fallen in on Tori's father. The older man was pinned under a beam, blood coming from a gash on his head, and his eyes were closed.

He knelt down and checked his pulse. "He's alive. Get out of here, Tori. Go for help."

"I'm not leaving either of you," she said, grabbing the beam. "We can move this together."

He had no time to argue, and he knew it wouldn't matter anyway. If they could move the beam even a little bit, they could rest it on the pile of debris and hopefully make enough room to pull her dad out.

"Hurry," Tori said, coughing at the end of her words.

He moved to the other side of her father. "On three," he told her. "One, two, three..." With a deep groan of effort, he pulled with all of his might as Tori did the same. They managed to slide the beam about six inches to the right, freeing her father's chest. He grabbed her dad's shoulders and pulled him free.

He still had a pulse but he wasn't moving.

"He's alive, isn't he?" Tori asked with fear in her voice.

"Yes. Let's get out of here."

With Tori's help, he was able to get her father up and over his shoulder. He moved toward the stairs, urging Tori in front of him. He just needed to get them out of the building.

Tori took one step and her foot crashed through the wooden stair. Flames were licking at the railing. In another minute they might not be able to get out.

"Stay to the right," he told her.

"I can do it," she said, finding enough solid wood to make it up to the landing.

He followed in her footsteps.

They'd just stepped through the doorway when the floor began to buckle under them.

Tori screamed. He pushed her forward, managing to get them both to safer ground as the floor behind them fell into the basement and the fire burned hotter from the added fuel.

Sirens blazed through the air and relief ran through him as they struggled through the thick smoke, trying to find the exit.

Yells suddenly lit up the air. "Fire department, call out."

"Here," he yelled.

A firefighter came through the smoke—Tom Franks, one of the men who worked the other shift at his house.

"Dylan," he said in shock. "What the hell? You need help?"

"I've got him," he said, not wanting to move Tori's dad any more than he had to. "Get her out."

Tom helped Tori to the door, and he followed close behind.

When they got to the street, two other firefighters came over to help. Together they placed her father on a stretcher and took him over to the ambulance where paramedics were waiting.

"He was pinned under a beam," he told Rachel, one of the paramedics who often worked his shift. "He might have a concussion, possible internal injuries."

"Got it," she said. "Are you two okay?" she asked, as her partner began work on Tori's father.

"We're fine," Tori said. "Just take care of my dad."

"We will," Rachel promised.

As Rachel went to work, Tori turned to him, her face covered in ash and smoke, her eyes wide with fear. "You think he has internal injuries?"

"I don't know, but that was a heavy beam on his chest."

She drew in a breath. "You're right. Oh, God." She put a hand to her mouth. "I can't lose him again, Dylan. I just got him back."

"Yeah, and I want to hear all about that."

"I want to tell you, but—"

"Not now," he said, cutting her off. "Just breathe, Tori." He put his arm around her shoulders, pulling her trembling body next to his. She was shocked, but she was whole. She was alive. He'd never felt so relieved in his life. "It's going to be okay," he added.

"That's what my dad said, right before everything blew up. He has to make it, Dylan. He has to survive. I have a lot more questions for him."

"I'll bet."

"We're taking him to California Lutheran if you want to meet us there," Rachel said, as her partner and another firefighter loaded Tori's dad into the ambulance.

"Should I go with them?" Tori asked.

"I'll take you." He didn't want Tori in the back of the ambulance if things went south for her father.

As the ambulance raced down the street, she lifted her hand to tuck her hair behind her ear, and he saw blood on her fingers.

"You're bleeding."

She looked at her hands in bemusement. "I didn't even realize. They don't hurt."

"Because you're in shock. I should have had the medics check you out."

"No, it's nothing. They're just scratched from trying to get my dad out. My father pushed me out of the way when the ceiling came down. I didn't think we were going to get out. I thought we were going to die down there. That damned locked door was the only thing that didn't break when the explosion went off."

"You're safe now."

"Because of you. If you hadn't broken down the door, we wouldn't have gotten out before the rest of the ceiling fell down. The firefighters might not have even known we were in there."

He didn't want to consider that possibility. "You're out now. That's all that matters."

"How did you know they kidnapped me? How did you know where to find me?"

"When you didn't call me or text me back, I got worried. I went to your apartment, and I saw your bag in the hall. I dug through it and found a map of possible fire sites. I figured that whoever took you needed a place to put you." He paused. "But seeing your dad…that was a shock."

"For me, too."

"I shouldn't have left you alone, Tori."

"None of this is your fault—none of it."

"Do you know whose fault it is?" he asked.

"Not exactly who set the fire, but I know the players. My dad says he's been putting together a case, but I don't know where the information is. He has to survive, so we can put them all in jail. Otherwise, we'll never be safe."

Twenty-One

For the second time that day, Dylan found himself in a hospital waiting room. This one was at California Lutheran, where Tori's father, Ben Hayden, had been taken into surgery. Tori had also been checked out, and her hands were now cleaned and bandaged. She'd also stopped in the restroom to wash her face, and as she sat down next to him, she still looked like she'd been to hell and back, but the color was starting to return to her face.

"Feeling better?" he asked.

She nodded. "But I won't be able to stop worrying until my dad gets out of surgery."

"I know."

She'd filled him in a little on her dad's sudden reappearance on the way to the hospital, and while he still had questions, he didn't want to stress her out by asking them.

She turned sideways in her chair so she was facing him. "Did you call anyone while I was in the examining room?"

"I spoke to Burke. Emma is stable now, and the doctor says she's going to be fine."

"Thank goodness," she said, letting out a sigh. "And the baby?"

"She's a tiny little thing, but Burke says she's a fighter like her mother. She'll need to stay in the hospital until she gets bigger, but the prognosis is good." He paused for a moment. "I told Burke what happened. He got Max on the phone."

"Oh, I hate to bother Max at this time."

"Emma was sleeping, so he had a minute. He's sending Sergeant Phillips to speak to us. Tony has been working with him on the case, so he won't be coming into this cold."

"That's good. I wasn't looking forward to trying to explain everything. What about Emma's attacker?"

"They've pulled security footage, and it's clear that it was Gary Kruger. The cops are looking for him."

"He'll be able to fill in some important information if they can get him to talk."

"He'll talk," he said decisively. "If he doesn't speak to the cops, I'm going to have a chat with him."

She gave him a faint smile. "He's just one of the players, you know."

"We'll give Sergeant Phillips the other names. Max told me that usually what happens in situations like this is that one person turns on the others and starts talking in order to cut a deal. They use the smaller fish as bait to catch the bigger fish."

"I hope that's true. Some of these men are very rich and powerful, with a lot of connections. I don't know how big the circle is." She paused. "But I do know that one of my coworkers, Jeff Crocker, is the one who betrayed my father— not just now, but seventeen years ago. My dad trusted the wrong man twice. And you know why he trusted him? Because he thought Jeff would fight for the truth as a journalist, not sell his soul to the highest bidder."

"Sounds like your dad has an idealistic streak—much like his daughter."

"I don't know how idealistic I'm going to be anymore."

"You will be. You can't help yourself, Tori. You'll always fight for the truth. That's who you are."

"Sometimes the truth hurts people." Shadows filled her eyes.

"You're thinking about how you're going to tell Scott and your mom that your dad is alive?"

"Yes. I'm torn between calling them now and getting them back here or waiting until I know he's going to make it. But what if he doesn't make it? What if they never get a chance to talk to him? Do I have the right to make the choice for them?"

"It will take Scott hours to get back here, Tori. And your mom is what—an hour away at a spa? It's your call, but I think you should wait until the surgery is over."

"I think so, too," she agreed. "But it's nice to hear you back that up. I can't imagine how they're going to react."

"Probably the way you did."

"I was angry. I was literally yelling at him. Seeing him drove everything else out of my mind. I forgot for a minute that I'd been kidnapped, that we were trapped in a basement, and that at any moment someone might try to kill us. I just couldn't take my eyes off his face. I know now that I followed him into that building because somewhere in my head, I knew it was him."

"I believe that, too," he said quietly. "You have good instincts."

"I don't know how you can say that. I got myself into a mess of trouble."

"On the way to bringing down a circle of criminals."

"I hope we can take them all down. I don't think we'll be safe until we do."

"About that—Max said he was also sending over an officer to stand outside your dad's door until they're sure they've got everyone in custody who could be a threat. He also wants to make sure you're safe, so he said to let him know when we leave here."

"I can't believe he's worrying about us when his wife and

daughter just came through a horrible time."

"I think it actually gives him something to take his mind off how close he came to losing them." He paused, looking into her eyes. "I know that feeling. I keep thinking that if I'd been a minute later..."

She drew in a breath. "I was thinking about you, too, Dylan. All the things I wish I'd said."

Now he was the one who needed to suck in some air. "We have some talking to do, but not now," he added, seeing a man in a suit, followed by a uniformed police officer, walk into the waiting room. "I have a feeling this is Sergeant Phillips."

He was right about his assumption as the sergeant introduced himself and the officer who would be outside her father's room when he came out of surgery.

They sat down in a corner of the empty waiting room. It was after nine o'clock at night and the only person still in surgery was Tori's father.

He listened while Tori related the story she'd shared with him earlier. The sergeant took detailed notes and asked a lot of questions. While they were wrapping things up, he went down to the cafeteria to get Tori a coffee and a snack. When he got back, Sergeant Phillips was on his feet.

"We're done for now," Sergeant Phillips said. "We'll be in touch when we know anything."

"Thanks," Tori said. "I know my father has more evidence, so when he wakes up..."

"We'll get it," the sergeant said. "If you're going to leave here, let the officer know, and he'll call someone to meet you at your apartment."

Dylan didn't like the thought that Tori could still be in danger, but he didn't plan on taking his eyes off her until she was completely safe.

"You always know what I need," Tori said, as he handed her a coffee.

She sat back down in her chair, and he took the seat next to her.

"I looked for ice cream, but they didn't have any, so I settled for a chocolate bar and some chips." He held out his offerings. "I would have liked to get you some real food."

"I'm not hungry," she said. "But if you are—"

"No. I'm not hungry, either, and I'm not leaving you."

She stared back at him, her beautiful blue eyes filling with emotion. "You're amazing, Dylan."

"I'm glad you think so."

"I do. I don't know how things got so serious between us, or at least for me, but the one regret I had when I thought I was going to die was that I hadn't told you how I really felt about you. I stayed silent, because I didn't want to scare you. It was supposed to be a sexy fling, a fun, one-night kind of deal, but the truth is I'm in love with you."

A knot grew in his throat. "Tori—"

She held up her hand. "Wait, let me finish. I've been in love with you since I was thirteen years old. I thought it was a crush. I'm sure you thought it was annoying. And when I went away to college and lived on the East Coast, I tried to put you behind me. But you were always this ideal guy in my head, and no one ever really lived up to you. I know this is the last thing you want to hear, because you don't like clingy women, and the last thing you wanted to be was my personal hero. But that's what you were tonight. I knew you'd rescue me. And you did."

"I just did what needed to be done. You would have done the same if I'd been the one in trouble."

"I would have. And if it didn't mean you being in some sort of danger, I'd tell you that I'd like to be your personal hero. But maybe it would be better if neither of us needed rescuing again."

He smiled, loving her candor, and how willing she was to put her feelings on the line. "You think I'm the brave one, but that's all you, Tori. You let yourself be vulnerable, and that takes a lot of guts."

"I just need you to know how much I care about you. I'm not expecting anything back. And maybe it's not fair to burden you with these revelations, but it seems like the right time to be completely honest."

"Then let me be honest, too. I did not fall in love with you when you were thirteen."

"Fair enough."

"You asked a million questions, and you had so many deep and mature interests. You wanted to change the school rules through lobbying and whistleblowing, and I just wanted to break the rules. I didn't know what to make of you."

"Okay, I can accept that."

"But I always liked you and I had a grudging respect for your energy and ambition when you were a teenager. Now, you knock me out with not just your looks—although you are beautiful, Tori—but also your intelligence, your drive, your kindness and generosity, and dammit, you're also sexy as hell and a lot of fun."

A smile curved her lips. "Glad you finally realized that."

"I think you grew into it."

"Maybe I did," she agreed. "You grew into who you are now, too. I did have a huge crush on you, but I didn't know you then the way I do now. You're a good guy and also sexy as hell and a lot of fun," she said, echoing his words. "But all that said, I don't want to lose you as a friend, so if the sexy fun part is over because I'm getting too serious, then I hope we can still at least be friends. We'll see each other over the years at Scott's house, and I don't want you to ever feel like you owe me anything. I don't have any regrets. I really don't."

He took her hands in his and gazed into her eyes. "I don't have any regrets, either, and I'm thinking we should keep the sexy fun going."

"I haven't scared you away?"

"Not a chance. Because I might not have fallen in love with you all those years ago, but I am in love with you now."

She sucked in a quick breath. "Really?"

"Really." He leaned over and gave her a long, promising kiss.

"So we'll see where this goes?"

"I already know where it's going, but if you need some time to figure it out, take as long as you want."

"You already know?"

He nodded. "I do."

She squeezed his fingers. "So do I. And I want you to know, Dylan, that while I am crazy about you, I'm not putting you up on a pedestal. You're not responsible for my happiness. I just think we make an awesome team, and we're better together."

"We are definitely better together. You are one of the strongest women I've ever met. And I do want to make you happy."

"You will."

He kissed her again, wishing they were anywhere else but here, so he could really show her how he felt, but there would be time for that later.

The doctor came into the room. "Excuse me."

They broke apart and jumped to their feet.

"How is he?" Tori asked.

"The surgery was successful," the doctor replied. "Your father has a concussion and a broken rib, but we've fixed the internal damage, and in time we expect a full recovery."

"Thank God," she breathed out. "Can I see him?"

"The nurse will tell you when he's in his room, but he'll be sleeping for hours. You might want to come back in the morning."

"I can't leave him," she said. "I want to be here when he wakes up."

The doctor nodded. "Let the nurses know if you need anything."

As the doctor left, Tori turned him, her eyes blurring with tears. "He's going to live."

"He is."

"I need to make calls—Scott, my mom, for sure, and maybe Joanie. We need to get Mitch and Jim back into town so they can corroborate my dad's story, and talk to the police..." She gulped, her words ending on a sob. "I don't have time to cry. I told myself I wasn't going to be weak."

"You are never weak, but it's okay to lean on someone once in a while." He pulled her up against his chest. "It's fine, Tori. Cry it out. You're due."

And that's exactly what she did.

———————

Her father woke up a little after eight on Thursday morning. He'd drifted in and out of consciousness a few times during the night, and she had tried to reassure him that he was okay, but she wasn't sure he'd heard her. Now, his gaze was much less fuzzy.

He blinked a few times, and she rose from the chair she'd pulled next to his bed, the chair where she'd spent the night. Dylan had stayed in another chair, refusing to leave no matter how many times she'd told him they would be fine. He had, however, agreed to get them coffee a few minutes earlier, so at the moment she was alone.

"Tori," her father murmured. His gaze darted around the room. "I'm in the hospital."

"Yes. Do you remember what happened?"

He stared back at her for a moment. "The smell of gas, the explosion, things falling down on my head."

"We got you out, but you had a concussion, some internal injuries and a broken rib. They took you into surgery and fixed you up. You're going to be all right, but maybe in a little pain for a few days."

"Are you okay?"

"I'm fine. Just some cuts. You pushed me out of the way when the ceiling caved in. You saved me from getting hurt."

"Well, at least I did something right," he said heavily. "How did we get out of the building?"

"Dylan figured out where they'd taken me from some notes I left in my bag. He got there just after the explosion. He was able to get the door open and we pulled you out of the rubble. It wasn't a second too soon. The building was falling down upon itself."

"God, Tori. I am so happy you're all right."

He lifted his hand, and she curled her fingers around his. "I was so scared," she said. "I didn't want to lose you a second time."

"I didn't want to lose you, either."

"I've spoken to the police. They're going to need whatever information or evidence you've put together to make a case, especially against men as powerful as Lundgren and Litton."

"My notes are on the boat."

"The boat?" she asked.

"Jim has a friend who is a fisherman. He's let me stay on his boat for the last few months. I didn't want to risk a hotel or motel. Credit cards and hotel clerks can trip you up."

"It's so strange to think you've been on the run all these years. You've led a life I don't know anything about."

"I hope we can catch up. I hope you'll give me the chance."

She looked into his eyes, realizing she was starting to get used to his face again. It was a different face than the one she remembered from her childhood. And she wasn't quite ready to let go of the anger she had for some of the choices he'd made, but love and life were complicated, and she was beginning to realize that nothing was black-and-white.

He cleared his throat. "Have you called your mother?"

"Yes, I talked to her late last night. It took me a while to convince her I wasn't out of my mind. Scott had pretty much the same reaction. He's coming back from his honeymoon, and Mom is driving down from the spa I sent her to a few days ago."

"You sent her away?"

"I had a bad feeling after Mitch and Jim disappeared. I didn't know if they were good guys or bad guys, but I did know that they had too much access to Mom. Speaking of your best friends, Mom said she was going to call Joanie. I think Mitch and Jim are about to feel the wrath of some very angry women."

"They don't deserve anger. I'm the one who was responsible for everything. My ambition, my drive to break the big story, put you all in jeopardy. And the sad thing is that I didn't even learn from my mistakes the first time around. I took a second swing at getting the story and it almost ended up killing you."

"I want to blame you for a lot of things, but as a journalist, I have to say that I understand why you wanted another chance to make things right. You had no way of knowing I'd follow you into an abandoned building like an impulsive idiot. I won't be doing that again."

He gave her a small smile. "Good. I really am proud of everything you've accomplished. You're a good reporter."

"I learned from the best. And sometimes you have to sacrifice to get the truth. We're going to write the story, Dad. We'll write it together. We'll put away everyone responsible and we're going to tell the truth for the whole world to see."

"You called me Dad," he said in bemusement.

"That's all you got out of what I just said?" she asked, feeling a little self-conscious.

"It's been a long time since I've heard the word," he said. "It feels good."

"I'm still mad at you. And I have a lot of questions."

"You always do. And I understand the anger. I don't know if you can ever forgive me, but I hope someday it will all make sense."

"This is going to make sense?" a male voice demanded, breaking into their conversation.

Tori whirled around as her brother Scott came into the room, followed by her mother. There was no sign of his new wife Monica, which was probably a good thing.

She stepped back as her brother and her mother approached the bed.

Her mom hadn't said anything yet. Her face was tense, her eyes bright with unshed tears.

Scott's expression was grim, his skin pale, his lips so

tight she wondered how he'd gotten any words through them.

She knew what they were feeling—the same shock and anger she'd experienced yesterday. But underneath that was something else...a remembrance of love, a miracle that this man they had once adored was alive.

"How could you stay away all these years?" Scott asked. "How could you lie to us, dupe us, play us for fools?"

They were the same questions Scott had asked her when she'd first told him their father was alive. She'd hoped his anger would have cooled on the flight home, but apparently not.

Her father drew in an uneasy breath, and she worried that he wasn't up for this. He'd almost died the night before.

"Well, what do you have to say?" Scott demanded.

"Give him a second," she said. "He's recovering from surgery."

Her brother barely glanced at her. "I think I have a right to ask."

"You have every right," her father said. "I'm sorry for everything, and I will explain. I'll answer all the questions you have." His gaze moved to his wife. "Pamela..."

She shook her head, putting a hand to her mouth. "I don't know what to say. I can't believe you're alive, Ben. I can't believe Mitch and Jim helped you fake your death."

"I did it to protect you—all of you."

"He's telling the truth," she put in. "Henry Lowell's whole family was killed, and Dad knew we could be next. That's why he left."

"I see you believe him," Scott said harshly.

"I've had a little more time to understand what was going on. I know the power of the men he was up against. I believe we were in danger back then. I don't know if he made the right decision. But I get it."

"You get it? Great, but I don't. Why not go to the police? Why not get us all protection?" Scott asked. "How could you even be sure we'd be safe after you died?"

"Because they wanted to shut me up—they didn't have

anything against you," her dad answered. "I did watch over you, though. And I made sure Mitch and Jim kept tabs on you."

"He was at your wedding, Scott," she interjected. "He was at your baseball games. You did feel his presence. It wasn't your imagination; he was there."

"You were?" Scott asked, his anger starting to cool as he gazed back at his father.

"I stayed away the first few years, then I'd sneak into town for a few days, for special occasions. I'd get out before anyone knew I was there." Her father turned to her mother. "I'm glad you found someone else, someone who could be there for you."

"Ray," her mother murmured, as if she'd just remembered she had a husband.

"I don't want to make trouble for you, Pam. I want you to be happy, to be loved. Because I loved you so much. I loved all of you."

Tears sprang into Tori's eyes as her mother put a hand on her father's arm.

"I don't understand this, Ben," her mom said. "But…"

"But?" he asked hopefully.

"I'm glad you're alive." Her mother paused. "I used to pray for a miracle. There was a tiny part of me that always wondered if there was some mistake. I think that came from not seeing your body. I guess you made sure of that with Mitch's help."

"The hardest part was seeing you all so sad," he said tersely. "But I had to let you go. I wanted you to be safe, and I hoped the sadness would pass."

"It never left me completely—never," her mom said. "Part of me is furious that you made me go through that. You changed the course of my entire life, Ben. You changed your kids forever. They mourned your loss, and they missed some of the joy of their childhood because of that pain. I could see it in their eyes every time they looked for you in a crowd, because they just couldn't help themselves."

Tori felt her heart break a little more at her mother's words.

"I'm sorry, Pam," her father said again, helplessness in his eyes. "I thought that as long as you were all alive and safe, it was worth it."

"I don't know if it was," her mom murmured. "But...maybe."

"Okay, I need more answers," Scott interrupted, squaring his shoulders, putting on his lawyer interrogation face. Dylan might think she was the only Hayden who could grill someone with questions, but her brother could be tough as well. She didn't know if her father was up to it.

"He's pretty weak, Scott," she said. "Maybe the questions can wait until we all calm down."

"I don't think they can," Scott said, folding his arms. "Not with a police officer outside the door. I need to know what we're dealing with."

"It's okay, Tori," her father said. "You go take a break. You've been here all night. Let me talk to your brother and your mom."

She hesitated, then decided to go along with that plan. "All right. I'm going to see if I can get an update from the police."

When she reached the corridor, she saw Dylan leaning against the wall with two coffees in his hands.

"I didn't want to intrude," he said, handing her a cup. "How did that go?"

"Rough. But it's getting better."

"I just talked to Sergeant Phillips. They've arrested Gary Kruger for Emma's assault."

"That's great news."

"Kruger started talking immediately. He said he was approached by Robert Walker on behalf of Peter Lundgren shortly after he got into the investigator's office. Walker told him how they'd worked with his father and showed him proof of the money his dad had been paid. They said they'd destroy his father's reputation if he didn't go along, and he didn't want that."

"Even though his dad was guilty of hiding an arsonist?"

Dylan shrugged. "That's what he said. We'll know more as they question him further."

"What else is happening? What about Jeff Crocker, my fellow news reporter? He's the one who set my father up yesterday and sent him to that building. I'm sure he knew about my kidnapping as well."

"They found Crocker at the airport last night, about to skip town. He was also eager to talk and share the blame. Based on the conversations they've had so far with Kruger and Crocker, they've brought in Peter Lundgren for questioning. Eric Litton will not be far behind."

"Really?" she asked, surprised it was all happening so fast.

"Yes. Lundgren has already gotten his very expensive attorney working on his case, but Phillips is hopeful they can mount a solid case against him, as well as Litton. He will be over this morning to talk to your father. And he'd like to talk to you again, but he said we could do that later. He's going to leave the guard here until they have a better handle on the situation, but he feels confident that shutting you or your father up is now the least of anyone's problems."

Relief ran through her. "That's the best news yet. And I'm glad I don't have to answer any more questions right now. I'm kind of tired."

"Kind of?" he asked with a small smile. "You didn't sleep all night, Tori."

"I drifted off a few times. And I'm sure you're exhausted, too. You didn't get any sleep, either."

"What do you say to going home for a few hours? Unless you want to be part of the reunion in there?"

"You know—I probably should be in there, but I need some time to catch my breath. I would like to get out of here for a while."

"And I would like to buy you breakfast. I'm over the vending machine snacks. Do you want to say good-bye to your family before we leave?"

She looked back at the room, seeing that her mom and brother had moved closer to the bed. "I'll talk to them later." The three of them were having the conversation they needed to have. She'd had her time with her father. Later, they would all catch up.

———➤➤◄◄——

Dylan thought about taking Tori home, but as he started the car, he didn't think either one of them wanted to go back to her apartment and remember the moment she'd been kidnapped and how close to death she'd come. Going to a restaurant didn't seem like the best idea, either. As he pulled out of the lot, he turned in the opposite direction.

Tori gave him a surprised smile. "Where are we going?"

"I think it's about time you saw my place."

"Your place, huh? I thought we were doing breakfast."

"The beauty of my place is that I actually have food in the refrigerator, not just ice cream."

"Can you make me pancakes and eggs and bacon?"

"I can do that," he said, happy that he'd stocked up a few days ago.

"Then you're on." She leaned her head back as she gazed out the window. "Everything looks so normal. The city just goes on. It reminds me of when my dad died. I'd see people laughing and talking and going to work, and I just thought how strange it was that no one else was sad or crying or lonely. It was just another day."

"You've got him back now," he reminded her. "Are you going to be able to forgive him?"

"It's difficult not to. His heart was in the right place. And it's not like he's been having a fabulous time without us. He's been alone for seventeen years. He told me there had never been another woman, another family. He's been on his own." She glanced over at him. "I want him back in my life. I want him to be there for the big moments, without hiding in the shadows, although I am touched that he was at my graduations, even if I didn't know it."

"And he was at Scott's baseball games. We all thought Scott was nuts."

"I know. Apparently, Scott was more intuitive than I was." She paused. "My dad gave me hell yesterday for following him in the first place. Maybe I did know it was him all along; I just couldn't believe it."

"Well, just don't do it again. You see someone watching you, call the police, call me, do anything but run after the guy."

"I will. I promise. But..."

He heard an odd note in her voice. "But what?"

"I just don't know if I can kick all the bad habits at once, Dylan. I am nosy and impulsive and reckless and sometimes get caught up in a story, and I don't think everything through. If you and I are going to work, you might need to realize that some of my not-so-charming traits aren't going to go away."

"I like that you're not perfect. It makes it easier on me."

"So you don't have to be perfect, either?"

"Exactly. Let's be imperfect together."

She smiled. "I've heard worse offers."

He grinned. "We make a good team. We bring out the best in each other."

"You have made me think a little more before I jump," she admitted. "Consider all the options instead of just choosing the first one. But what have I done for you?"

"That's easy. You've shown me what courage is really about."

Her smile faded and her gaze grew serious. "What do you mean?"

"You're not just brave about fighting off kidnappers or staying in a burning building to save someone else's life. You have the courage to be vulnerable, Tori, to put your heart on the line. That's the one thing I've never been able to risk."

"I promise if you risk your heart with me, I'll take good care of it."

"I know you will," he said, reaching out his hand for hers.

She curled her fingers around his. "I can hardly believe the biggest crush of my life is going to be the biggest love of my life."

"And I can hardly believe how many questions I'm going to have to answer every day," he said dryly.

She laughed and let go of his hand to playfully punch him in the arm. "You are going to love talking to me."

"I already do." He turned down his street. "This is me."

"Nice," she said approvingly as she eyed the two-story, old Victorian house. "Do you have a view of the bay?"

"Unfortunately, no. The top floor was out of my price range. But it's a short run to the water. We should go sometime."

She groaned. "Oh, man, if we start dating, you're going to make me run, aren't you?"

"There's no *if* about it—at least not the dating part." He paused. "Things have been moving fast."

"Well, maybe," she agreed. "But it did take us more than ten years to get here, so fast is good for me, at least some of the time."

He laughed at her wicked smile. "We are definitely on the same page."

A moment later, he pulled into his garage. After parking the car, he took her up a short flight of stairs and into his first floor-apartment.

Tori walked around the living room, noting the two big leather recliner chairs and the super comfortable couch, all set up around a big-screen TV. "This is definitely a bachelor pad," she said.

"It certainly has been, but I'm happy to put those days behind me. Hunter used to live here, but when he decided to travel, he moved his stuff out, and I am thrilled about that."

"I can see wanting to live alone, but are you really done with bachelor days?"

He pulled her into his arms. "Yes. I think I've just been

waiting for you, Tori."

"I like that. You didn't really have to wait this long, though."

He laughed at that. "Yes, I did. We weren't ready before."

"But we are now." She licked her lips. "What do you think Scott is going to say about us dating?"

"I don't know, but I don't care. You were right. This was never about him. He's just going to have to deal, because I'm not letting you go."

She put her arms around his back. "I'm not letting you go, either." She leaned in and pressed her mouth against his.

The brief taste of her lips was all he needed to want a lot more. But he forced himself to breathe past the rush of desire. "Let me cook you breakfast, Tori. You need to eat. And then you need to sleep."

She shook her head, her eyes glittering with humor and desire and love. "What I need right now is you. Everything else can wait. Love me, Dylan."

"For the rest of my life," he murmured, as he took her into the bedroom.

Epilogue

*E*ight weeks later...

"So what do you think?" Tori asked impatiently, looking at her father across the kitchen table in her apartment.

"One second," he said, holding up a hand, as his gaze moved across the hard copy version of the news article they'd been working on the past two months. She knew it was good, but she wasn't sure it was great. And anything that her father was going to put his name on had to be excellent.

As she waited for him to finish reading, she couldn't help thinking how much better he looked now. He'd recovered from the injuries he'd sustained during the fire, and since he'd started to reclaim his life, he'd gotten his hair cut, bought better-fitting clothes, and rented an apartment. He was slowly becoming Ben Hayden again.

He still seemed to spend a lot of time looking over his shoulder, but with the cases building against Peter Lundgren, Litton, and the others, he'd finally started to believe that justice was going to win out after all these years.

Soon everyone would know the story, because this article would be the first of three in a series that would cover the long-running, multi-million-dollar scheme that had been cooked up and carried out by some of San Francisco's most prominent citizens off and on for twenty years. The crimes had carried through two generations, but they were officially done and the entire truth could be told.

Her father set down the paper and gave her a smile. "It's perfect."

"Are you sure? Nothing is perfect." Her heart was swelling with pride at not just her achievement but theirs.

"This is. You told this story better than I could have told it."

"I have a bit more objectivity—"

"No," he said, cutting her off. "You have a way with words that's magical."

She loved the compliment, but she thought he might be a little biased. "If I do, I got it from you."

"Let's just agree that we're both great."

She laughed. They'd gotten to know each other again through the research and writing of the article, and he felt like her dad again. They'd even had a few arguments, having managed to get past the point of tiptoeing around each other to just be themselves. "Fine. I agree. We're awesome. And the *Examiner* is going to sell a lot of copies and get a lot of online traffic with this series. It's the scoop of all scoops."

"Truly a career-making story," he said. "It only took seventeen years. But I'm glad we did it together. I wish you'd consider taking my name off it, though, unless you think it will help you generate more traffic."

"I want your name on it, because it's your story more than it is mine."

"You might get a bigger cubicle after this."

"Stacey already gave me Jeff's cubicle. He's not going to need it since he's in jail." Jeff had made a deal to save himself from a trial and a list of charges going all the way up to accessory for murder. He hadn't gotten completely off, though. He would still be in jail for at least ten years, and Tori was very happy about that.

The rest of the staff at the *Examiner* had been cleared of any involvement, and Jeff had insisted that he'd had no idea Tori had applied or gotten the job until she showed up for work. At first, Jeff had thought she was there to spy on him, but quickly had realized she didn't even know her father was still alive. He'd decided to keep an eye on her and wait for a chance to use her to his advantage.

"Crocker was my biggest mistake," her father said. "I thought I could read people, but he played me from the very beginning. I thought I was giving him the chance to help me on a big story. But he didn't care about that. He was the one who told Lundgren seventeen years ago that I was on to him. He was the one who also gave up Henry's name, which led to the death of four innocent people. And he did it all for cash and access to the power players. They fed him stories over the years. He made his name through their exclusives."

"But even with their help, he was never that successful," she said. "He couldn't even buy his way to greatness. And when you came back to life, and he realized you might eventually discover his betrayal along with everything else, so he had to get rid of you. Taking care of me as well was added protection. But I think he also wanted me off the paper. I was going to be competition. It's always about greed— whether it's money or position or power, isn't it?"

"Maybe not always, but often," he agreed.

Her doorbell rang.

"Is that Dylan?" her dad asked. "I thought you were meeting him at his parents' house for the engagement party."

"I am," she said, pushing the button for the speaker. "Hello?"

"It's Scott."

"Why are you here?" she asked in surprise.

"Just let me in."

She buzzed her brother in, then glanced over at her dad. "Do you know what this is about?"

"Maybe he doesn't want me to go to the party," he said heavily. "He's probably worried it's going to be hard on your mother, and I completely understand where he's coming from."

She understood, too. Her mom had been torn up and conflicted since her father had come back from the dead. She worried about hurting Ray and also worried about hurting Ben. Her mother was torn between the two men, because she loved both of them.

Tori couldn't imagine what her mom was going through. It was easier for her and Scott. Ben was still their father. They'd never replaced him, not even with Ray. But her mom had fallen in love with someone else, and she'd told Ben that she wasn't going to walk away from her second husband of fourteen years, because her first one turned out to be alive. It wouldn't be fair to Ray.

Her father had wished her well, but there had still been a lot of tension between them, and they hadn't been able to get together just the four of them since that first day in the hospital. But she needed that to change.

"I want all of you at my party," she said. "There will be a ton of Callaways, and I need the Haydens to be out in full force, so no one is bailing." She opened the door, getting ready to tell her brother he needed to get over whatever problem he had. But he wasn't alone; her mom was with him.

"What are you both doing here? Is something wrong?" she asked.

"No, but we need to talk," Scott said. "The four of us."

As Scott and her mother entered her apartment, her dad got to his feet. For a moment, the four of them just stared at one another.

"Okay, this is weird," she said, breaking the tense silence. "What's going on?"

"I don't want to say the wrong thing," her mother said, a pained look on her face. "I told Scott this was a bad idea."

"No, it's a good idea," Scott argued. "I didn't want this tension to be at Tori's party. It's too big of a night for her."

"That was considerate of you," she said, knowing that Scott hadn't been completely thrilled with the idea of her and Dylan getting together, but he'd come around when he realized how much in love they were.

She waited for Scott to keep talking, but he seemed like he'd already run out of things he wanted to say. Time for the baby of the family to take the lead.

"It can't ever be the same," she said. "We need to stop looking back and start looking forward. We've all lived a lot of years without this particular foursome being together, but there's love here. I can feel it. I know each of you can, too. Sure, there's lingering anger and resentment, and we'll need to keep talking and keep trying to work things out, but the bottom line is that we should be happy that we're all together again. We have years ahead of us, big moments that we'll finally get to celebrate together. And tonight is one of those." She paused, glancing at her brother. "As usual, you were right, Scott. We did need to get together before we're in the middle of a party."

"And you're right, Tori," her mother said. "The tension is mostly my fault. You and Scott are trying not to choose sides, but you're worried about me, and you don't need to be."

Her mother walked across the room, stopping in front of Ben. She gave him a sad smile. "I have nothing but great memories about the years we spent together, about the love we shared, and the children we brought into this world. I miss the way we were, but I know we can't go back there. We've both changed. We have to let the past be the past. We've all missed out on so many great moments that we should have shared together. I don't want that to happen even one more time. So I think we should get rid of the *weirdness*..." She flashed Tori a smile. "And celebrate because we can, and because we should."

"I agree," her dad said.

"Me, too," she said. "Scott?"

"I'm on board," he agreed. "It will be a lot easier if we're all getting along when the baby comes."

"What?" she asked with a squeal. "You and Monica are having a baby?"

"We are," he said with a grin that spread across his face. "We were going to tell you together, but we didn't want to ruin tonight's big event, and I probably should have kept my mouth shut until another day."

"Don't be ridiculous," she said, giving him a hug. "I'm so happy for you."

"I can't believe I'm going to be a grandmother," her mom said, following up with a hug as well.

"Congratulations, Son," her dad said.

There was a moment's hesitation, and then Scott walked across the room and hugged their dad. It was the first time they'd embraced.

Happy tears rushed to her eyes. Her family was back together.

"So, is the article done?" her mom asked.

"It's finished," she replied.

"And it's better than good," her dad said.

"I'll upload it on Monday morning and we'll see what happens," she added.

"It's going to shake the city," Scott predicted. "But that's what you do best, Tori. I hope Dylan knows what he's in for."

"I'm pretty sure he does," she said with a laugh. "So who's driving me to the party?"

"I am," Scott said. "I'm driving all of us, if that's okay with everyone?"

"Ray is going to meet us at the party," her mom put in.

"He's a good guy," Ben told her mother. "I'm glad you found him."

"Me, too," her mom said. "Now, let's go celebrate Tori's engagement. Then we can start planning a wedding. I can't wait." Pamela gave them all a happy smile. "This time, I get to be the mom in charge."

Scott groaned. "I almost feel sorry for you, Tori."

She wasn't sorry at all. She was going to love planning her wedding with her mom, and knowing that her dad would be there to walk her down the aisle filled her heart with happiness. But even more importantly, she was going to spend the rest of her life with Dylan.

———◦◦◦◦◦———

His parents' house was packed with Callaways, Dylan thought, as he greeted Aiden and his wife Sara and sent them into the family room, where his dad was tending bar. Even his grandparents had made it, his grandfather Patrick standing like a sentinel over his wife Eleanor while she chatted with his Aunt Lynda and his Uncle Jack.

Mia, her husband Jeremy, and their daughter Ashlyn had come up from Angel's Bay, and Kate and Devin had flown in from DC for the weekend so they could finally meet Tori. His sister Annie and his brother Hunter had taken a break in their travels to come home, too. The only person missing was the most important person—Tori.

He walked into the kitchen and glanced out the window. Tori should have been here by now. As much as he wanted to believe all the problems were behind them, he still didn't like it when she was late.

His brother Ian came up next to him and gave him a knowing smile. "She'll be here."

"I know. She's just going over the article she's writing with her dad about everything that happened. They probably got caught up in it."

"Probably. It's quite a story. Why don't you come join the party?"

"I'll be there in a second."

The kitchen door opened, and relief ran through him as Tori walked into the room.

She wore a dark-red, short lacy dress that clung to her body, her dark hair falling in clouds of brown silky waves over her shoulders, her lips bright and pink, her blue eyes sparkling with happiness. "You're late," he said.

She laughed. "It wasn't my fault. Blame your best friend,

Scott. He wanted to have a family heart-to-heart before we came over here." She paused. "Hi, Ian."

"Tori," Ian said. "I'll leave you two alone, but don't take too long. We're ready to drink some champagne."

"We'll be right there," Dylan promised. As his brother left, he grabbed Tori's hand and pulled her in for a kiss. "I missed you."

"I saw you like four hours ago," she said with a laugh.

He grinned back at her. They'd been spending every second together, but it still wasn't enough. "It seems like longer. Did you get the article finished?"

"Yes, and it's good."

"I had no doubt. And the family heart-to-heart?"

"Better than good. It's going to be okay, Dylan. We're going to find a new way to be a family."

He knew how much that meant to her. "I'm really happy for you."

"I'm happy for me, too. Oh, and by the way, Scott and Monica are pregnant."

"That was fast."

"This time next year there will be a baby in the family. It's going to be wonderful." She paused as the kitchen door opened, and Emma and Max came into the room with their new baby.

Nora, named after Eleanor Callaway, had spent the first two weeks of her life in the hospital, but looking at her now, a plump, bright-eyed and smiling child, there was no sign of her dramatic entrance into the world.

"Oh, Nora looks so cute in that little dress," Tori said.

"I couldn't resist," Emma replied, giving her daughter a hug.

"She has trouble resisting a lot of pretty dresses," Max said with a teasing smile for his wife. "Both in Nora's size and in Shannon's size."

"Can I go see Kyle and Brandon?" Shannon asked, tugging on Max's hand.

"Sure," Max said, as the little girl ran into the other room.

"It's good to see you, Emma," Dylan said. "You look well."

"I am well. So the three of you can stop worrying and feeling guilty," Emma said, her gaze encompassing her husband as well as him and Tori. "I'm only going to say this one more time. I was the one who made the impulsive decision to look through Gary's files. I certainly didn't anticipate he was going to shove me down the stairs, but it was a risk I took on my own. I don't want to hear any more apologies from any of you. Gary is paying for what he did, and thanks to my brilliant husband, and the hard work the two of you have put in, so will everyone else. All is well that ends well."

"We do appreciate your help—both of you," he said.

"We're Callaways," Emma said. "Taking care of each other is what we do. Now, we're going to go show off Nora to the rest of the family. I hope we didn't miss the big announcement."

"That's still coming, along with the champagne," he assured them. "Tori and I will be there in a minute."

When Emma and Max and their daughter had moved out of the kitchen, he took Tori into his arms again. Gazing down into her blue eyes, he said, "I just want you to know how happy I am."

"Me, too. We're going to have a great life together. I have a feeling it might get exciting at times."

"I'm counting on that."

"So shall we go out there and make it official?"

"Not before I kiss you."

"Or I kiss you," she teased. "I wonder if you would have ever made a move if I hadn't kissed you first?"

"I definitely would have. I only hesitated because I knew even then how special you were, and how important you were going to be to me."

Her gaze filled with emotion. "I love you, Dylan."

"And I love you back."

They sealed their promises with a long, passionate,

heartfelt kiss, and then they walked into the living room together.

Surrounded by his siblings, his parents, his cousins, and his friends, as well as Tori's family and their friends, he felt incredibly lucky and excited to be bringing their two families together.

"For those of you who haven't met her yet, this is the love of my life," he said, putting his arm around Tori. "And very soon she's going to be my wife."

"Welcome to the family, Tori," Emma said.

As Tori was surrounded by well-wishers, Scott came over to him and shook his hand.

"I always thought we were brothers," Scott said. "Now it's official. You better take care of her. It won't be easy. She's a handful."

He laughed. "I will watch over her every day of my life. She has made me the luckiest man on earth."

Scott smiled. "She's lucky, too. And I'm just glad you'll be the one planning a wedding this year."

"I'm looking forward to it. It's certainly a lot less scary than having a baby," he said pointedly.

"Tori told you," Scott said.

"She did. Congratulations."

"Thanks. It's an exciting time—for both of us."

"We need some champagne," he said.

As if on cue, Tori handed him a glass and slid her arm around his waist.

"Time for a toast," she said.

He clinked his glass against hers, not caring that there were dozens of people waiting for some romantic and well-spoken toast. He only had two words, and they were everything. "To us," he said.

"To us," she echoed, as they gazed into each other's eyes.

They each took a sip of champagne and then came together in a kiss that would start the rest of their lives.

THE END

About The Author

 Barbara Freethy is a #1 New York Times Bestselling Author of 63 novels ranging from contemporary romance to romantic suspense and women's fiction. Traditionally published for many years, Barbara opened her own publishing company in 2011 and has since sold over 7 million books! Twenty of her titles have appeared on the New York Times and USA Today Bestseller Lists.

Known for her emotional and compelling stories of love, family, mystery and romance, Barbara enjoys writing about ordinary people caught up in extraordinary adventures. Barbara's books have won numerous awards. She is a six-time finalist for the RITA for best contemporary romance from Romance Writers of America and a two-time winner for DANIEL'S GIFT and THE WAY BACK HOME.

Barbara has lived all over the state of California and currently resides in Northern California where she draws much of her inspiration from the beautiful bay area.

For a complete listing of books, as well as excerpts and contests, and to connect with Barbara:

Visit Barbara's Website:
www.barbarafreethy.com

Join Barbara on Facebook:
www.facebook.com/barbarafreethybooks

Follow Barbara on Twitter:
www.twitter.com/barbarafreethy

CPSIA information can be obtained
at www.ICGtesting.com
Printed in the USA
LVOW12*1557090817
544390LV00006B/58/P